# SWANSONG

## ALSO BY DAMIEN BOYD

*As the Crow Flies*

*Head in the Sand*

*Kickback*

DAMIEN BOYD

# SWANSONG

This is a work of fiction. Names, characters, organizations, places, events, and incidents are either products of the author's imagination or are used fictitiously.



Published by Thomas & Mercer, Seattle

www.apub.com



ISBN-13: 978-1477828601
ISBN-10: 1477828605

Cover design by bürosüd° München, www.buerosued.de

Library of Congress Control Number: 2014955142

Printed in the United States of America

*For my brother, Geoffrey*

# Prologue

*A glass of wine? What harm can it do? He's a harmless old duffer.*

*'Yes, please.'*

*'Red or white?'*

*'Red, please.'*

*She watched him pour a large glass from an open bottle.*

*'Cheers.'*

*'Down the hatch. Now, about this test of yours . . .'*

*It was after that things got a bit muddled. The conversation started well but tailed off when her eyes began to glaze over. Then she dropped her glass of wine and slumped back onto the leather sofa. She tried to apologise for spilling the wine but the words wouldn't come. Some did. She heard them. But they weren't in the right order and she didn't recognise the voice.*

*'Have another drink.'*

*The glass, refilled now, was thrust into her hand. She felt another hand behind her back sitting her up. The glass held to her lips.*

*The wine tasted bitter. She hadn't noticed it before.*

*Then he was gone and she fell back onto the sofa. She rubbed her eyes. She could hear noises behind her, in the kitchen, but could see nothing.*

*Her left hand felt wet. It was hanging over the edge of the sofa, resting on the floor. She held it up and looked at it. Red wine was running down her arm, staining the sleeve of her blouse.*

*'How are you getting on in there?'*

*She couldn't reply. She was going to be sick any minute. How embarrassing was that?*

*What's happening to me?*

*She closed her eyes. When she opened them again she was looking down at a girl lying on a leather sofa, her left arm hanging over the side and her hand resting in a puddle of red wine that was gradually seeping away through a crack in the floorboards.*

*Wake up. It's me, you idiot.*

*No response, no movement. Nothing.*

*The man reappeared. He looked different this time. Cold, black eyes.*

*She watched him kneel down next to the girl on the sofa. He took her hand, turned it over and placed it flat on the floor, palm down. Then he reached up and took something off the arm of the sofa.*

*What the . . . ?*

*She screamed but there was no sound. The girl on the sofa lay motionless.*

*She watched. Mesmerised.*

*He picked up her hand. The girl on the sofa didn't flinch. She flinched for her. She felt the sharp edges of the blades bite into her flesh as he closed them around her ring finger.*

*Wake up . . . please wake up . . .*

*Sobbing now.*

*She saw him grasp the yellow handles in both hands, at the same time checking the blades were lined up with the base of her finger.*

*Did he know she was watching?*

*Then he snapped the handles shut. Hard. She heard the crunching of the bone.*

*Blood, so much blood. Pumping. But she felt no pain.*
*She looked down at her left hand and tried to count her fingers.*
*One, two . . .*

# Chapter One

Dixon leaned against a pillar and closed his eyes. He was fighting to stay awake and it was a battle he was losing. He had been up since 8 a.m. the previous morning and now not even the bright strip lights could keep him awake. There were people everywhere, jostling for position, some of them shouting, but it was no good, he had to get some sleep. Even a few minutes would do.

Suddenly, he felt a hand on his shoulder.

'You missed 'em.'

'What?'

'The bags. They've gone round again.'

It was just after 4 a.m. on a Friday morning in early December and Detective Inspector Nick Dixon was waiting by the bag carousel in Gatwick North Terminal. He had just arrived back from a week in Cyprus with his girlfriend, Detective Constable Jane Winter. She had persuaded him that a week in the sun would do them good, and it would have done had the sun shone. She had also said it wasn't worth paying the upgrade for daytime flights, which was something Dixon could not forgive. Why they hadn't flown from Bristol was also a mystery to him.

'Now all we need is for that old heap of yours to conk out on us,' said Jane.

They caught the bus out to the long stay car park. Dixon handed his car keys to Jane as they stepped off the bus into the early morning rain.

'You can drive.'

'Why me?'

'You slept on the plane.'

Much to their surprise, his old Land Rover Defender started first time.

'Old car, new battery,' said Dixon, grinning.

Jane switched the headlights to full beam as she drove down the slip road onto a deserted M23. Ahead of them lay four hours in the car listening to the clunk of the windscreen wipers, the only consolation being breakfast in the Little Chef at Amesbury.

It was mid-morning by the time they arrived home in Brent Knoll. Dixon had driven from Amesbury, taking the old route cross-country from Stonehenge that he had always used when going home for the weekend during his days in the Met. They had taken a short detour via Jane's parents' to collect Monty, who had started barking as soon as he heard the diesel engine, and Dixon was looking forward to a walk on the beach followed by lunch and a few beers in the Red Cow.

'You switched your phone on yet?' asked Jane.

'No.'

'Me neither. Maybe we should?'

'No fear.'

Dixon picked up the landline and listened. He could tell from the intermittent dialling tone that a message was waiting. He replaced the handset and turned to Jane.

'Coming to the beach?'

'No. You go. I'm gonna have a shower. Be back in time for lunch.'

'OK.' Dixon looked at Monty. 'Where's your ball?'

Monty ran into the kitchen and began scrabbling at the back door. Dixon ran to pick him up and carry him out to the Land Rover before the powerful Staffordshire terrier could damage the door, which had only just been replaced following a recent break in. The terms of his tenancy didn't allow pets either so he wanted to keep signs of Monty's presence to a minimum.

Dixon was deep in thought as he drove out of Brent Knoll towards Berrow. It struck him as an oddly routine domestic scene. Odd for him, at least. Walking the dog, Jane in the shower, lunch in the pub. While they had been away they had talked about getting a place together, but instead decided that Jane would rent out her flat and move into Dixon's cottage. His landlord had been very understanding about the incident with the shotgun and they felt sure he had known about Monty all along.

It had crept up on him, this relationship, but maybe that was the best way. It had been a long time since he had felt anything for anyone, but as he drove along Coast Road towards the beach, he decided that he liked it.

They knew it meant they would be separated at work, but then that was inevitable when Jane passed her sergeant's exams. They should have been split up before now and had only got away with it for their last investigation because there had been no one else available. Perhaps it was for the best? Living together and working together. It didn't bear thinking about.

He parked on the beach beyond the Sundowner Café and walked towards Brean Down. They had left the rain behind on Salisbury Plain and it was a glorious morning, cold and crisp with a clear blue sky. The tide was on its way out, making for a pleasant walk on firm, wet sand. He watched a horse lorry unload three large and very lively horses that clearly knew they were in for a gallop along the beach. Dixon hardly dared watch while the riders mounted, and was relieved when they galloped off in the opposite direction.

Brean Down jutted out into the Bristol Channel ahead of him with its limestone cliffs towering over the beach, and he was getting close enough now to pick out some climbers in Boulder Cove. There were a few dog walkers around too; he recognised some of them, but most gave Monty a wide berth. They saw a large white Staffie and arrived at the wrong conclusion every time.

Dixon was beginning to think about turning round and heading home. Monty had long since lost interest in his tennis ball and was sniffing the lines of seaweed and other debris left behind by the tide. Dixon thought about Jane in the shower and it dawned on him that walking the dog might have been the wrong option.

He was watching the sand yachts racing along the flats off to his left when he heard a car horn in the distance and turned to see a small red car speeding towards him along the beach. He quickly put Monty on his lead and watched the car approach. It was less than two hundred yards away before he realised it was Jane. She slid to a halt next to him and wound down the window.

'What's up?' asked Dixon.

'Get in.'

'What's going on?'

'I switched my phone on.'

'But . . .'

'And I suggest you do the same.'

The message was short and to the point.

'Ring me as soon as you get this. I don't care what time it is.'

The caller hadn't left his name or number but then he didn't need to.

'He's left the same message on mine and on the home phone. You'd better ring him.'

Dixon checked his watch while he waited for Detective Chief Inspector Lewis to answer his phone. It was just after midday.

'Where the bloody hell have you been?'

'Cyprus.'

'I know that. Your flight was due in at four o'clock.'

Dixon turned to Jane and raised his eyebrows.

'Well, you're here now. There's a meeting this afternoon at Taunton Police Station, 2 p.m. Be there.'

'What's it all about?'

'Get there a bit early and I'll fill you in. And the assistant chief con will be chairing it, so put a tie on.'

Lewis rang off.

Dixon looked at his phone.

'Yes, I had a lovely holiday, thank you, Sir.'

'Well?' asked Jane.

'Taunton at 2 p.m.'

'Bang goes lunch and an afternoon with our feet up.'

'I have a horrible feeling our holiday's going to seem a very long time ago, very soon,' said Dixon.

'Shall we leave your car where it is?'

'Don't be daft, the tide'll get it.'

Jane grinned.

'Cheeky sod.'

---

Dixon turned into the car park behind Taunton Police Station just after 1.30 p.m. to find DCI Lewis waiting for him.

'Good holiday?' asked Lewis, opening the car door before Dixon had switched the engine off.

'Yes, thanks.'

'Don't think much of your tan.'

'Too cold for that.'

'Well, you're going to wish you'd stayed there, I'm afraid.'

'Sounds ominous.'

'It is.'

Dixon followed DCI Lewis up to the CID Room on the first floor and waited while Lewis got two coffees from the machine. The CID Room was busy but quiet, which struck Dixon as odd, although he had his back to the officers sitting at their desks. He remembered that the assistant chief constable was in the building. Perhaps that was it? There was a good deal of whispering going on and he felt sure he heard the words 'Dixon' and 'Bridgwater' over the noise of the coffee machine.

'We'll use this room,' said Lewis, gesturing to a vacant office. 'Sit down.'

Lewis handed a coffee to Dixon. It was in a light brown plastic cup and neither looked nor smelt much like coffee. The layer of powdered milk still floating on the top prompted Dixon to take a biro off the desk and stir it.

'Have you ironed that shirt?' asked Lewis.

'Collars and cuffs.'

Lewis rolled his eyes. 'Don't take your jacket off, for God's sake.'

'What's it all about, then?' asked Dixon.

'Isobel Swan. Aged seventeen. A sixth form student at a local boarding school. Brunel. Have you read about it?'

'No.'

'It happened just before you went on holiday, I think. She was found in a ditch that runs around the perimeter of the playing fields . . .' Lewis stopped and waited. He was watching Dixon. 'Are you listening?'

No reply.

'Nick?'

Dixon wasn't listening. He had done what they had told him to do. He had placed all the memories in a box, locked it and put it on a shelf in a storage cupboard at the back of his mind. It had gathered dust there ever since, this box. From time to time he had seen it, stared at it, paused and then moved on. But he had never opened it. Now he could feel a hand on it, dragging it off the shelf.

'Nick?'

'Yes, Sir.'

'Are you all right?'

'Fine, yes, sorry, you were saying?'

'Isobel Swan. Her throat had been cut and her ring finger severed. Roger Poland thinks it was bolt cutters or something like that.'

Dixon could feel his shirt clinging to a cold sweat in the small of his back. He realised that it was his own hand on the box, doing exactly what he had been told not to do, all those years ago.

'*Counselling? That's not me, but thank you for the offer.*'

Then had come the advice.

'*Box it up; put it to the back of your mind.*'

'*Wouldn't that be the same as forgetting?*'

'*No, entirely different. You'll never forget.*'

And he hadn't.

'Nick, are you all right?'

'Fine, really.'

'Well, we'd better get down to the conference room. And make sure you only speak when you're spoken to. OK?'

'Yes, Sir.'

The meeting began at 2 p.m. sharp. Sitting at the head of the conference table was Assistant Chief Constable David Charlesworth. Dixon thought him unusually young to have such a thick head of grey hair. He wore dark horn rimmed spectacles and was in uniform.

'I think it's fair to say that this is a crisis meeting,' he began. 'We're nine days into a high profile murder investigation. We've made no progress whatsoever and the commissioner's going up the pole. The victim was a brilliant student, by all accounts, from a poor background at a posh school on some sort of scholarship, so you'll understand the media interest. It's a recipe for disaster. Now, how can I put this politely?' Charlesworth threw his pen onto the table for dramatic effect. 'What the bloody hell's going on?'

'Well, Sir . . .'

'Identify yourself for those around the table, will you, Simon?'

'Simon Chard, Detective Chief Inspector, Taunton. My team are running the investigation.' He turned to his left. 'This is Detective Inspector Margaret Baldwin, leading the team, and to her left is DS Tom Bryan.'

'You know DCI Lewis?' asked Charlesworth.

'Yes, Sir. I don't know the officer to his left, I'm afraid.'

'That's DI Dixon,' replied Charlesworth.

'What's he . . . ?'

'He's here at my request. We'll come onto why in a minute. You all know Vicky Thomas, Public Relations, don't you?' continued Charlesworth, gesturing at the remaining figure seated at the table.

Chard nodded.

'That's everyone, then. Now, what's going on, Simon?'

'We've got no CCTV, no DNA and no witnesses . . .'

'Perhaps you'd better start by telling us what you have got, then,' said Charlesworth.

'A seventeen year old female student in the lower sixth, that's the first year of two A Level years. Her ring finger's been cut off and her throat cut. No evidence of a struggle. Roger Poland found a large quantity of ketamine and red wine in her body so she'd been drugged. Probably didn't feel a thing, if that's any consolation.'

'It isn't,' said Charlesworth. 'Where was she found?'

'In a ditch at the bottom of the playing fields. There was a large quantity of blood on a small footbridge over the ditch so it looks like her throat was cut on the bridge before she was pushed in.'

'What else?'

'Several witnesses report seeing a car in the car park behind the Bishop Sutton Hall they'd not seen before or since. It had been there a few days and then disappeared.'

'Make, model?'

'They couldn't say. Only that it was blue and small with a boot. Definitely not a hatchback. The obvious inference is that it was for moving her and the killer was disturbed.'

'Why is that obvious?'

'There's CCTV covering the main car park at the front of the school, but none on this car park. It's also adjacent to the playing fields. I'm guessing now, but it's possible he was carrying her across to the car when he was disturbed and had to drop down onto the playing fields. There's a line of leylandii he could have hidden behind and it leads out to where she was found.'

'Who uses it?' asked Dixon. Lewis glared at him.

'What?' asked Chard.

'The car park,' replied Dixon.

Chard looked at his notes. 'Parents visiting Bishop Knox, Markham and Tuckerman houses. Staff as well. And anyone visiting the sports hall.'

'Any CCTV of the car?' asked Charlesworth.

'None, Sir. We've checked the town cameras but if you come out of the school and turn left you're straight out into the country.'

'What about her friends? What do they say?'

'We've talked to her two best friends, Emily Setter and Susannah Bower. They say it was just an ordinary Saturday afternoon, really. They'd watched the 1st XV rugby match. They beat Millfield 22–10 . . .'

'I'm not interested in the bloody score, Simon.'

'Sorry, Sir. Then they went into town after Isobel's driving lesson.'

'Into town?'

'Sixth formers are allowed into town, Sir.'

'Last sighting?'

'Just before ten at the main entrance. Emily and Susannah went back to Tuckerman and Isobel headed for Gardenhurst House. Different directions.'

'Is there a boyfriend?'

'She was friendly with a lad called . . .' Chard began thumbing through a notebook, '. . . Ben Masterson, but there's no evidence they were boyfriend and girlfriend.'

'What about the driving instructor?' asked Dixon.

'He checks out. He picked her up at 5.30 p.m. for a half hour lesson and then dropped her back.'

'Dropped her back where?'

Chard looked at DI Baldwin.

'The car park behind the Bishop Sutton Hall,' said Baldwin.

'So, apart from some guesswork about an otherwise unidentified car, we've got no leads at all. Is that right?' asked Charlesworth.

'We're going to be doing a public appeal, Sir. I've already spoken to Vicky about it,' replied Chard.

'Appeal for what?'

'Information about the car. Sightings, anyone who can report it missing.'

'I've set up a press conference for Monday morning,' said Vicky Thomas.

'Well, go ahead with that, by all means; you never know what might turn up. In the meantime, we've another plan, thankfully.' Charlesworth turned to Lewis. 'I'm assuming you've told Dixon why he's here?'

'Not specifically, Sir, no. I briefed him about the investigation, not his part in it.'

Dixon sat up. He had spent much of the last ten minutes brushing the dust off a box of memories and wondering whether the time had come to open it. And whether he could face it. He had drifted in and out of the conversation, blurting out the odd question when it had occurred to him, if only to make it look as if he had been paying attention. The mention of his name brought him back to the present with a jolt.

'Dixon.'

'Yes, Sir.'

'Fancy trying your hand at a bit of teaching?'

'Teaching?'

'Yes. Get in there and find out what the bloody hell's been going on in that place.'

'Undercover?'

'You'll be a student teacher doing a Postgraduate Certificate in Education at Bristol University. Two weeks' work experience before the end of term. It's all been set up with the headmaster.'

'But . . .'

'You won't have to do any real teaching. Just sit in on a few lessons, that's all. The head teaches law A Level. You can sit in with him to make it look genuine.'

'Why me?'

'Two reasons. Firstly, you went to one of these places.'

'I went to St Dunstan's, Sir. On the other side of town.'

'They're all the same, and you know how they work. None of us have got a bloody clue.'

Dixon noticed the sneer on Chard's face.

'And, secondly,' continued Charlesworth, 'DCI Lewis tells me you're the best we've got.'

'Remind me to thank him later, Sir,' said Dixon, glaring at Lewis.

'I asked for a copy of the investigation file to be made available.'

'It's here, Sir,' said Chard, offering a green document wallet to Charlesworth in his outstretched hand.

'I don't want it. Give it to Dixon.'

Chard slid the folder across the table. Dixon opened it and flicked through the contents. There was a bundle of witness statements, from which he did not expect to learn much, Roger Poland's post mortem report and then, at the back, a bundle of photographs. He started with the post mortem report.

'Take it away and read it, but for God's sake don't take it into the school with you,' said Charlesworth.

'Yes, Sir,' replied Dixon, without looking up.

'The headmaster's expecting you this evening. One of the masters is away on a sabbatical in the Far East so you'll be using his rooms in the main school.'

'Yes, Sir.'

'What about liaison?' asked Charlesworth.

'I thought we might assign Jane Winter to Simon's team for the duration of the investigation, Sir,' replied Lewis. 'She could act as Nick's contact. After all, what could be more plausible than his real girlfriend?'

'A relationship with a fellow officer, Dixon?' asked Charlesworth.

'Yes, Sir.'

'Well, it makes sense, I suppose.'

Dixon began flicking through the bundle of photographs. It started with shots of Isobel Swan lying face down and naked in a shallow stream, her hair waving in the current. Her left arm was resting on the bank with her right arm underneath her. Dixon could see that the ring finger was missing from her left hand. The photographs had been taken from above, the photographer standing on the bank and also on the small footbridge that crossed the stream and led through a gap in the hedge into the adjacent field, where the all weather hockey pitches were.

Dixon recognised the spot. Memories came flooding back. Of away hockey matches and the walk down to the all weather pitch; there had been only one back then. Of times he had chosen not to think about since.

The last photograph in the album showed Isobel Swan lying on the slab in the mortuary. Dixon stared at it. There was no going back now. The box was open and the memories were running wild. People, places, sounds, smells, laughter, tears. He was reliving his school days in a split second as the images flashed across his mind.

He could hear voices but was no longer listening to the conversation going on around him. Then he felt a hand on his shoulder, shaking him.

'Dixon.'

He closed the photograph album and looked up. All eyes in the room were on him. Watching and waiting. He took a deep breath and exhaled slowly through his nose. Then he looked at Charlesworth.

'It is a consolation, Sir.'

'What is?'

'To know that she didn't suffer.'

*The day began much like any other Sunday during term time. He had remembered to adjust the time for the lost hour in bed now that the clocks had gone forward and his alarm had gone off just after 7 a.m., as usual. Then it was a quick shower, a shave and over to breakfast in the main school. After breakfast came chapel, hence the Sunday suit; regulation dark grey with a white shirt and navy blue tie.*

*The shave was not strictly necessary but he had bought the cheap plastic razors and a can of foam the day before, so he thought he'd give it a try.*

*They always had breakfast together at 8 a.m. Always. Without fail. But then they did everything together and had done since they had first met. They were inseparable, or so it seemed to the rest of the school. She watched him play rugby and hockey and he watched her play netball and tennis. They never missed a match. They even studied together in the school library.*

*They had got used to the constant jibes and whistles from the other pupils. Romeo and Juliet, Bonnie and Clyde, even Pinky and Perky, they had heard it all. But he didn't care. She was beautiful and he knew they were just jealous.*

*It had been love at first sight for her and a little longer for him, perhaps an hour. They used to joke about it. She always said he was a bit slower.*

*They had got it all mapped out. They were engaged to be married, they just hadn't told anyone yet. Next came the same university to study the same subject. It didn't matter what. Then they would get married. Earlier if they summoned up the courage to defy their parents. They had talked about Gretna Green many times but they knew they had the rest of their lives ahead of them. Time was on their side and all that mattered was that they would never be apart again.*

*But today she wasn't there.*

*8 a.m. came and went. He waited. It had never happened before and he knew straight away that something was wrong.*

*The night before they had gone to the wine bar in the High Street. The one that never asked your age. She had passed her driving test and they were celebrating.*

*Then they crept over the wall at the bottom of the playing fields and across the new AstroTurf hockey pitch to the car park. They had said goodnight on the steps of the girls' house, as usual, and their kiss had attracted several wolf whistles and shouts of 'get a room' from the students piling out of the 287 Club. Full of watered down beer, the lot of them.*

*That was the last time he saw her.*

*He looked around the dining room, which was starting to empty now. 8.15 a.m. came and went and breakfast was over. She had never missed it before. He was starting to panic. Then he noticed that none of the girls were there.*

*He ran out of the dining room and along the corridor towards the girls' house. He took the flight of steps halfway along in two bounds and then stopped abruptly when he saw his housemaster and the headmaster's wife walking towards him.*

*He heard his name and felt an arm around his shoulder. They were talking quickly and he noticed that the headmaster's wife was crying. He couldn't remember much of what was said but two words from his housemaster got through.*

*'She's gone.'*

# Chapter Two

Roger Poland was waiting outside the pathology lab at Musgrove Park Hospital when Dixon arrived, his large frame blocking the doorway. Dixon watched him rubbing his huge hands together and blowing on them for warmth. Poland always joked that he was too clumsy to be let loose on patients while they were still alive.

'Good holiday?'

'Yes, thanks.'

'How come you're involved in this one, then?' asked Poland, opening the back door to the lab.

'You wouldn't believe me if I told you.'

'Try me.'

'I'm going undercover as a trainee teacher . . .'

Poland roared with laughter. 'You?'

'What's so funny about that?'

'I'd love to be a fly on the wall.'

'I'm not going to do any real teaching,' said Dixon, following Poland along the corridor. 'Just sitting in on a few lessons to make it look real.'

'Why you?'

'I've got the right old school tie, apparently.'

'Which one did you go to, then?' asked Poland.

'St Dunstan's.'

'When was that?'

'I left seventeen years ago.'

'And the dead girl was at Brunel?'

'She was.'

'Chances are no one will recognise you, then.'

'I hope not.'

'You know Brunel, though?'

'I played away matches there. Hockey and rugby. I was useless at cricket.'

'You played rugby?'

'Not very well.'

Dixon sat down on the corner of a desk in the lab while Poland fetched Isobel Swan's file from the cabinet in his office.

'You've read my report?' asked Poland, appearing through the swing doors.

'Just the summary. Tell me about ketamine.'

'It's an anaesthetic. It causes hallucinations, so it's not first choice these days, but it's still used in certain situations. Vets use it a lot too, on horses, mainly. Powerful stuff.'

'And druggies?'

'They use it, or rather abuse it, for the hallucinatory effect. It's a dissociative too so they get an out of body experience and hallucinations at the same time. Not my cup of tea.'

'How long does it take?'

'It's quick, maybe ten minutes or so and it tastes bitter, which explains the red wine in her system.'

'How much had she had?'

'Enough to stop a horse. She'd have been unconscious pretty quickly, thank God.'

'Why thank . . . ?'

'You haven't read that bit?'

Dixon shook his head.

'Her finger was cut off while she was still alive,' said Poland. 'Through the proximal phalanx, just about where a ring would sit. Bolt cutters, I think . . .'

Dixon stood up and walked over to the window. Sitting on a bench under a large tree on the far side of the lawn was a man smoking a cigarette. He wore a raincoat and was sheltering under an umbrella. Next to him was an oxygen bottle, the tube connected to his nose. Dixon watched him for several seconds before he shook his head.

'Makes you wonder, doesn't it?'

'What does?'

'A young life snuffed out in here and he's over there . . .'

'Are you all right, Nick?'

When he turned back to Poland, Dixon's face was ashen. He was gritting his teeth so hard he could feel them creaking in his jaw and could taste blood.

'You look like you've seen a ghost,' said Poland.

'Something like that, Roger,' replied Dixon.

Dixon sucked the blood from in between his teeth and swallowed hard.

'Can I see her?'

'Er, yes, give me a minute.'

Dixon turned back to the window and watched the man finish his cigarette and then light another. But Dixon was elsewhere, delving into a box of memories, all of them good this time. He was brought back to the present by the crash of a trolley into the swing doors on the far side of the lab.

'Here she is,' said Poland.

Dixon walked over and stood next to Poland.

'Ready?'

Dixon nodded.

Poland turned back the green sheet as far as her chin and no further.

'D'you know her?' he asked.

Dixon stared at Isobel Swan, lying on the trolley in front of him with her blonde hair swept back, her eyes closed and her skin a deathly grey.

'What colour are her eyes?'

'Green,' replied Poland.

'No, I don't know her.'

'What's up, then? I've never seen you react like this before.'

Dixon took a deep breath and looked at Poland. Then he uttered the three words he knew changed everything.

'He's killed before.'

Dixon was sitting on a chair in Poland's office watching him rummage in the back of the top drawer of his filing cabinet. Then, with a flourish, Poland produced a half empty bottle of Famous Grouse and poured two large drinks into white plastic cups that he had taken from the water tower.

'No one must know about this, Roger . . .'

'Hang on a minute. You're telling me the killer's done it before and no one must know?'

'That's right. I never told you. You never knew.'

'Why?'

'If anyone finds out, I'll be taken off the case. That can't happen.'

'Let's have it, then,' said Poland, handing a plastic cup to Dixon.

'This one's personal.'

'Personal?'

'I was sixteen. My parents sent me to St Dunstan's to study for my A Levels. There were girls in the sixth form back then and . . . there was one . . .' Dixon's voice tailed off. He took a large swig of Scotch. He was staring into the bottom of the plastic cup and spoke without looking up. '. . . And . . . we were . . .' He took another swig of Scotch.

Poland smiled at Dixon and nodded.

'Then one day she disappeared,' said Dixon.

'Disappeared?'

'Not a trace. Not a bloody thing. They never even found a body. It was all over the news at the time.'

'I was in Birmingham back then,' said Poland. 'What happened?'

'I was all over the place. Bombed all my exams. Had to resit them at some grotty tutorial college in Oxford.'

'You poor sod.'

'It's why I joined the police and came back to Somerset.'

'Does Jane know about this?'

'No.'

'Are you going to tell her?'

'I haven't got that far yet.'

'But . . .'

'I've waited seventeen years to come face to face with this son of a . . .'

'All right, all right, I get it. No one will hear it from me. But don't you do anything stupid.'

'I won't.'

'Answer me this, though. If a body was never found, how d'you know it's the same killer?'

'They're identical.'

'Who are?'

'Both girls,' replied Dixon. 'They could be twins, identical twins, and I don't believe in coincidence.'

Poland had the last word, as usual, and as Dixon drove north on the M5, it was ringing in his ears.

'Tell Jane.'

And he knew that he would. After all, if he couldn't trust Jane, who could he trust?

He glanced across at the copy of Isobel Swan's investigation file on the passenger seat. Find her killer and he would find out what happened to Fran. At last. Then maybe he could move on.

He had already begun to, if he was honest, despite having always sworn that he wouldn't. He had met Jane and their relationship had crept up on him. That phrase again. He smiled at the idea of Jane creeping anywhere. Yes, he would tell her and she would help him. He didn't doubt it for a minute.

He glanced up at the stars and wondered whether Fran was looking down at him. He had felt her presence from time to time over the years, but less so in recent months. Anyway, one way or the other, he was determined that she would soon be able to rest in peace. So would her family and so would he.

Dixon grimaced. A car on the southbound carriageway with its lights on full beam dazzled him. He blinked and shook his head. Suddenly, the image of Fran having her ring finger cut off flashed across his mind. He saw her screaming. He blinked again and she was gone.

It was a question he knew he had to answer. He would find out soon enough and had no real idea how he would react when he did. He had promised Poland that he wouldn't do anything stupid, but finding out that Fran had suffered as Isobel Swan had done might just change that.

Dixon arrived home just after 6 p.m. to find Jane cooking a spaghetti bolognese. She was standing by the cooker stirring the onions and minced beef, which sizzled in the pan. Monty was sitting at her feet hoping for something, anything, to drop on the floor.

'Hello, Mr Chips,' said Jane.

'Very funny.'

'Hungry?'

'Yes,' replied Dixon, lying. 'How d'you . . .'

'Lewis rang me. There's some beer in the fridge.'

'I'd better not. Roger filled me up with whiskey.'

Dixon stood behind Jane and put his arms around her waist. She turned her head and kissed him, all the time looking into his eyes.

'What's up?'

'Long story.'

Jane switched off the gas under the pan and turned round to face Dixon, his arms still around her waist.

'Something's up. I know it is. Tell me.'

'It's . . .' Dixon hesitated, '. . . difficult.'

'Is it to do with Isobel Swan?'

'Sort of.'

'Did you know her?'

'No. Look, let's go and sit down.'

'You're worrying me now,' said Jane.

Dixon took her by the hand and led her into the sitting room. She sat down on the sofa, while Dixon paced up and down in front of the television.

'Just start at the beginning and tell me, for heaven's sake.'

'Everyone's got a past. You've got one, I've got one.'

'Of course we have.'

'This is about mine. I'm just going to blurt it all out and then you can let me know what you think when I've finished.'

'Fine.'

Dixon took a deep breath.

'You remember me telling you I went to St Dunstan's College to study for my A Levels?'

'The posh school?'

'That's the one. I'd never been to boarding school before and I was like a fish out of water, in amongst all these kids who'd been there for years. Sink or swim, it was. Anyway, I swam.'

Jane nodded.

'Then I met Fran,' continued Dixon. 'Fran Sawyer. She was in the lower sixth too. It was like walking into a brick wall. Bang. And that was it. Love's young dream.' Dixon smiled. 'They tried separating us. Fran was switched to a different class but it didn't work. In the end, they gave up.'

Dixon looked at Jane, sitting on the sofa, listening intently.

'It's never occurred to me before, but she'd probably look much like you now. She was beautiful. Blonde hair in a ponytail, green eyes.'

Jane smiled.

'And she had a beautiful smile too,' said Dixon. 'We even got engaged. Told no one, of course, but we were going to be married. Till death us do part and all that.' Dixon turned to face the television. 'I loved her, Jane.'

'Go on.'

'Anyway, just before Easter, at the end of the Lent term, before our final exams, she disappeared. All hell broke loose. There was a huge investigation but they never found her. Not a trace. And that was that.'

Dixon sat on the arm of the sofa next to Jane. She reached up and put her arm around him.

'The sad part about it is she wasn't even supposed to be there.'

'Where?' asked Jane.

'She should've gone on a hockey tour to Holland but her parents blocked it. Too close to her exams, they said.'

Jane shook her head.

'Looking back, it's why I took up rock climbing, I think,' continued Dixon. 'Hanging on by your fingertips three hundred feet up a cliff takes your mind off most things. It's why I joined the police too and why I came back to Somerset. One day I was going to get the chance to find out what happened to her.'

'And now you have?'

'And now I have. Isobel Swan is identical in almost every way except two. Different school and her body's been found. Same age, profile, looks, everything. This bastard's killed before.'

'You're personally involved . . .'

'No one must know. They'll take me off the case. Someone in that school knows what happened to Isobel and if I find her killer, I find Fran's killer too.'

Dixon stood up and walked over to the window. He opened the curtains and looked out. 'It's down to you now. I couldn't do it without telling you and I can't do it without you.'

Jane stood up, walked over to Dixon and put her arms around him.

'What d'you want me to do?'

'What're you going to wear?' asked Jane.

'I thought about that brown sports jacket my old man gave me.'

'That's tweed.'

'Don't start.'

'And there's that wool tie . . .'

'You can go off people, you know,' said Dixon, taking the plates out to the kitchen.

'We'll have a look in the wardrobe.'

'No, it's fine. I can . . .'

Dixon dropped the plates in the sink and ran upstairs, arriving in the bedroom just in time to watch Jane unzip the cover on the 'wardrobe'. She was being generous. It was a clothes rail with a canvas cover on it that Dixon had got for twenty quid online. It had served its purpose but would soon be going to the tip when Jane moved in with all her furniture. They had intended to hire a van the following weekend, but those plans were on hold now.

'Is that it?'

There were several pairs of trousers, a couple of shirts and a suit that he wore for court appearances. Behind that was the sports jacket.

'It'll have to do,' said Jane, flicking the dust off the shoulders. 'What about shirts?'

Dixon opened a suitcase that was lying on the floor and produced two shirts that were still in their plastic bags. 'Brand new, with tags,' he said.

'eBay?'

Dixon shrugged his shoulders.

'I am not living with someone who buys their clothes on eBay,' said Jane.

'You'll get used to it,' said Dixon, putting the sports jacket on. Then he did up the top button on his shirt and straightened his tie. 'How do I look?'

'Like a trainee teacher going to a boarding school for two weeks' work experience.'

'You know just what to say.'

'Thanks,' replied Jane.

Dixon threw the shirts and some clean underwear into his sports bag and then went into the bathroom.

'What's the plan, then?' shouted Jane, sitting on the end of the bed.

'Haven't got one yet,' came the reply. Dixon reappeared in the doorway carrying his toothbrush, razor, a can of shaving gel and a towel, which he stuffed into the top of his bag. 'I'm just gonna play it by ear to begin with.'

'And me?'

'You've got the difficult job. I need details of anyone arriving at Brunel within the last seventeen years. Teachers and support staff.'

'Support staff?'

'Kitchen and grounds staff, bursar, secretaries, the lot. Look for anyone who was at St Dunstan's seventeen years ago and moved to Brunel. It'd be useful to have details of anyone who left St Dunstan's within the last seventeen years too.'

'Bloody hell.'

'It'll be easy to get the Brunel stuff. Chard should've done full background checks on all of them anyway. Just look for the dates they arrived.'

'What about St Dunstan's?'

'That won't be so easy.'

'What reason can I give without giving away the connection?'

'I know. For now, just focus on the Brunel staff and where they were before. We can worry about the rest later if we come up with nothing.'

'Wait a minute,' said Jane. 'If someone was at St Dunstan's and killed Fran and is now at Brunel and killed Isobel then they might recognise you, surely?'

'I doubt it. Anyway, it's a chance I've got to take.'

'You'd have been at St Dunstan's at the same time.'

'I know.'

'Bloody hell.'

'I was only there for two years and it was seventeen years ago. I'll be using a different name as well, don't forget.'

'It's too risky,' said Jane, shaking her head.

'I'll be fine, really. I'm the hunter, not the hunted.'

'You'd better be.'

'The driving instructor,' said Dixon, changing the subject. 'I haven't got a copy of his statement.'

'I'll get it.'

'Fran passed her test the day she disappeared.'

'What about her file?'

'My name'll be all over it so we'd best leave it in store for the time being.'

Jane followed Dixon down the stairs. Monty was curled up on the sofa so Dixon sat next to him and scratched him behind the ears. 'Keep an eye on her, matey. I'm relying on you.'

Jane rolled her eyes.

'Routine stuff on the usual number, OK? They'll expect that. Get a pay as you go SIM card for anything else, just in case,' said Dixon.

'OK.'

Dixon opened the back door of his cottage. It was still raining. He turned back to Jane and kissed her.

'Don't do anything stu . . .'

He reached up and put his fingers over Jane's lips, stopping her mid-sentence.

'Once upon a time, maybe, but I've got too much to lose now,' he said.

# Chapter Three

The rain had been replaced by sleet, which danced in the headlights of Dixon's Land Rover as he drove south on a quiet M5. He had stopped at the supermarket just off the motorway roundabout and paid cash for a pay as you go SIM card with twenty pounds of credit, which was safely tucked into his inside jacket pocket.

He turned off West Road into the main entrance of Brunel School, and parked on the far side of the car park, opposite the main school building, to take in the scene. To the left of the car park was a large single storey building that looked as if it had once been the school chapel. Stained glass windows revealed rows of bookshelves inside, telling Dixon that it was now the library. The main building itself was set over three floors with leaded windows and old weathered brickwork. The top floor had dormer windows and there was a large tower in the centre above the entrance. Two large carved oak doors were set side by side in an ornate stone porch.

Dixon could not see a single room that was unoccupied. Either that or someone had left the lights on. He winced at the thought of the electricity bill. The view was familiar to him from visits with hockey and rugby teams from St Dunstan's and it hadn't changed. He knew that the playing fields and sports hall were behind the main school and he remembered the long corridor with the tiled floor that ran the full length of the building. The only other thing he knew was where the dining room was.

To the right of the school, as he looked up at it, was a smaller two storey building with a private garden enclosed by a high box hedge. This was the headmaster's house. Dixon drove across the car park and parked in the corner close to the front door. He stepped out of the Land Rover and pulled up the collar of his coat before walking over and ringing the front doorbell.

The door was opened by a woman in a tweed suit. Dixon smiled. At least he wouldn't look out of place in his tweed jacket.

'I'm looking for the headmaster. I believe he's expecting me.'

'Yes, of course. Won't you come in? I'm Miranda Hatton, the headmaster's wife.'

Dixon stepped into the hall. As he did so a man, presumably the headmaster, appeared from behind the door opposite. A small springer spaniel ran out from behind him and began jumping up at Dixon. Mrs Hatton took hold of it by the collar.

'Sorry about that,' she said.

'You'll be Dixon,' the man snapped.

'Yes, Sir.'

'You're late.'

'I wasn't aware I had to be here at a specific time. Just as soon as I could.'

'And this is as soon as you could, is it?'

'Yes.'

'Well, it'll have to do. Follow me.'

Dixon followed the man along the corridor and into a room at the far end.

'Sit down.'

Dixon sat down on a leather sofa. The man poured himself a drink from a decanter on the sideboard. At the far end of the room was a desk.

'Drink?'

'No, thank you.'

'My name's Hatton. I'm the headmaster,' said the man, sitting down in a leather armchair opposite Dixon. 'Charlesworth tells me you're St Dunstan's?'

'A long time ago, Sir.'

'They're not a bad lot.'

'We used to say the same about Brunel.'

'I bet you did,' said Hatton, smiling. 'I'm sorry about . . . well, anyway, this is all incredibly difficult for me. There's nothing in the manual about dealing with a murder and the school governors are getting very jumpy. The idea that there's someone running around out there who's killed one of our pupils . . .'

'Out there?'

'Yes, of course. They're not going to be in here, are they?'

Dixon did not reply.

'It stands to reason. You're not seriously suggesting someone in the school did it?'

'I really don't know, Sir.'

'Is that why Charlesworth sent you in here?'

'I don't think he knows either.'

'Inspires confidence, doesn't it?'

'It's my job to find out . . .'

'Well, for God's sake, be discreet about it. Whatever you find, we don't want to see it ending up in the papers. It could be devastating for the school.'

'A girl is dead . . .'

'I know that,' said Hatton. 'We just need to be careful how it's handled, that's all.'

Dixon nodded. He could hear his mother's voice ringing in his ears, '*If you haven't got anything useful to say, say nothing at all.*'

'Now, I've arranged for you to work with Mr Phillips. He teaches chemistry but is also in charge of school discipline, so it'll give you a good insight into what's going on,' continued Hatton. 'He doesn't know who you are, of course.'

'Good.'

'I did send an email to all staff letting them know you'd be here until the end of term.'

'What name did you use?'

'Dickson, but I spelt it with a "cks" instead of an "x" just in case anyone saw the news the other day. That was quite a show you put on at Taunton Racecourse.'

Dixon rolled his eyes. 'You heard about that?'

'I was there,' replied Hatton.

'Not much of a false ID, is it?'

'Sorry, Charlesworth never . . .'

'It'll have to do. Did you mention which school I went to?'

'No, why? Is that a problem?'

'I wouldn't want anyone knowing I'd gone to a school in Taunton. If anyone asks, we can say I went to King Alfred's in Burnham-on-Sea.'

'Fine. I've got a couple of lessons tomorrow morning that you can sit in on. The first one's at 10 a.m. so be here just before that. Robin Phillips is expecting you in the masters' common room at 9 a.m. and he'll give you a tour of the school. You'll be with him for the rest of the weekend after lunch.'

'Yes, Sir.'

'This is a letter I've written confirming who you are and what you're doing here,' said Hatton, handing an envelope to Dixon. 'Just in case anyone asks.'

'Thank you.'

'Come along, then, and I'll show you to your rooms. They're Haskill's, actually, but he's on sabbatical. He won't mind. Laos or Cambodia, somewhere like that, I think. We go past the MCR on the way too.'

The door at the back of Hatton's office led to a small corridor that connected directly to the main corridor inside the school building. Dixon followed Hatton along it, past the main entrance hall towards the library. He looked at the green felt notice boards that lined both sides of the corridor above the dado rail, each with any number of different bits of paper pinned to it, and tried to read them as he went past. Various drama groups, the canoe club, team sheets for all sorts of different sports, martial arts he had not even heard of, the debating society, computer club. He gave up halfway along.

'Everyone's studying now until 9 p.m., so it should be pretty quiet. There's the odd thing going on. Father Anthony has a confirmation class in the Lady Chapel and there's a rehearsal for the school play in the Bishop Sutton Hall. That's it, I think.'

Hatton stopped at the bottom of a flight of stairs.

'That's the library,' he said, looking at two large doors opposite. 'And that's the MCR over there,' pointing to a smaller door further along the corridor. There were more notice boards in between the two. A door at the end of the corridor led outside and a flight of steps opposite the MCR led down to a corridor running at right angles to the main corridor. 'That takes you down to the dining room. Turn left along the cloisters for the chapel.'

Hatton then turned and went up the stairs. He paused at the top.

'Those are the physics labs over there,' he said, pointing to three doors on the far side of the large landing. 'Locked at this time of night, as you might imagine. And those are Mr Small's rooms. Classics and ancient history.' He began rummaging in his trouser pocket and produced a Yale key. 'Haskill's.'

Dixon followed Hatton through a door that led into a dark corridor, with wood panelling that made it gloomy even after Hatton switched the lights on. There was a small kitchen on the right as Dixon went in, then a shower room with no window and, at the end of the small corridor, a larger room with a small lounge area in front of the door and a single bed at the far end. The whole of the wall to his left was covered in bookshelves and the furniture consisted of a coffee table, a two seater sofa and a small armchair.

'I asked Matron to change the bed, so you should be all right. Here's the key and I'll see you in the morning.'

'Yes, Sir. Thank you.'

Dixon heard the door slam. He looked around the room but could not see a television so he looked at the books on the shelves. He decided that he wasn't in the mood for Homer or Plato so he took out his phone and sent Jane a text message.

*No effing telly x*

Dixon waited five minutes to give the headmaster time to get back to his house and then walked down the stairs and across to the library. The left of the two large oak doors creaked as he opened it. He could see rows of bookshelves either side and desks at the far end, some of them occupied. Presumably working in the library rather than your own study was allowed. It had been at St Dunstan's. Just inside the door was a sloping newspaper table, with various newspapers laid out on it, each secured in place by brass clips. All of them were open at the sports pages and all of the crosswords had been done.

He went back out to the main corridor, which was eerily quiet, and then down the steps leading to the cloisters. He stopped halfway along and looked out of the window at the school war memorial in the centre of a manicured and immaculate lawn. Gravel paths led from each corner to the memorial itself in the centre and it was completely enclosed by the school buildings. Several wreaths were still lying on the plinth at the base, no doubt placed there on Remembrance Sunday only a few weeks before. It had been the tradition at St Dunstan's for the school to gather at the war memorial and for the headmaster to call the roll of those who had not come back. It looked as though Brunel held the same tradition.

Dixon shook his head. He was looking back on a part of his life that he had shut out for years and the memories were flooding back. Not all of them good. He remembered the one thing he had done in his life of which he was truly ashamed. He had been presented with a petition calling for the abolition of the Remembrance Sunday service and he had signed it. It was the one and only time he had bowed to peer pressure, the first and last time, and he had been haunted and embarrassed by the memory. It didn't matter that the headmaster had ignored it. What mattered to Dixon was that he had signed it. He had been to see the headmaster to withdraw his name from the petition and he winced at his words, which hit home again.

'*I was surprised and disappointed to see your name on it, Dixon.*'

'*Yes, Sir.*'

'*But at least you've had the courage to put it right now. Well done.*'

'*Thank you, Sir.*'

'*An important lesson learnt?*'

'*Yes, Sir.*'

Dixon heard a door bang at the end of the corridor and looked to his left to see a crowd of younger pupils streaming out of the chapel and along the cloisters towards him. He stepped back and allowed them to pass, which they did at speed and noisily, none of them appearing to notice that he was there.

The door at the end of the cloisters had been left standing open, so Dixon walked into the chapel and stood at the back. Huge banners were hanging either side, each depicting a scene from the Bible. At the far end was the altar and behind that a large and ornate stained glass window. Dixon could see a smaller chapel off to the side, adjacent to the altar, presumably the Lady Chapel. He gave up trying to count the pews but there must have been enough to fit everyone in.

He was about to leave when he realised he had been spotted by the chaplain, who was striding towards him along the aisle. He was dressed in black robes with a dog collar and had thinning white hair, a grey beard and thick horn rimmed glasses.

'Can I help you?'

'I was just looking around, Father. Getting to know the lie of the land.'

'You'll be Dickson, then?'

'Yes.'

'How did we manage before email?' asked the chaplain, shaking Dixon's hand. 'Welcome. I'm Father Anthony. I'm afraid you've arrived at a very bad time for the school.'

'So I gather.'

'It's been terrible. Knocked everyone for six.'

'I can imagine.'

'Dreadful. God bless her. She was a lovely girl.' Father Anthony shook his head. 'Makes you wonder why these things happen sometimes, doesn't it?'

'It does.'

'I even found myself doubting my faith . . .' Father Anthony's voice tailed off. 'Will you be joining us for worship?'

'Er, yes,' replied Dixon. 'If I can.'

'Jolly good. There's evening prayers tomorrow at six and then Sunday morning at ten for Communion.'

'Can you get everyone in?'

'Just about. There's always a few stragglers. It's a sport for some of them, missing chapel,' replied Father Anthony. 'And it's been extended over the years. There's a stone in the floor halfway along the aisle marking where the altar used to be in the old days.'

'I assumed that the library . . .'

'No, that was the assembly hall until the Bishop Sutton Hall was built.'

Dixon nodded.

'Anyway, I must lock up. Nice talking to you,' continued Father Anthony. 'Let me know if you need anything.'

Suddenly, they heard footsteps running along the cloisters behind them and Dixon turned to see three girls rushing into the chapel, tears streaming down their faces.

'Can we talk to you about Isobel, Father?' spluttered one.

'Of course, of course. Let's sit over here,' replied Father Anthony, gesturing to the pews at the back of the chapel.

'I'll leave you to it,' said Dixon.

Father Anthony smiled and nodded.

Dixon walked back along the cloisters and had reached the steps at the end before he could no longer hear the girls crying. He opened the door to the masters' common room and looked in. It was pretty much as he imagined it would be. Old armchairs and sofas with a small kitchen area against the back wall. There was no one at home so he looked at the notice boards to the left of the door, which displayed the team sheets for the various rugby matches the following day. The 1st XV were playing St Dunstan's at home so Dixon made a mental note to keep away from the rugby pitches, just in case.

He fetched his overnight bag from his Land Rover and then went back up to his rooms on the first floor, in amongst the physics labs. He smiled when he remembered sitting a physics multiple choice paper and scoring four out of fifty. Physics had never been one of his better subjects and he could hear the teacher's voice even now.

'*Dixon, a monkey could've got more than that.*'

Needless to say, physics hadn't been his first choice at A Level.

There was a small jug of milk in the fridge so he made himself a cup of tea. Then he threw his overnight bag on the bed and unzipped a pocket in the bottom. He pulled out the file on Isobel Swan, which he had wrapped in a towel, and began flicking through the witness statements. There were twenty-one in all, from her parents, the headmaster, her housemaster, teachers and various friends who had seen her at some point that evening. She had her own study/bedroom in Gardenhurst and no one had seen her arrive back, her disappearance only coming to light when her body had been found the following morning by one of the ground staff. Dixon thought it odd there was no statement from the groundsman who had found her. He made a mental note to ask Jane about that.

Isobel had been studying maths, physics and chemistry and had been expected to sail through her exams on her way to medical school. She was one of those lucky students for whom studying and passing exams came easily. Dixon had been one of them too, until Fran had disappeared.

He turned to the statements of Emily Setter and Susannah Bower and read them again. After Isobel's driving lesson they had gone to the cinema and then called in at Pizza Hut for a bite to eat. Susannah had driven and they had got back just after 10 p.m., leaving her car in Conway Road, a small residential cul-de-sac opposite the school. They had last seen Isobel in the hall at the main entrance when they had gone in different directions along the main corridor, Emily and Susannah turning left and Isobel turning right. Nothing that Isobel had said had given either of them any cause for concern or reason to believe that she might run away. Dixon thought about his last night with Fran and it all sounded a little bit too familiar.

The officer who had taken Susannah's statement had been more thorough, having asked her to describe Isobel's route to Gardenhurst from the main entrance. Dixon read Susannah's statement several times before putting all of them back in the file and hiding them under the mattress. Then he walked back down to the main entrance and followed Isobel's route back to Gardenhurst.

Once past the headmaster's house the corridor narrowed and at the far end double doors led into the boys' toilets. There were also doors either side of the corridor: a pair of large double doors to the left, leading to the back of the school, opposite a smaller door leading to the front. Dixon looked out of the window in the smaller door. It was almost dark this way, illuminated only by the glow from the lights at the back of the headmaster's house.

Once through the door Dixon found himself in a small car park, which he took to be the headmaster's private parking area. There were flowerbeds on three sides with large bushes that gave it an intimidating feel. If Isobel had been anything like Fran there was no way she would have come this way, even if it was a shortcut.

Dixon walked back to the side door, into the main corridor and then out of the swing doors opposite. The area behind the school was well lit with several outside lights and there were a number of students milling around, two throwing an American football to each other on a lawn to the left. Dixon walked around the side of the toilet block and into the bright lights coming from a large building set at right angles to the main school. The sign above the door told him it was the Underwood Building, and it was a hive of activity. Every light was on and all of the rooms were occupied.

In front of Dixon was the Bishop Sutton Hall. He could hear the school play rehearsal going on inside and, judging by the noise, it was a musical. He followed the path around to the left. It was wide, well lit by lamps along the side of the hall and overlooked by all of the windows along the side of the Underwood Building. Isobel would've come this way.

'Can I help you, Sir?'

'And you are?'

'Chamberlain, Sir. I'm a prefect.'

'My name's Dickson. I'm a trainee teacher here for two weeks' work experience before the end of term.'

'Do you have any identification, please, Sir?'

'A letter from the headmaster.' Dixon reached into his inside jacket pocket and handed the letter to the boy. He read it and handed it back.

'Thank you, Sir. I'm sorry . . .'

'Don't be,' replied Dixon, 'and well done.'

At the far end of the hall was a door with a sign on it. 'Sixth Form Bar.' Dixon shook his head. At that time of night on a Saturday there would have been students everywhere, surely? He could see Gardenhurst a short distance away and the car park off to the left, down a slope. She would have been in plain view of any number of different people if she had come this way just after 10 p.m. on a Saturday night. Dixon felt sure that she would have done, which left only one alternative. She was intercepted before she got here.

He walked back to the end of the corridor and stood outside the toilets, in between the two exit doors. It was possible that Isobel had been snatched by an assailant waiting in the darkness behind the smaller door. Possible but unlikely. The noise would have alerted anyone in the toilets to her abduction, and certainly if she had screamed. She would also have been taken to a waiting car and, in all probability, have simply disappeared. Like Fran.

The exercise had confirmed what Dixon already knew. Isobel had been taken by someone familiar to her and who presented no obvious threat. Someone she trusted. There would have been no sound, no scream, and it would explain the red wine in her system.

Dixon looked back down the corridor towards the entrance hall. There were several doors on either side, one leading to the headmaster's house, and two flights of stairs, one leading up to Reynell House and the other to Neales. Dixon checked the time. It was almost 11 p.m. and no time to be creeping about a boarding school, unless he wanted to get himself arrested.

Dixon sat down on the end of his bed and rang Jane.

'You still awake?'

'I am now,' replied Jane. 'What's it like?'

'Pretty much as I expected, really. I've had a look at the route she'd have taken back to Gardenhurst. It's well lit and would've been buzzing with students at that time on a Saturday night so it's unlikely she was snatched. I reckon she went with somebody she knew.'

'One of the teachers?'

'Don't know yet. I've only met the headmaster and the chaplain so far. And one prefect who wanted to know who I was. He asked me for ID and I nearly gave him my warrant card.'

'That would've been a great start.'

'I remembered in the nick of time.'

'Did he fall for it?'

'What?'

'The trainee teacher bit.'

'Seemed to.'

'He'll go far.'

'I've got a letter from the headmaster. My get out of jail free card.'

'I've got to be in Taunton at 8 a.m. so I may see you tomorrow.'

'Watch out for Chard. Wouldn't trust him as far as I could throw him. The DI seems all right, though. Baldwin's her name.'

'I know her. We worked together on a fraud case a couple of years ago.'

'Good.'

'I'll get a copy of the driving instructor's statement and see about the other stuff.'

'OK. I'll catch up with you over the weekend, if I get the chance,' said Dixon.

'And be careful,' replied Jane. 'Remember . . .'

'I know.'

Dixon rang off. He picked up the wooden wedge propping open the living room door and pushed it under the front door from the inside. Then he dropped the catch on the Yale lock. The previous night spent travelling home from Cyprus, despite seeming like a lifetime ago, was beginning to catch up with him so he lay back on the bed, set the alarm on his iPhone for 7.30 a.m. and was asleep before its backlight went out.

# Chapter Four

Dixon found a box of stale cornflakes in the cupboard and used the last of the milk in the jug. Skipping breakfast hadn't been an option since he had been told that he was diabetic. He had thought about going down to the dining room but decided it would be best to avoid answering awkward questions, if he could. After all, it was his job to ask them and he didn't want to risk his cover before he had to.

He managed to negotiate the crowd of pupils waiting on the landing for the physics lab to be unlocked and dropped down to the masters' common room for 9 a.m., as instructed. A small crowd had gathered around the notice board to look at the various team sheets for the day's rugby matches but it soon dispersed when a loud bell rang. He knocked on the door and went in.

'Are you Dickson?'

'Yes.'

'For heaven's sake, don't knock. Come in. I'm Phillips. Robin Phillips.' He was tall and wore a blazer, which seemed to be the acceptable alternative to tweed, a white shirt and a tie Dixon didn't recognise.

'You're looking at my tie?'

'Yes.'

'Royal Artillery.'

Dixon nodded.

'Work experience, is it?'

'Yes.'

'Wish I'd had the chance when I was training.'

'Really?'

'Yes. I'd never have become a bloody teacher if I'd known what it was like.' Phillips laughed loudly, revealing yellow teeth. 'Let me finish this, then I'll show you around.' He was pushing a small amount of tobacco into a pipe, which explained the teeth. Dixon looked around the room. All but two of the chairs were empty, classes for the day having started.

'How rude of me. Let me introduce you,' said Phillips. 'That's Keith Foster, maths, and that's Janet Parkin, art and drama.'

Neither stirred from their chairs but they did at least acknowledge Dixon's presence.

'C'mon, let's leave these miserable buggers to it. We'll start outside seeing as it's not raining.'

Dixon followed Phillips out of the masters' common room.

'How long've we got?'

'I've got a class with the headmaster at 10 a.m.'

'Lucky you,' replied Phillips. 'This way.'

They went out of the door at the end of the corridor and down a flight of stone steps. Once outside, Phillips paused to light his pipe.

'That's Geldard over there,' said Phillips, pointing to a detached building off to the left. 'Day pupils only.'

Dixon nodded.

'And that's the old gym. Rather surplus to requirements now we've got the sports hall. Plan is to knock it down and replace it with new classrooms. The gym and those prefabs you can see. They're getting a bit tired now. The rifle range is down that alleyway too.'

Dixon looked across at two blocks of single storey prefabricated buildings that had clearly seen better days. The gap between them was presumably the alleyway that Phillips had been referring to.

'Rifle range?'

'Small bore target stuff. We do quite well in the competitions. Miss Weatherly's our crack shot.'

'What are the main disciplinary issues you have, then?' asked Dixon.

'You mean apart from murder?'

'Yes.'

'Sorry. My little joke. Bloody mess it is, really. And the fucking police are useless. Haven't got a bloody thing to go on, by all accounts.'

'It's early days.'

'If you say so,' said Phillips, sucking hard on his pipe, which he was struggling to light in the wind.

'You were going to tell me about the other . . .'

'Yes, sorry. We've got the usual, really. Nothing too dramatic. A bit of pot smoking. Sometimes something harder gets in. We know who it is but can never catch the little shits. What irks is that it's getting to the younger pupils these days and that's the worry. There's some home brewing going on and occasionally a bit of petty pilfering.'

Nothing much had changed since Dixon's school days if that were the case. Except the casual attitude to hard drugs, perhaps.

'Do you try and catch them?'

'Yes.'

'What about smoking?'

'Sixth formers are allowed to but few do. Catching the younger ones at it is good sport.'

Dixon could see lessons going on in the classrooms to his right.

'Classics,' said Phillips. 'That's Small in there. Latin. And in the next one is Griffiths. Ancient history. He's filling in for Haskill, who's buggered off to the Far East on holiday.'

'A supply teacher?' asked Dixon.

'Yes.'

Dixon followed Phillips around the side of the chapel. He could see lessons going on in the prefabs across the lawn.

'French and German in there. Mr Clarke and Miss Heath.' Phillips stopped. 'We're round the back of the dining room now. Those are the kitchens.'

Dixon looked across to see a van unloading boxes of frozen food. Several porters wearing blue overalls were standing in a small group, all smoking.

'Where does that alleyway go?' asked Dixon, pointing to the back of the dining room.

'It leads to the Memorial Quadrangle. Always a good spot for catching smokers. We'll have a go later.'

They continued along a path until it met a service road at the back of the school. Dixon recognised the cricket pavilion and the squash courts off to the left. The old cricket nets had gone and been replaced with new buildings all along the boundary of the cricket pitch.

'Two new houses over there. Havens and Hardwicke,' said Phillips.

They turned right along the road and Dixon could see that they were now walking towards the Underwood Building, which was directly in front of them. He looked down across the playing fields and could just about make out an area cordoned off with police tape on the far hedge line. That was where Isobel Swan had been found.

Phillips stopped to light his pipe again.

'That's the Underwood Building there. Biology labs at the far end. History above them. Bishop Knox and Markham are in there too. The sports hall's behind it.'

'What do you teach?' asked Dixon.

'Chemistry.'

'How long've you been here?'

'Twenty years. Ever since I came out of the army. And that's the Bishop Sutton Hall,' continued Phillips, 'school plays, assemblies, that sort of thing.'

Phillips stared into the bowl of his pipe.

'Bloody thing's gone out again. C'mon, let's go and get a cup of tea.'

'Did you know her well?' asked Dixon, once they were back in the staff room.

'Who?'

'The girl who was murdered?'

'I taught her chemistry,' replied Phillips, handing Dixon a mug of tea. 'She was very bright.'

'What happened?'

'I got the call before breakfast on the Sunday. She'd been found in the ditch at the bottom of the playing fields and the police were on their way. We put the school on total lockdown. Everyone confined to barracks on pain of . . . well, you know what I mean.'

'I do.'

'They were here for two days taking statements from everyone and anyone who knew her. Looking at the CCTV too. We've got some but not much and probably not as much as we should. No doubt the governors will stump up the cash for that now.'

'I wouldn't want to have been the one to tell her parents,' said Dixon.

'The police offered to do it but the head did it in the end. Admired him for that. Couldn't have been easy.'

'Are they local?'

'Yes. Yeovil, I think. He's a bus driver.'

'How . . .'

'She was here on a scholarship, if that's what you're wondering. Bright girl. She'd have gone far.'

*So would Fran.*

Dixon took a swig of tea. Just as he did so the door flew open and three teachers rushed into the common room. They each threw a pile of books onto a chair and then headed for the kettle at the back of the room.

'That's McCulloch. Scottish but he teaches English lit. The others are Whitmore and Rowena Weatherly, both history.'

Dixon nodded.

'You'll never remember everyone's name so I wouldn't even bother to try,' said Phillips.

'Who's this, then?' asked McCulloch. He was small with a closely cropped grey beard and smelt strongly of cigarettes, which Dixon noticed even over Phillips' stale pipe tobacco.

'Dickson,' replied Phillips. 'Two weeks' work experience.'

'Bugger me. I wish I'd had the chance. I'd never have . . .'

'I've already used that line, William,' said Phillips.

'Git.'

Phillips smiled. 'You'd have thought a teacher of English literature would have a better vocabulary, wouldn't you?'

'Knob.'

'Ignore him, he's like this with everyone.'

Dixon was ignoring him. He was watching Rowena Weatherly. She was sitting on a window seat on the other side of the room sipping from a mug of coffee. He knew from the statements that she was in charge of girls' hockey and that Isobel played in the team. So did Emily Setter and Susannah Bower.

'You'd better go,' said Phillips. 'Don't want to keep His Lordship waiting.'

'No, thanks,' replied Dixon, getting up from his chair.

'Back here oneish and we'll go off and get some lunch.'

Dixon stopped outside the masters' common room and looked again at the rugby team sheets. He still needed to track down Ben Masterson, Isobel's boyfriend, or perhaps he wasn't? Chard hadn't known and neither Emily nor Susannah had confirmed it in their statements. Dixon spotted Ben's name on the 2nd XV sheet, playing away at St Dunstan's. Next he checked the girls' hockey notices to find that both Emily and Susannah were playing in a home match against Roedean. He frowned. It was going to be a long day catching smokers with Robin Phillips.

Dixon was no stranger to difficult and stressful situations. He had found himself in a few in his time and had even gone undercover before, although he hadn't mentioned it. It had been several years ago when he was in the Met, but there seemed a world of difference between a trainee teacher in a murder investigation and a shop assistant in a newsagent trying to catch shoplifters. It was hardly relevant experience. But now he faced, more than anything else, the part of his current situation that he dreaded the most. Even more than coming face to face with Fran's killer.

He had been introduced to the class by the headmaster and was sitting by the window trying to look as though he knew what Hatton was talking about. He had not let on that he was a qualified solicitor, not least because it had been years ago and he had neither studied nor practised law since, except perhaps criminal law. Today, however, the class were learning about the law of tort.

Dixon could remember that it had something to do with negligence and he could even recall a case involving a snail in a bottle.

But that was the extent of his knowledge. Jane would wet herself laughing if she knew.

He looked at the pupils, most of whom appeared to be looking out of the window. Dixon counted nineteen, none of them studying law A Level, but the headmaster had decreed that all students in the sixth form would have one law class each week, presumably to broaden their general knowledge. Dixon thought it might be useful if they ever appeared on *Who Wants to Be a Millionaire?* but that was about it. The next class was for the A Level students and there were only eight of them.

'So, which part of the law of tort do we think is most commonly encountered in daily life?'

Dixon knew the answer to that one but managed to resist the urge to put his hand up.

'Anyone?'

A hand went up at the back of the class.

'Yes, Jenkins.'

Dixon looked at the boy with his hand up. He had dark curly hair and was tall, judging by his height when sitting. Probably played in the second row, he thought, recognising the boy's name from the 1st XV team sheet.

'Accident compo, Sir,' he said, in a strong Welsh accent.

'That's right, Darren.'

'Where there's blame, there's a claim, Sir.'

'Yes, I think we've got the idea, Darren, thank you,' said the headmaster. 'Accident compensation. So, what three elements do we have to prove to succeed in a claim for damages?'

Dixon knew this one too. It was all coming flooding back.

'Masterson, what about you?'

Dixon watched the pupils at the front of the class turn as one and look at the boy sitting next to Jenkins. He had ginger hair and the top button of his shirt was undone. He looked up, slowly.

'I . . .'

'You weren't listening were you, Ben?'

'No, Sir. Sorry, Sir.'

'All right, don't worry about it. We were talking about negligence and what you have to prove to succeed in a claim for damages,' said the headmaster. 'Mr Dickson, what about you? You're a solicitor, I'm told.'

*Oh, shit.*

'Liability, causation and quantum,' he replied, dredging up the knowledge just in time. 'That it was someone else's fault, their negligence caused the injury and then the extent of the injury itself so the damages can be quantified.'

'Perfect.'

Dixon nodded. He knew that he had just been tested. And that he had passed. He looked across at Ben Masterson, sitting at the back with his head bowed, once again. He was still hurting, mourning even, which told Dixon that he and Isobel had been more than just friends, at least as far as Ben was concerned. Maybe his feelings for Isobel had not been reciprocated? Dixon had seen the effect of unrequited love before and knew it could be toxic. He would need to have a talk with Ben but, in the meantime, there was one thing of which he could be sure. Ben Masterson would have been a babe in arms when Fran disappeared.

Dixon hadn't appreciated that Phillips meant a liquid lunch but the Winchester Arms at Trull was clearly a popular spot with the teachers at Brunel. Dixon could see McCulloch, Small and the supply teacher, Griffiths, at the bar.

'A few beers and a toastie'll set us up for the afternoon,' said Phillips, 'unless you'd rather watch the rugby.'

'No, I'm fine. Whatever you'd usually be doing and I'll tag along.'

'How did you get on in class?'

'I haven't had so much fun since I had my wisdom teeth out,' replied Dixon.

Phillips roared with laughter.

'No, it wasn't too bad,' continued Dixon. 'They were quite subdued, really. Hardly surprising, I suppose.'

'The whole school is.'

'One boy seemed worse than the rest. Ben Masterson, I think his name is.'

'Isobel's boyfriend. Poor lad. Seems a bit lost to me.'

'He will be.' *Take it from me, he will be.*

'Another?'

'It must be my round, surely?' replied Dixon.

'Good God, no. We can't have a student teacher putting his hand in his pocket for the beers. Wouldn't hear of it.'

Dixon watched Phillips go to the bar and could see him telling Small and Griffiths who he was. The inevitable glance across from them both gave it away. They saw him watching and raised their glasses. Dixon smiled and nodded in acknowledgement. He looked for any glimmer of recognition on their faces and saw none. Nor did he recognise them.

He thought about everyone he had met so far. Phillips had been right. He couldn't put names to all of the faces, despite his best efforts. More importantly, perhaps, he recognised none of them from St Dunstan's, but then it had been a long time ago. If Isobel's killer had also killed Fran seventeen years ago then he or she might well have changed their appearance over the years.

He hadn't yet got a look at the kitchen staff and porters either. He'd need to engineer a tour of the kitchens this afternoon, and perhaps eat in the dining room at some point too. But would he recognise a kitchen porter anyway after all this time? Some of them, possibly, but it would not be easy.

He needed the names of anyone arriving at Brunel in the last seventeen years who had previously worked at St Dunstan's. That would, at least, narrow it down. Or it should.

'Here you go,' said Phillips, placing a pint of bitter on the table in front of Dixon.

'Thank you.'

'Why teaching, then?' asked Phillips.

Dixon had prepared for this one. 'I qualified as a solicitor then realised it was the academic study of the law that fascinated me rather than the practice of it. So, here I am. I plan on teaching history too . . .'

'What period?'

'Early twentieth century. The Great War is my specialist subject.'

'Fascinating stuff,' replied Phillips. 'Any connection?'

'My great grandfather served in the Somerset Light Infantry.'

'Never got the hang of history. Still, you're either scientific or arty farty, aren't you?'

'I suppose so.'

Their toasted sandwiches arrived but a mouthful of food did not stop Phillips continuing the conversation.

'What did you study at A Level, then?'

'English, history and biology.'

'An odd combination . . .'

'They seemed the easiest. The ones I was most likely to pass.'

'And did you?'

'Just.'

'University?'

'Staffordshire.'

'Why there?'

'Chosen mainly for its proximity to the Peak District, I think. I spent most of my time rock climbing and just enough studying.'

'A climber? You should come on Easter Camp in the Lakes.'

Dixon smiled. He had done that very thing with St Dunstan's, although it had been Snowdonia that year.

'I'd love to.'

'C'mon, let's get back. We can finish that guided tour and perhaps catch some of the rugby. I'll just nip to the . . . er . . .'

Dixon took the opportunity to send Jane a text message.

*Meet me at the Greyhound Staple Fitzpaine at 6 x*

It was just before 2.30 p.m. when Phillips turned right off West Road into the main entrance of the school. Dixon could see three coaches from St Dunstan's College parked in a line on the other side of the car park, adjacent to the library at the front of the main school building. The visiting teams had arrived and so had some visiting schoolteachers who might recognise him, thought Dixon. Unlikely out of context, of course, but he'd need to be careful all the same.

Phillips followed the drive around to the right rather than forking left into the main car park and parked in the smaller car park in front of Gardenhurst, where the suspicious car had been left for several days, according to the witness statements. No one had been able to identify the make or model. Dixon thought it an odd place to hide a car, if indeed it had been hidden. Although there was no CCTV coverage, the car park was in full view of just about everyone in the school. Either it was a red herring or the killer would have no further use for it after the murder. Dixon suspected the latter. No doubt it would turn up in a remote field somewhere, burnt out.

It was a cold and crisp afternoon. Dixon could see spectators gathering along the touch lines of several rugby pitches down on the playing fields. The corner flags were fluttering in the gentle breeze and red and black padding had been put in place around the base of the posts. Both AstroTurf hockey pitches were also already in use, the matches having started earlier to allow for another game on the same pitch before dark.

Dixon looked up at Gardenhurst. It was a modern building, with stone cladding and large windows. A service road ran along the front and around to the far side. Several students were milling around.

'They'll be off into town in a few minutes, that lot,' said Phillips. 'Two till five on a Saturday, they're allowed out.'

Dixon nodded. He watched a small group of three girls appear through a gate in the red brick wall that he had thought marked the boundary of the school.

'What's through there?'

'The old convent,' replied Phillips. 'We bought it in the seventies and it houses Woodward and Breward. About two hundred pupils in all. C'mon, I'll show you round.'

Dixon followed Phillips through the gate.

'That road goes round to the front and there's an entrance off West Road too.'

A large oak door led into an entrance hall. Off to the left was an old cloister with a tiled floor and stained glass windows. It was being used as a bike store now. Racks had been fitted along the inner wall and Dixon counted at least forty bicycles before he gave up trying.

'Seems a shame to use it as a bike rack, doesn't it?' asked Phillips.

'Progress,' replied Dixon.

'C'mon, let me show you the old chapel.'

Dixon listened to the click of their heels on the tiled floor as they walked along behind the bicycles. Phillips had metal caps on his heels that made a distinctive sound. Anyone up to no good would hear him coming and have plenty of time to make good their escape. Dixon suspected that was the idea. At the end of the cloisters a short flight of stairs led up to a doorway. The corridor continued around to the right.

'That takes you round to the accommodation block,' said Phillips. 'This is the bit I wanted to show you.'

He took a large bundle of keys out his pocket, selected one and then opened the door.

'The old convent chapel. We use it as a storeroom now, as you can see.'

Dixon ignored the junk and looked instead at the building itself. It was small, by comparison with the school chapel, and had a high vaulted ceiling with ornate carved woodwork, stained glass windows and a large galleried landing at the far end. There was a door at the back of the gallery but no steps leading up to it.

'Sad, isn't it?' asked Phillips.

Dixon treated it as a rhetorical question. He looked around at the piles of old mattresses, desks and chairs, folding tables and wardrobes. It was possible to walk in only a few paces. It would then be necessary to climb over old furniture to make any further progress, such was the extent of the clutter.

'We know the little buggers are getting in here somehow,' said Phillips, 'we just don't know how.'

'Is it used much?'

'Occasionally.'

'The easy answer is to wait until someone comes in, sneak in and hide, then when they go just creep out and leave the door on the latch. It's only got a Yale lock on it, hasn't it?'

'That's right. You crafty devil.'

'Still young enough to think like a schoolboy,' said Dixon.

He looked at the entrance. It was a timber framed internal lobby with the door set back to allow the corridor outside to continue around to the right and up to the accommodation area. Dixon thought it a temporary measure, possibly put in when the building had been converted for use by the school in the seventies. He spotted two glass windows in the ceiling outside and above the door.

'There'll be another way by the looks of things.'

'What?'

'Come out for a minute and lock the door,' said Dixon.

'Now what?'

Dixon looked up. The panes of glass above him were just out of reach so he walked down the stairs, round the corner and reappeared a few seconds later carrying a bicycle.

'Hold this, will you?'

Phillips held the handlebars while Dixon stood on the pedals. He reached up and pushed the glass. It moved.

'What the f . . . ?' said Phillips, his voice tailing off.

Dixon pushed the pane up with both hands. It was thick safety glass, heavy and with wire mesh set into it. He lifted it clear and pushed it to one side. Then he stood up on the crossbar of the bicycle with his hands either side of the opening and jumped up. It took only a few seconds then to replace the glass, drop down on the inside and open the door.

'You missed your vocation,' said Phillips.

'Possibly.'

'Certainly. You should've been a policeman.'

Dixon smiled. 'Good pension, I suppose, but that's about it.'

He looked at Phillips for any sign of recognition but there was none.

'Let's see what we can find, then,' said Phillips, 'while we're here. I'll get maintenance to nail down that glass on Monday and put another lock on the door.'

'What about up there?' asked Dixon, pointing to the gallery at the far end of the disused chapel.

'No way up. The only access is through that door, which I know is locked.'

Against the far wall beneath the gallery was a chest of drawers next to a wardrobe. On top of the chest of drawers, upside down, was a wooden chair.

'Really?'

Dixon stepped up onto a pile of mattresses and then onto another before arriving at a line of tables that he was able to use as stepping stones across to the chest of drawers. He stepped up onto the wardrobe, taking the wooden chair with him. He then stood on the chair and was able to reach the balustrade. A short step up and across and he was on the gallery. Those days spent crossing glaciers in the Alps hadn't been wasted after all.

Dixon was not impressed by what he saw. It reminded him of certain alleyways he'd walked down, never alone, whilst in the Met. He counted ten syringes, a pile of discarded silver foil and at least three blackened dessert spoons. Cigarette butts and empty bottles of vodka completed the picture.

*Try not to act like a policeman.*

'Can you get up here?'

'Yes, I think so. I'll give it a go.'

Phillips was clearly not as agile as he had once been but, after a good deal of huffing and puffing, he made it as far as the wooden chair. He lost his nerve at the step across to the gallery but got a clear view of the scene through the balustrade.

'Oh, fuck.'

'Quite,' said Dixon.

'The headmaster'll do his nut.'

'Do you know who it is?'

'I've got a pretty good idea.'

'A webcam, then. Set up over there . . .'

'What about the police? Shouldn't we tell them?' asked Phillips.

'Was Isobel . . . er . . .'

'Swan.'

'That's it. Was she involved in it?'

'God, no. Squeaky clean, that one.'

'Needn't trouble the police, then. It's hardly relevant. An internal matter for the school.'

'Perfect,' said Phillips. 'I'll get our computer studies boffin to sort out the webcam next week.'

Dixon was last out of the old chapel and closed the door behind him.

'Let's go and watch the rugger,' said Phillips.

Dixon scanned the touchlines of the four rugby pitches he could see for anyone from St Dunstan's who might recognise him, and saw only one teacher he'd need to steer clear of watching a team of younger boys, probably the junior colts. He'd also need to give the AstroTurf hockey pitches a wide berth. His old housemaster was watching one game and his biology teacher, Miss Macpherson, was watching the other.

'Let's give the thirds a bit of support,' said Phillips. 'Everybody and their dog watches the firsts.'

'OK.'

Dixon looked across the car park in front of Gardenhurst to the far corner where the mysterious small car had been parked. The four minibuses that were usually parked there had gone, taking students to the away matches at St Dunstan's and Roedean, no doubt.

According to the various witness statements, the car had been reversed into the corner space, adjacent to the wall, with its boot facing the playing fields. The wall that ran along the far side of the car park dropped away in the corner down the slope and then along the outer perimeter of the sports field. Just inside the wall was a line of mature and very large leylandii that would have provided more than enough cover for the killer to disappear into had he been disturbed. The leylandii ended at a hedge that then continued the outer boundary at right angles. According to the file the whole area, including the gap between the wall and the trees, had been the subject of a fingertip search, but nothing had been found except cigarette butts and empty bottles. Dixon would have a look for himself later.

In the meantime, he followed Phillips around the back of the sports hall and down through a line of trees to the 3rd XV rugby pitch. A small crowd was assembled along the near touchline at the halfway line. Phillips looked at his watch. It was just after 3.30 p.m.

'Second half must be under way.'

He spoke to a boy standing at the end of the crowd.

'What's the score, Thompson?'

'15–9, Sir.'

'Who to?'

'Them.'

'What about over there?' he asked, nodding in the direction of the 1st XV pitch.

'We're winning, 21–0,' came the reply.

'That's better,' said Phillips. 'Want to watch that game instead?'

'Sounds like this lot need our support more,' replied Dixon.

'You'll go far,' replied Phillips, smiling and lighting his pipe at the same time.

'Not watching the firsts, Robin?' The voice came from behind them.

'Ah, Rowena, how did your girls get on?' asked Phillips, turning around.

'We won, 3–0.'

'Well done.' Phillips pointed at Dixon with his pipe. 'This is our trainee teacher. You got the email?'

'I did,' replied Rowena.

'Nick, this is the Miss Weatherly I was telling you about.'

They shook hands.

'All good, I hope,' said Rowena.

'Yes,' replied Dixon.

Rowena Weatherly was tall and slim with short hair, dyed jet black. She looked every inch the hockey coach in a red and black Brunel tracksuit with a Grays hockey stick bag slung over her shoulder.

'How long are you here for?' she asked.

'Till the end of term.'

'Having fun?'

'He's sitting in on His Lordship's law classes,' said Phillips, rolling his eyes.

'Oh. Still, it could be worse. It could be chemistry . . .'

'Yes, thank you, Rowena.'

'It's not that bad, really,' said Dixon.

'Well, a change is as good as a rest. I must dash. Got another match starting in ten minutes.'

Dixon turned back to the rugby match. He felt odd cheering for a team he had always thought of as the opposition but did his best to sound enthusiastic, even remembering to limit his reaction to a St Dunstan's try under the posts to polite applause. At one point he thought he had been spotted by his old housemaster, who had come across from the hockey pitches and was walking along the far touchline, but he turned away just in time and his housemaster continued over to the 1st XV pitch.

The ditch where Isobel had been found was still cordoned off with blue tape and attracted a good deal of attention from students, teachers and parents walking to and from the hockey pitches in the far field. It seemed that no one was capable of crossing the footbridge over the ditch without stopping to look in.

The game ended in a resounding victory for St Dunstan's, 33–15. Dixon watched the Brunel players shake hands with their opposite numbers and then trudge back to the changing rooms in the sports hall.

'Tea?' asked Phillips.

'Yes, please,' replied Dixon

They walked back up through the treeline and then along a path that led to the dining room. It was starting to get dark now and Dixon could see lights on in various rooms in the main school and in the Underwood Building.

'That's the sanatorium up there,' said Phillips, pointing to a door off to the right, 'and behind that is where the kitchen staff live. Those who live in, anyway.'

'Right,' said Dixon.

Once through the double doors, a short passageway led to the main corridor. Dixon turned left and headed towards the masters' common room.

'No, this way, old chap,' said Phillips, 'tea's in the dining room.'

Dixon smiled. This was his chance to get a look at the kitchen staff, or at least some of them. At best, he could remember perhaps three or four from St Dunstan's, so the chances were likely to be very slim that he would recognise any now, and that was assuming that the ones he could remember had moved to Brunel. The more he thought about it, the more it seemed to be a pointless exercise. If progress was to be made in this section of the school then he would need the names of any kitchen staff working at Brunel who had previously been at St Dunstan's. He checked his watch. It was just after 4.30 p.m. Plenty of time for tea, then he would make his excuses and get over to the Greyhound to meet Jane.

Phillips handed Dixon a tray as they approached the front of the queue.

'Not for me, thanks.'

'What, no cake?'

'Diabetic. Just a mug of tea for me.'

'You poor sod.'

Phillips helped himself to some bread and jam, two jam tarts and a piece of fruit cake. 'I'll have yours then.'

'You carry on,' replied Dixon.

He recognised none of the kitchen porters on duty behind the counter but there were only three, one serving the tea and the others topping up the supply of bread and cakes.

At the end of the counter, two steps up led into the dining room. It was larger than St Dunstan's with long tables, bench seating and walls covered with small shields, each listing in gold lettering the names of the first team members for the relevant year. Green for cricket, red for hockey and black for rugby. Dixon found the rugby shield for the team he had played against seventeen years ago. He recognised none of the names now but could still remember the score.

At the far end of the dining room, near the exit, was a counter where trays were collected by a kitchen porter, any rubbish tipped into large bins and the dirty crockery stacked for washing. Dixon stared at the man standing behind the counter. He was immediately familiar to him; older, of course, and with grey hair and moustache rather than black, but he definitely recognised him. It had been a standing joke at St Dunstan's: two kitchen porters who always worked together called Derek and Clive. Dixon did not know whether this was Derek or Clive. In fact he could not recall ever having known who was who, but he did remember that the man standing at the counter in the Brunel dining room had been a big Beatles fan. He used to say he had even seen them live in the Cavern Club and everyone had believed him.

Dixon watched Phillips eating his cake. At the same time, he was watching the kitchen porter on the far side of the dining room. There was no chance that Dixon would be recognised, he was sure of that, but he now had positive identification of at least one person who had been at St Dunstan's when Fran disappeared and at Brunel when Isobel had been murdered. He wondered how many more there might be. Taunton was a small place, after all.

As soon as Phillips finished his cake, Dixon picked up the tray.

'I'll take that.'

'Oh, thanks.'

He joined the back of the small queue and waited. When he got closer to the counter, he began whistling 'Norwegian Wood', a suitably obscure song that would only be recognised by a real Beatles fan. He waited for a reaction and the man did not disappoint, turning sharply to look at Dixon.

'You a Beatles fan?'

'Is there anyone else?' replied Dixon.

'John or Paul?'

'John.'

The man smiled. 'Good taste.'

'Thanks.'

'We've had this conversation before.'

'Have we?' replied Dixon.

'I never forget a face.'

*Fuck it.*

Dixon handed the man his tray and walked out of the dining room. Phillips was just getting up, giving him a few seconds. He tapped the student in front of him on the shoulder.

'What's that man's name?'

'Derek.'

'Thanks.'

Dixon stepped out of the line filing out of the dining room and waited for Phillips to catch him up.

'Right, that's me off duty. I'm going home,' said Phillips. 'What are you up to this evening?'

'I said I'd meet my girlfriend for a bite to eat in town.'

'Fine. See you in the morning for chapel patrol?'

'What time?'

'Nine o'clock.'

'See you then.'

# Chapter Five

Jane arrived at the Greyhound Inn at Staple Fitzpaine to find Dixon's Land Rover already in the car park behind the pub. She parked next to it and ran across the gravel car park to the back door, sheltering under her handbag. The last few red leaves still clinging to a large Virginia creeper were visible in the light streaming from the windows. The rest were on the ground or being blown around by the wind.

Once inside the door she wiped the raindrops from her nose and looked in the mirror on the wall. She was grateful that her mascara was waterproof. Then she spotted Dixon at the bar, tiptoed over and stood next to him. He was sitting on a bar stool, staring into his beer and did not notice her arrive. She nudged his arm and he looked up. There were tears in his eyes.

'You all right?'

'Miles away,' said Dixon, shaking his head.

He put his arm around Jane's waist, pulled her towards him and kissed her.

'We do rooms,' said the barman. The look on Dixon's face stopped him in his tracks. 'Sorry.'

'Gin and tonic, please,' said Dixon.

'Yes, Sir.'

'How's it been?' asked Jane.

'Teaching is definitely out.'

Dixon paid for Jane's drink and they sat down in the far corner of an otherwise deserted lounge bar.

'Apart from two law lessons that I sat in on, God help me, I've spent the day with Phillips, the school gamekeeper. Please tell me he's not on your list.'

Jane shook her head.

'He's got an oddly relaxed attitude to drug taking at the school but, apart from that, he's . . .'

'Drug taking?'

'I found the drug den but my guess is he knew it was there all along and just never wanted to look.'

'Why not?'

'School's reputation, I expect.'

'Well, that's buggered now anyway, isn't it?'

Dixon nodded. 'How many on your list?' he asked.

'Four.'

'I've spotted one. Derek somebody. A kitchen porter.'

'Derek Phelps. Left St Dunstan's ten years ago and then popped up at Brunel a year or so later.'

'He said he knew me.'

'Really?'

'Yeah, it's nothing to worry about. He'd have no idea from where.'

'Are you sure?' asked Jane.

'Yes. Does he live in?'

Jane took a plastic wallet out of her handbag and passed it to Dixon.

'Copies?'

Jane nodded.

Dixon slid the papers out of the wallet and then flicked through them until he found the ones he was looking for. Jane watched his eyes scanning the pages.

'He does,' said Dixon, nodding. He looked up. 'At St Dunstan's he used to work with a man called Clive . . .'

'Derek and Clive?'

'I know. Find out what became of him, will you?'

'What was his surname?'

'No idea.'

Jane took her notebook out of her handbag and began making notes.

'Who else've we got?' asked Dixon, turning back to the bundle of papers. 'Marcus Haskill. I don't remember him.' Dixon shook his head.

'Isn't he the one on sabbatical?' asked Jane.

'Yes, I'm using his bloody rooms, for heaven's sake.'

'He only taught at St Dunstan's for your last year.'

'I see that. And ancient history wasn't exactly on my radar.'

'Do you want me to check him out?'

'Yes. See if he's really gone to the Far East,' replied Dixon. He was speed reading Haskill's employment history. 'Ex-army. Did the old SSLC, saw active service in the Falklands and then went into teaching.'

'What's an SSLC?' asked Jane.

'Short Service Limited Commission. Three to five years then you're out. Don't think it exists any more. That's odd . . .'

'What is?'

'You'd expect him to be involved in the Cadets, wouldn't you? With his background . . .'

'I'll find out if there's a reason why not.'

Dixon was reading the next set of papers.

'Rowena Weatherly?'

'She was a contemporary of yours,' said Jane.

'But I don't . . .' Dixon closed his eyes. 'Rowena Abbot, of course. She was in the year below us. Played hockey with Fran. Must've got married, I suppose. I was only introduced to her this afternoon, for heaven's sake.'

'Did she recognise you?'

'"A change is as good as a rest", my . . .'

'Eh?'

'Yes, she recognised me. But I sure as hell didn't recognise her.'

'Why not?'

'She's dyed her hair, for a start. And we only overlapped for a year, I suppose.' Dixon shook his head. 'I wonder why she didn't say anything?'

He turned to the last set of copy documents. Jane waited for the inevitable expletives to follow.

'What the f . . . ?' Dixon looked at Jane and then back to the papers in front of him. 'The headmaster?'

'Seems so.'

'I don't remember him being there . . .'

'It was just the one term. He was doing the Oxbridge entrance exams. It would've been your first term too. And he'd been gone for over a year by the time Fran disappeared.'

'He never let on he'd been to St Dunstan's.'

'It means he must know about Fran, surely?' asked Jane.

'Not necessarily, if he'd left by then.'

'I suppose so. Wouldn't he have been there at the same time as her, though?'

'She'd have been a couple of years below him,' replied Dixon.

'If you assume he knows, then there can be only two reasons why he's said nothing. One, he doesn't want the added scandal or, two, he's in it up to his neck,' said Jane.

'Get his school records, will you. I want to know what sort of pupil he was.'

'Why?'

'There are two types. Those who leave and never look back and those who wear the old school tie every chance they get. If he was one of the never look back lot then it's possible he doesn't know about Fran.'

'Which were you?'

'Never looked back. Not once.'

Dixon glanced around the bar. It was filling up, so they ordered some food before the kitchen became too busy.

'Did you get a pay as you go SIM card?'

'Yes,' replied Jane.

They exchanged numbers and agreed a code. Any reference to Monty in a text message would trigger a switch to the new numbers.

'What about alibis?'

'They've all been checked. The headmaster was with his wife, Derek Phelps was in the Dolphin. The barman remembers him, or rather the barman would remember if he hadn't been there because he always is. Haskill's abroad, but I'll check that, and Rowena Weatherly was home alone. Well, in her rooms in Gardenhurst.'

'And the driving instructor?'

'Arnold Davies. He was at Bible study earlier in the evening then at home with his wife.'

'Have you come across anything on a supply teacher called Griffiths?' asked Dixon.

'No.'

'Chard is a useless tosser. Well, there is one. Filling in for Haskill. Better get his records.'

'Will do,' replied Jane, scribbling in her notebook.

'It's quite possible he's been to St Dunstan's in the past and he's certainly old enough to have been teaching seventeen years ago.'

'OK.'

'What about Isobel's father? Has he been checked?'

'Not by me.'

'Do so. See if he's ever had anything to do with St Dunstan's.'

'OK.'

'And the groundsman who found Isobel. I've not seen his statement. Better check it for anything unusual.'

'Listen, I was thinking. Isobel had her ring finger cut off,' said Jane.

'She did.'

'So, perhaps the killer has an issue with marriage?'

Dixon nodded.

'Why else cut off that particular finger?'

'And keep it,' added Dixon.

'Quite.'

'Good thinking. Look for anyone who's been divorced. Let's have a look at the school governors too. Full background checks on the current lot. Look for any who were at St Dunstan's seventeen years ago.'

'All of them?'

'It'll keep you out of trouble,' said Dixon, smiling.

'And what's gonna keep you out of trouble?'

The answer to that one was 'nothing'. Dixon fully expected to get into trouble but he thought it best not to worry Jane with that now.

They left the Greyhound just before 8 p.m. A lone figure was standing under the smokers' gazebo, sheltering from the rain. Neither Dixon nor Jane noticed him step back into the shadows. Nor did they notice that he wasn't smoking.

Dixon followed Jane back towards Taunton and flashed his lights at her when she turned off towards the M5. Then he pulled into the front entrance of the convent and parked behind a line of garages.

He tried the door of the old chapel. It was still on the latch, just as he had left it. He opened the door a crack and listened. Nothing, so he crept inside, dropped the latch, holding it with both hands to ensure there was no sound, and then closed the door behind him. He stopped to put on his shoes, which he had carried along the cloisters, and then looked around. Just enough light was coming in through the stained glass windows that he could make out the gallery at the far end and the outline of the junk that had to be negotiated to get there. It took a moment for his eyes to adjust to the darkness. He fumbled for the light switches on the wall just inside the door but did not turn them on. He just needed to know where they were. Then he looked for a suitable place to hide.

Three large piles of mattresses where the altar had once been offered the perfect spot, not far from the lights and ensuring that Dixon would be between the gallery and the door. He moved two of them to form a screen of sorts, switched his phone to 'silent' mode and then lay back with his hands behind his head. He did not expect to have to wait long.

He allowed his mind to wander back to days at St Dunstan's, some of them sad, others not so. When he tried to picture Fran's face he couldn't see her. Just her outline and a blank face. It had been that way for a long time but it was not unusual, or so people said. 'Think about doing something together and it'll come to you.' He thought about their first kiss and could see her right in front of him, just as she had been all those years ago. He could see her now, giggling. He had thought it had been nerves until months later when she told him he'd overdone the Extra Strong Mints.

Then there was the time they bunked off to see U2 at Wembley Stadium. They had spent the night at her sister's flat in Teddington.

*'Are you supposed to be here?' 'We've got permission, it's fine.'* They hadn't, of course, but they got away with it. The first train out of Paddington on the Sunday morning got them back to Taunton in time for Fran's tennis match. They missed chapel but Dixon could live with that.

His mind jumped from memory to memory, scene to scene. Smiles, laughter, tears, he saw them all. Again. He remembered his housemaster, in the corridor at St Dunstan's that Sunday morning. He could see his lips moving but even now he could only hear two words, '*She's gone.*'

Back to the business in hand. He thought about Jane's marriage theory and liked it more and more. It would explain the missing ring finger. Then there was the prospect of finding Fran's body with her ring finger missing. Or of finding her ring finger and not her body.

Dixon grimaced. He took his phone out of his pocket and checked the time. It was just after 9 p.m. and he had received one text message from Jane.

*Missing you x*

He was halfway through tapping out a reply when he heard voices outside the chapel. He slipped his phone back into his inside jacket pocket and listened. The door handle moved, more voices, then someone running. Wooden chair legs on the tiled floor. More voices. Seconds later he heard the pane of glass in the ceiling above the door start to slide across the wooden frame. He waited.

Dixon sat up just enough to see over the mattresses that he had piled in front of him. A head appeared through the opening above the door. Dixon watched him look down and speak to those waiting below him. It reminded him of Steve McQueen opening up the tunnel in *The Great Escape*. Then the boy hopped up inside the chapel and looked around. Dixon lay back and listened to the boy climbing down inside the door and then opening it. A short pause and then the door was closed again. Dixon lay still and listened. He was unsure whether there were three or four of them. He heard only two voices and so concentrated on the footsteps. No more than four, certainly. More whispering and then light. He thought that they were probably using their smartphones as torches. He had meant to download that app himself.

Then the scrambling began. Furniture moving under the weight of the boys clambering across it, knocking together, creaking and clunking. They were doing their best to be quiet but it was always going to be difficult. Every now and then Dixon could hear someone 'ssshhhhh' the others and the occasional 'shut the fuck up' but that was to be expected. They reached the gallery with a final crescendo of clattering, banging and muttering. Quite how nobody had caught these idiots before was beyond Dixon.

He waited. The group was well out of earshot now up on the gallery but he could make out whispering and glass bottles clinking. Then he saw what he had been waiting for. A flame flickering.

He slid down off the mattresses and ran the few steps across to the light switches, hitting all four at once with his left hand. Three lines of large strip lights, each running the length of the chapel, came on one by one. Dixon looked up at the gallery. There was no movement and no sound, the occupants clearly hoping that they had not been seen.

'Either you come down or I'm coming up there. It's up to you,' shouted Dixon.

Silence.

'I'm going to count to three.'

One boy stood up. Dixon recognised him immediately. It was Ben Masterson, Isobel's boyfriend. He frowned. Ben had not looked the type to do drugs but then he could be forgiven for going off the rails, perhaps. Dixon had very nearly done so.

'And the others.'

Two more boys stood up. They tried to hide under hoodies, which they pulled down over their faces. Only Ben didn't bother.

'Don't just stand there, come down,' said Dixon.

He watched them step across from the gallery to the top of the wardrobe and then scramble across the assorted furniture and junk. They lined up side by side in front of Dixon in the small space just inside the door, all of them looking at the floor.

'Names.'

'Ben Masterson, Sir.'

'And you?'

'Gittens, Sir.'

'Lloyd, Sir.'

'Well, I know you, Ben. You were in the law class this morning. But you two could be anybody. Take those hoods off.'

Gittens and Lloyd threw back the hoods on their tops, revealing their faces. Dixon took out his iPhone and took photographs of them both.

'Now, empty your pockets.'

Gittens and Lloyd looked at each other and hesitated.

'Pockets. On the floor. Now.'

All three boys emptied the contents of their pockets onto the floor in front of them. Dixon watched them to ensure that each pocket was emptied and that none were left out.

'What've you left up there?'

'Nothing, Sir,' replied Gittens.

Dixon looked at the small piles of belongings on the floor. Ben Masterson's consisted of a packet of chewing gum, a small amount of change, a pocket diary, a pen and a wallet. Gittens' and Lloyd's was much the same, except for the addition of cigarettes, a Zippo lighter each, a small plastic bag containing white powder and an even smaller piece of tin foil. Dixon picked up the powder and the tin foil.

'What about the bottles?'

No reply.

'Do I look like an idiot?'

'No, Sir.'

'That's the right answer. Now piss off, the pair of you. And if I see you near this place again, you'll be in deep trouble.'

Gittens and Lloyd looked at each other and then back to Dixon.

'That's right, go. Now.'

All three boys picked up their belongings and turned to go to the door.

'Not you, Ben,' said Dixon.

He waited for Gittens and Lloyd to leave the chapel.

'What happens now?' asked Ben.

'Nothing.'

'You're not going to report us?'

'I'd like to report them. They deserve it. But I can't do that without dropping you in the shit too, can I?'

'But . . .'

'Everyone says they know exactly what you're going through, right?'

'Yes.'

'Well, they're full of shit. Only someone who's been through it knows.'

'And you've been through it?'

'I was your age when my girlfriend disappeared. They never even found a body. I fell apart just like you're doing now. Failed all my exams. Got in with the wrong crowd. But I got out of it and so will you.'

'Will I?'

'Yes, you will. But you won't if you get expelled for taking drugs with those two fuckwits.'

'I don't care.'

'I didn't either.'

'Did they find out what happened to her?' asked Ben.

'No. They never did.'

'So, she could still be out there somewhere?'

'That's crossed my mind. I know she'd have got in touch with me, though. Somehow.'

'If she could,' said Ben.

'You certainly know how to cheer someone up, don't you?'

Ben smiled.

'Tell me about Isobel,' said Dixon.

'She was beautiful. Funny. Perfect. I loved her.'

'Did she feel the same about you?'

'No. She wanted to be friends. And that was enough for me, you know. Just good friends.' Ben shook his head. 'It was better than nothing.' Tears began rolling down his cheeks.

'Who'd she hang around with?'

'Emily and Susannah, mainly. And me.'

'You'll get through this,' continued Dixon. 'Just don't do something you'll regret for the rest of your life. All right?'

'Yes.'

'One day at a time and it will get easier.'

Ben nodded.

'And you know where I am if you need to talk.'

'Yes, Sir.'

'Now, hop it.'

Ben left the chapel and closed the door behind him. Dixon waited until he had gone before picking up the foil and the bag of white powder and putting them in his pocket. Then he went back up to the gallery and collected another bag of powder and two full bottles of cheap vodka.

Dixon unwrapped the foil to reveal about an eighth of an ounce of marijuana resin. Twenty quid's worth. It would be interesting to know where they had bought it. Then he threw it into the bushes outside the chapel. Next he poured the vodka down the sink and flushed the powder down the toilet. It was another line crossed for Dixon, but it was worth it if it kept Ben Masterson out of trouble.

By 10 p.m. Dixon was standing in the main entrance to the school. At the same time exactly two weeks before, Isobel Swan had last been seen alive by Emily Setter and Susannah Bower, and he wanted a clear understanding of just how busy the school would have been at that time of night on a Saturday.

A few boys came and went from the computer room. Dixon opened the door and looked in. All but two of the seats were empty.

'Where is everybody?'

Two boys sitting in front of one computer both turned to look at Dixon.

'Don't know, Sir,' said one.

Dixon closed the door behind him. Most of the younger boys would be in bed and, thinking about it, where would he have been on a Saturday night? In town with Fran. Most of the pupils would have their own computers too, of course. Laptops and iPads. Dixon rolled his eyes. He suddenly felt old.

A group of smaller boys ran along the corridor from Dixon's left and up a flight of stairs. Late for bed, no doubt. Apart from that, it was much quieter than he had expected and certainly quieter than the night before. You could hear a pin drop, let alone a girl scream.

Dixon followed Isobel's route back to Gardenhurst again. He turned left at the end of the corridor, out through the double doors and around to the front of the Underwood Building. Most of the ground floor lights were off except for those in the corridor and there was no sound coming from the Bishop Sutton Hall opposite either. He followed the path around to the sixth form bar and peered in through the window. He could hear music and see students enjoying a drink, some sitting at a table with the headmaster. Dixon counted thirty-two in all. He checked the opening hours on the door. It closed at 10.30 p.m. on a Saturday, after which all of them would come piling out into the cold.

Dixon walked back to the main entrance and sat on the window seat in the foyer. He had underestimated just how quiet the school would be and had forgotten how quiet St Dunstan's was on a Saturday night too. There would have been plenty of opportunity for someone to intercept Isobel and, if done carefully, very little chance of being seen.

Dixon stood at the bottom of one of the flights of stairs leading up to the accommodation and typed out a text message to Jane.

*Missing you too. Need a floor plan of the main school asap x*

Then he walked along the corridor back to his rooms. He listened to the sound of his heels clicking on the tiled floor. At the bottom of the stairs opposite the library, he turned and looked back down the full length of the corridor. It occurred to him that in the last twenty minutes while he had been sitting on the window seat, not a soul had walked past. Not one.

# Chapter Six

Dixon was shaving when there was a loud bang on the door of the flat. It was just before 7 a.m. and breakfast wasn't due to start for another hour.

'Nick?'

It was Phillips. Dixon opened the door, his face still covered in shaving foam.

'Can I come in?' Phillips didn't wait for the answer and stepped forward. Dixon closed the door behind him. Phillips was sweating profusely and out of breath.

'What's up?'

'There's another body.'

'Where?'

'Behind the sports hall.'

'Who is it, do we know?'

'One of the porters.'

'Which one?'

'The headmaster didn't say.'

'How . . . ?'

'He didn't say that either.'

'Have the police been called?'

'They're on the way now. The head's ringing around putting the houses on lockdown.'

'Give me a second.'

Dixon wiped the shaving foam off his face with his towel and then put on his shirt and tie.

'Our job is to find any stragglers,' continued Phillips. 'Some may be in the pool and a few go running. I need you to sit in the dining room and send back any who turn up for breakfast. Sports hall first, though, and check the pool.'

'What about breakfast?'

'It'll be sent over to the houses.'

Dixon picked up his jacket and followed Phillips down to the sports hall. Once outside, they cut across the grass, which appeared white in the lights from the Underwood Building. The crunching sound beneath his feet told Dixon it was frost rather than a trick of the light. He could just about make out the first light of dawn on the horizon and a small group of people standing on the corner of the hall, looking along the back.

'Who's that?'

'The head porter and the catering manager, Mrs Weston,' replied Phillips.

Dixon looked across to the car park in front of Gardenhurst. Only two patrol cars were there so far but he could hear sirens in the distance. No doubt some disgruntled CID officers, including Jane, were getting the call right now.

The sports hall was empty apart from two boys playing squash who were sent back to their house by Phillips. The swimming pool was still locked and the changing rooms empty. Phillips' mobile phone rang as they walked back out into the cold morning air.

'Phillips . . . yes . . . yes, Sir. Leave it with me.'

Phillips rang off and turned to Dixon.

'We've got two missing from Markham. Their housemaster thinks they've probably gone for a run. And two scrotums from Reynell who'll be up to no good, I expect.'

'Who . . . ?'

'Gittens and Lloyd. Probably lying drunk somewhere, if they haven't frozen to death.'

'What about the old chapel?' asked Dixon.

'Good thinking. I'll try there. You head back to the dining room. Anyone turns up for breakfast, just send them back where they came from.'

'OK.'

Dixon waited until Phillips had gone through the gate in the wall to the old convent and then walked along the side of the sports hall to the back corner. He arrived just as the head porter and Mrs Weston were being moved away by a uniformed police constable. Dixon thought it best not to pull rank and risk his cover. Besides, he had left his warrant card at home. He managed to get a glimpse along the back wall of the hall before he too was moved along, but it was enough to confirm what he had suspected.

Derek Phelps was sitting up against the back wall of the sports hall, although slumped forwards. It was impossible to know whether he had been left in that position or whether he had managed to crawl there under his own steam. Dixon would need to wait for Roger's report before he would know the answer to that question. The glimpse had been enough to answer Dixon's main question, though. Both Phelps, and the congealed blood on the back of his head, were covered in frost.

By 8.30 a.m. Dixon had sent five pupils back to their houses. Three swore blind that nobody had told them and the other two said that they had been in the shower. Dixon felt a little bit guilty sending them away with empty stomachs while sitting there tucking into a bowl of Weetabix, but he reminded himself that he was diabetic and had to eat on medical grounds. He just wished he could get 'Norwegian Wood' out of his head. A pleasant tune under different circumstances, perhaps, but today it felt unusually sombre.

He put his empty bowl on the side in the far corner of the dining room and looked up to see Gittens and Lloyd standing in the doorway. They turned to run away.

'Oi.'

They stopped and turned to Dixon when they realised he had seen them.

'Where the hell have you been?'

Neither of them looked as if they had been to bed. Their eyes were bloodshot and their pupils dilated.

'Never mind,' said Dixon. 'The whole school's gated so get back to your house straight away.'

'Gated?'

'Yes. Everyone's out looking for you so get back there now.'

'Are we . . . ?'

'It's not about you, no. But it will be if you don't get back.'

Dixon handed them his apple and banana.

'Well, don't just stand there, get going.'

'Yes, Sir.'

'Thank you, Sir.'

It was past 9.15 a.m. and Dixon thought it unlikely that any more pupils would turn up now. Noises from the kitchen and the smell of toast told him that breakfast was being prepared to be taken out to the various houses, and he watched two porters push trolleys past the door of the dining room. They were accompanied by a police constable. A second officer saw Dixon sitting in the dining room and walked over to him.

'May I ask who you are, please, Sir?'

'I'm a trainee teacher here on two weeks' work experience, officer. I've been asked to sit here and send anyone who turns up for breakfast back to their house.'

'Mr Dickson, is it?'

'Yes. I've got a letter . . .' replied Dixon, fumbling in his inside jacket pocket.

'There's no need for that, Sir.'

The officer winked at Dixon and then handed him a note.

'I'll leave you to it, Sir.'

Dixon looked at the note.

'Your phone's off. Can you get over to the sports hall? J'

He checked his phone, which was still on silent mode, and switched alerts back on. He had missed five calls and three text messages. All of them from Jane and all asking if he could get over to the sports hall. He tapped out a reply to the last message.

*On way. What's up?*

The reply came in seconds.

*Chard's made an arrest Jx*

Dixon resisted the temptation to race straight over to the sports hall. First he checked the chapel, which was empty, the message having clearly got through to the chaplain that Holy Communion was cancelled for the day. Next he checked the library and then the masters' common room. Both were deserted. Then he walked back down to the dining room, out of the side door and along the path that formed the boundary of the cricket pitch. This would take him straight around the end of the Underwood Building and across to the sports hall whilst at the same time reducing the chances that he would bump into anyone on the way.

He stopped at the end of the Underwood Building, stood on the steps leading up to the biology labs and looked across to the end of the sports hall. He could see DI Baldwin and Jane standing outside a Scientific Services tent talking to Roger Poland. Camera flashes were going off inside the tent despite the spot lamps.

Dixon looked up. Students were peering out of every window along that side of the Underwood Building overlooking the scene. Bored, no doubt. Or maybe they would grow up to slow down and gawp at car accidents.

Dixon sent Jane a text message.

*Behind you x*

He watched her take her phone out of her pocket, look at it and then look over her shoulder. She spoke to DI Baldwin and then walked over to him.

'You look cold,' said Dixon.

'Freezing,' replied Jane, her teeth chattering.

'C'mon, let's go and get a cup of tea.'

They walked back along the path to the dining room, in the side entrance and then turned left along the corridor to the masters' common room.

'What're you doing out and about, then? I thought the school was on lockdown?'

'I'm a teacher, don't forget,' replied Dixon.

Jane smiled.

'The dead man was at St Dunstan's . . .' she said.

'I know. Derek Phelps, the KP. Did you find out what happened to Clive?'

'Not yet.'

'Who's Chard arrested?'

'Keith Foster, maths teacher. D'you know him?'

'I've met him.'

'Well?'

'Not a chance,' replied Dixon. He put the kettle on and rinsed two mugs under the tap. 'He wasn't at St Dunstan's, was he?'

'No.'

'Why the arrest, then?'

'Written in the mud next to the body are the letters "K" and "F". Chard thinks Phelps was blackmailing Foster and he killed him.'

'Investigation by numbers . . .' Dixon's voice tailed off. He handed Jane a mug of tea. 'What does Roger say?'

'Hit over the head, several times, and left for dead. He's not sure yet if the head injury got him or the cold, but he'll let us know.'

'Where was he killed?'

'At the scene.'

'That means he knew his killer, surely? To follow him to the back of the sports hall.'

'I suppose so.'

'Must've been late last night. Phelps was covered in ice when I saw him this morning.'

'What time was that?' asked Jane. She was sitting in an armchair holding her mug of tea in both hands.

'Sevenish.'

'I'll let Roger know.'

'Well, it narrows it down a bit, doesn't it? Haskill, Rowena Weatherly and the headmaster are the only ones left who were at St Dunstan's.'

'I've still got to check Isobel's father and the supply teacher, Griffiths.'

'Check their alibis for last night too.'

'Will do,' replied Jane.

Dixon turned to look out of the window and sighed. 'Keith Foster. It just doesn't work.'

Jane nodded.

'Where is he now?' asked Dixon.

'At the station. Chard's interviewing him this morning.'

Dixon was stirring his tea. He was looking at the mug but his mind was elsewhere. And Jane knew better than to interrupt his train of thought. Unless she had to, of course.

'You're gonna spill your . . .' Jane rolled her eyes.

Dixon spilt his tea on his leg but didn't flinch. He put down his mug and took out his iPhone, holding it horizontally. Jane guessed he was searching for something online.

'There's a restaurant in town that stays open until 2 a.m. on a Sunday morning. Always used to and still does, according to this. Go in and look at their CCTV footage and get me stills of every customer in there between, say, 11 p.m. and closing time. Get it for the night of Isobel's murder too.'

'Why?'

'Let's just say I'm clutching at straws.'

Jane frowned at him. 'Can I tell Chard?'

'If you have to.'

'What're you looking for?'

'Some things never change, do they?'

'What things?'

'Every generation thinks they're the first to do it when the reality is it's been going on for years.'

'What?'

'Every Saturday night at midnight we'd tie a rope to the radiator and abseil out the window. Then someone'd let us in through the fire escape when we got back.' Dixon smiled. 'I remember one time my housemaster walked right under me. I only just pulled the rope up in time.'

'Why not just go out through the fire escape?' asked Jane.

'Not nearly as much fun.'

'You needed to get out more.'

'Less, actually, if you think about it,' replied Dixon.

'Where were you going?'

'Get a takeaway.'

'Chinese?'

'Kentucky Fried.'

'Ah, there you are,' said Phillips, climbing the steps opposite the masters' common room, just as Dixon came out of the library. 'Everyone's been accounted for, thank God.'

'What about those on weekend exeat?' asked Dixon.

'The parents are being contacted now and told to keep their little darlings at home until further notice. All Sunday leave is cancelled. Housemaster's job, that one.'

'So, what happens now?'

'We wait for the police. Last time they were here a couple of days. The head's called a staff meeting for first thing tomorrow morning. I expect we'll end up circulating coursework on the intranet like we did last time. Keeps everybody busy.'

'And what do we do?'

'We've done our bit for the day. I suppose we might get a call if someone slinks off but that's about it. Police may want to speak to us too. Fancy a cup of tea?'

'No, thanks,' replied Dixon. 'The headmaster's asked to see me.' It was a lie but it was the best he could think of on the spot.

'Not in the best of moods today, the old man. Be careful.'

'I will, thanks.'

Dixon waited until Phillips had gone into the masters' common room and then went up to his rooms. Once inside he rang Roger Poland.

'Hello, Nick.'

'Where are you, Roger?'

'Still on site.'

'What does it look like?'

'No struggle. I'm guessing he knew his killer, perhaps followed him around the back of the sports hall and then wallop.'

'I saw blood on the back of his head,' said Dixon.

'Yes, there's plenty of it. At least three separate blows. Blunt object of some sort.'

'Jane said he'd written the letters "K" and "F" in the mud next to him.'

'Yes, they're legible. Just. There's mud on the end of his right index finger too.'

'Is it just a "K" and an "F" or had he made any other mark?'

'Not that I can see.'

'A partially formed third letter?'

'SOCO have taken plenty of photos so you'll be able to see for yourself.'

'What time . . . ?'

'Early hours. Can't say any more than that at this stage.'

'OK, thanks.'

'How's teaching?'

'Don't ask.'

Dixon rang off. He looked out of the small window and across the playing fields. A line of uniformed police officers was shuffling across the rugby pitch, all of them staring at the ground in front of them, and several police dogs were weaving in and out of the leylandii at the bottom of the playing fields. Dixon could not see the sports hall, which was off to the right, hidden behind the Underwood Building.

He thought about the killer of Derek Phelps. Someone Phelps knew, according to Roger. But was it someone Phelps trusted? Keith

Foster was the obvious suspect for no other reason than he had the right initials, but that assumed that Phelps had been trying to identify his killer. Surely then he would have written 'K' and 'E' or 'F' and 'O' before he died, his message incomplete? Dixon still liked his hunch that Phelps had been writing 'KFC'. He needed to see the photographs of the scene. He also needed to see the CCTV footage from the restaurant. If they'd had it seventeen years ago, he'd have been on it most Saturday nights and he knew boys from Brunel went there too.

Dixon's phone rang.

'Nick, it's Jane. I'm with the headmaster. Can you come to his office?'

'Come in, Nick,' said Hatton, standing to one side to allow Dixon into his office. Jane was standing with her back to a gas fire and smiled at him. He got a frostier reception from DCI Chard and DI Baldwin, who were sitting on the leather sofa opposite Jane. Hatton walked around and sat behind his desk.

'You know we've got Keith Foster in custody?' asked Chard.

'I do,' replied Dixon.

'And?'

'It's the obvious conclusion. Pick him up, interview him, tick the box, then let him go . . .'

'He's got nothing to do with it?' asked Hatton.

'No.'

'How can you be so sure?' asked Chard.

'I can't be sure. So check. But look at it logically. Phelps is well over six feet tall and well built. Does manual work so is likely to be fit and strong too. Foster wouldn't stand a chance . . .'

'Unless he took him by surprise,' said Baldwin.

'And if Phelps was blackmailing Foster and they'd arranged to meet, they'd have done it miles away, surely? Not right in the middle of the bloody school.'

'Not necessarily,' said Chard. 'It was late enough.'

'Constable Winter tells us you have another theory about the writing in the mud,' said Hatton.

'We know that it was a Saturday night when Isobel was murdered. We think she was being carried to a car and that the killer was disturbed and took refuge down on the playing fields where he killed her and dumped her body in the stream. Then, three weeks later, we have another murder on a Saturday night at almost exactly the same time and very close to the scene of Isobel's murder.'

'So far you haven't told us anything we don't know,' said Baldwin.

'I haven't, but it's how you interpret what you do know that matters.'

'Go on,' said Chard.

'The killer was disturbed when he was carrying Isobel to the car. Who by?'

'We don't know,' replied Baldwin.

'Then let's find out,' said Dixon. 'It's the early hours of Sunday morning in a boarding school in Taunton and my guess is one or more boys were coming back from town with a takeaway . . .'

'Oh, come on. What restaurant is open at that time of night?'

'The Kentucky Fried. It's open till 2 a.m. on a Saturday night. Everyone knows that. Or anyone who's been to a boarding school in Taunton.'

'Are you saying that pupils from this school have been going to the Kentucky Fried Chicken in East Reach in the early hours of Sunday morning?' asked Hatton.

'Yes, Sir.'

'What the bloody hell's Phillips playing at?'

'It's not his fault, Sir. They've been doing it for years. I used to meet some of them there . . .'

'Go on, Dixon,' said Chard.

'I used to cycle down and come back with a rucksack full of the stuff so if they'd done the same, these boys, they'd have been carrying bags of it, possibly.'

'And that's what Phelps was writing in the mud?'

'It's worth a look at the CCTV, surely?'

'Yes, it is,' replied Chard.

'If I'm right, we could have another problem,' said Dixon.

'What?' asked Hatton.

'It's possible that the killer thinks these boys can identify him. Maybe that's why he was after them last night . . .'

'After them?' exclaimed Hatton.

'Possibly, and Phelps stepped in . . .'

'You think Phelps intervened . . .' Chard's voice tailed off.

'It's one explanation of what we've got.'

Chard turned to Jane. 'Get onto the KFC and get the footage.'

'The quickest way would be for you to go to the police station, if you'd be able to watch the film and identify anyone, Sir?' asked Dixon.

'Of course,' replied Hatton.

Jane left the room holding her phone to her ear.

'I think you should know,' continued Hatton, 'there's a meeting of the school governors on Tuesday afternoon. I'm proposing that we bring forward the end of term by one week. The carol service will take place this Thursday evening instead of next Thursday and then everyone goes home for Christmas on Friday morning. I don't really see that we can do anything else.'

'I understand, Sir,' said Chard.

'It may be that the governors will wish to postpone the start of next term too. Possibly until this whole sordid business is sorted out.'

Chard nodded.

'You've got four days, Nick,' said Hatton.

Dixon nodded.

'Where will I find Rowena Weatherly?'

# Chapter Seven

Jane had telephoned ahead but still faced a two hour wait for the manager to arrive before she was able to get hold of the CCTV footage from the Kentucky Fried Chicken takeaway in East Reach. He had checked with his head office but once that formality was out of the way he was keen to help. The manager confirmed that pupils from all three of the Taunton boarding schools were regular customers, particularly at weekends. It had always been the same and was part of the reason why it was worthwhile for them to remain open late on a Saturday. Their CCTV retention policy required the footage to be kept for thirty days and so Jane was able to leave with two DVDs, one from the night Isobel was murdered and the other from the previous night.

A car had been sent to collect Mr Hatton from Brunel and Jane fast forwarded through the film while she waited for him in an interview room at Taunton Police Station. Dixon had been right. It showed a succession of teenage boys, most arriving on bicycles and some on foot. One was even in school uniform. Some bought a single meal while others filled rucksacks full of boxes and buckets.

Jane thought about a young Dixon abseiling out of the window at St Dunstan's. She smiled and shook her head.

By the time Hatton arrived, Jane had been through most of the footage from the previous night and had identified fourteen boys she thought to be of interest, all but two arriving in pairs. She had made a note of the times that each appeared and began by fast forwarding to the relevant point in the film and showing Hatton a freeze frame shot of each possible pupil. Hatton identified three of them. One came as an unpleasant surprise: the head boy, Gabriel White. The other two were no surprise at all: Simon Gittens and Nigel Lloyd.

Hatton was unable to identify any of the others boys either from those singled out by Jane or from a trawl through the rest of the film.

'I suppose I should be grateful there's only three of them,' said Hatton.

Jane then loaded the DVD from the night Isobel Swan had been murdered. This time there were four, including two girls, but only two of them had been in on both nights. Gittens and Lloyd.

'It seems Inspector Dixon was right.'

'It does,' replied Jane.

'I gather that you and he are a couple?' asked Hatton.

'Yes.'

'I didn't think that sort of thing was allowed in the police.'

'It isn't. We're only working together now because of the unusual . . .' Jane hesitated, '. . . situation.'

'David Charlesworth told me he went to St Dunstan's?'

'He did.'

'Was he there when the girl disappeared?'

'You'd need to ask him that,' replied Jane.

'Come now, Constable Winter, we both know the answer to that question, don't we?'

Jane blushed. 'Were you?'

'I left the year before,' said Hatton, smiling. 'Been checking me out, I see.'

'We check everyone out, Sir.'

'Of course you do. I'm guessing now but I imagine that David Charlesworth doesn't know about Nick's personal connection to the case?'

Jane stared at him.

'I'll take that as a "no", then. Well, he won't hear it from me. From where I'm sitting it makes him the ideal man for the job.' Hatton stood up. 'Is there a car available to take me back to the school?'

'I'll organise that now, Mr Hatton.'

'And you'll be sending a car for Gittens and Lloyd, I suppose?'

'Yes. We'll need to speak to the others too but we can do that at the school.'

'I'd better let their parents know.'

Jane waited until Hatton had left the station and then ran into the ladies toilet. She sat in a cubicle and took her phone out of her pocket. First she sent a text message to Dixon, then she switched to the pay as you go SIM card and sent another.

'I think you and I need to have a chat, don't you?'

'We do,' replied Rowena Weatherly. She looked at Dixon and smiled. 'How're you getting on these days?'

'OK.'

'You haven't changed much.'

'You certainly have,' replied Dixon.

'Well, I'm older and fatter, for a start. Married and divorced too.'

'You've been busy. Children?'

'No.'

'How did you end up here?'

'In the wrong place at the wrong time.'

'I'm assuming you know why I'm here?' asked Dixon.

'I looked you up on the Internet. Hope you don't mind.'

'So, why didn't you say anything?'

'Figured I wasn't supposed to let on. The hero of the hour at Taunton Racecourse. It's on YouTube.'

'Oh, no, is it?'

'It was in the papers too. And if I've spotted it . . .'

'That's a chance I've got to take.'

'What happened to you after you left St Dunstan's?' asked Rowena.

'It's a long story but I got there in the end.'

'Where?'

'Now, there's a question. Not over it. I just came to terms with it, they said, which is bullshit for just getting on with it.'

'Fran was a good friend.'

Dixon smiled. *She was more than that to me.*

'And you think the two cases are connected?' asked Rowena.

'I'm hoping they are. Because then I come face to face with whoever took Fran.'

'You've spotted the others from St Dunstan's?'

'Derek Phelps?'

'Yes. And the head. Griffiths too. He taught me ancient history.'

'Anyone else?'

'Haskill, but he's in the Far East.'

'Miss Weatherly.' The shout came from inside Gardenhurst.

'I'd better go. Good luck, Nick. We'll speak again, I'm sure.'

'We will. Thanks.'

Dixon turned and walked down the steps. He had reached the corner of the Bishop Sutton Hall before his phone bleeped. It was a text message from Jane.

*Taking Monty for a walk later*

Dixon recognised the code and switched to his pay as you go SIM card. Seconds later his phone bleeped again to announce another text message.

*Hatton knows about you and Fran*

Dixon dialled the number and waited.

'Hello?'

'Where are you? It sounds echoey.'

'In the loo.'

'What'd he say?'

'Just that he knew.'

'And what's he gonna do about it?'

'Nothing.'

'Odd. Still if he was up to no good he'd hardly let on he knows, would he?'

'I suppose not.'

'Any luck with the CCTV from the KFC?' asked Dixon.

'Two were there on both nights. Boys . . . er . . .'

Dixon could hear Jane turning pages in her notebook.

'Gittens and Lloyd . . .'

Dixon laughed.

'D'you know 'em?' asked Jane.

'I do. Think Laurel and Hardy on drugs and you'll not be far off the mark.'

'We're sending a car for them now.'

'I'm on my way.'

The interview with Simon Gittens was already under way by the time Dixon arrived at Taunton Police Station. Simon's family lived locally and his father, Brian Gittens, had got there in a matter of minutes when he got the call from the headmaster. Nigel Lloyd was waiting patiently in an interview room. His parents lived in America and had asked that the chaplain sit in as an appropriate adult when he was interviewed. Father Anthony was on his way but it would be at least another hour before he was able to get there.

Dixon watched the interview unfold on a small television screen in an adjacent room. DCI Chard and Jane were sitting on a table behind him. The interview was conducted by DI Baldwin, who had been at pains to point out that Simon was not under arrest and that he was simply helping with enquiries. Either way, his father did not seem impressed that his son was mixed up in the current enquiry in any shape or form.

'Let's start with the night Isobel Swan was murdered,' said Baldwin. 'What did you get up to that night, Simon?'

'I was in the sixth form bar with Nigel.'

Baldwin looked at him and raised her eyebrows. She did not reply.

'For God's sake, just tell her the bloody truth, Simon,' said Brian Gittens. 'It's not as if you murdered the girl, is it?'

Silence.

'Is it?'

'No.'

'Well, spit it out, then.'

'We'd gone into town. The Half Moon and the New Inn. We got back late and then someone suggested a takeaway so we borrowed a couple of bikes and went down the KFC.'

'Who suggested it?' asked Baldwin.

'Adam.'

'Adam who?'

'Adam Edwards.'

Brian Gittens shook his head.

'Who went?'

'Nigel and me.'

'Not Adam?'

'He paid for it in return for getting him some.'

'Anyone else?'

'No.'

'What time was this?'

'Just gone midnight, I think.'

'So, why didn't you mention this before?'

'I didn't think it was relevant.'

'Didn't want to get in trouble, more like,' said Brian. 'Idiot.'

'Which way did you go?' asked Baldwin.

'We used the path behind the housing estate opposite the school. It comes out down the side of Vivary Park. Then we cut down behind the car park to the top of East Reach. It's off road most of the way.'

'Where were the bikes?'

'In the bike rack at the side of Gardenhurst.'

'Not in the old cloisters?'

'No, it's locked at that time of night.'

'And how did you get out of the school?'

'We went along the front of Gardenhurst and then down the drive. It brings you out opposite Conway Road. The path's down there off to the right.'

'Why did you go that way?'

'There were no lights on my bike.'

'How long did it take you to get there?'

'About fifteen minutes or so.'

Baldwin took out a black and white photograph and placed it on the table in front of Simon.

'This is a still from the CCTV in the KFC. Identify the boys in the photograph for me.'

'That's me and that's Nigel,' replied Simon, pointing to the figures in the photograph in turn.

'And the timestamp?' asked Baldwin.

'It says 12.27 a.m.'

'What time did you get back to the school?'

'Maybe ten to one. Something like that.'

'Which route did you take?'

'We went the same way.'

'All the way?'

'No, we left the bikes in the bushes at the bottom of the drive and went on foot the rest of the way.'

'Why?'

'Less likely to be seen.'

'What was the weather like that night?'

'Clear sky, windy.'

'Lights?'

'The lights were on outside Gardenhurst and the light on the corner of the Bishop Sutton Hall.'

'So, what did you see when you got back to the school?'

'Nothing.'

'Think, Simon, this is very important. Did you see anything unusual at all?'

Simon was looking at the table and shaking his head. 'No, nothing.'

'Did anyone see you?'

'No.'

'What about the car park in front of Gardenhurst? Did you see anything down there?'

'No.'

'Hear anything?'

Simon hesitated. 'I . . .'

'Go on,' said Baldwin.

'Nigel thought he heard something and we froze where we were for a split second before we scarpered. He said it was on the far side the car park but we couldn't see anything. It was pitch dark down there.'

'And that was it?'

'Yes.'

'What was this noise?'

'Nigel heard it, not me. Could've been anything.'

'Or nothing,' said Brian.

'OK, what about last night?' asked Baldwin.

'Same, really, but we went on foot. We ate it in Vivary Park and got back about oneish.'

'And what did you see?'

'Nothing.'

'Or hear?'

'Nothing.'

'I've seen enough,' said Chard, leaning forward and switching off the television. 'Where the hell's that vicar?'

'Father Anthony Johns. And he's the chaplain,' replied Dixon.

'Is there a difference?'

'Yes.'

'Whatever.' Chard pulled a chair out from under the table and sat down. 'The fact is that we're no further forward, are we? They saw nothing and think they might've heard something but don't know what it was. It could've been a bloody fox . . .'

'If they could identify the killer then they'd have done so before now,' replied Dixon. 'Not even these two idiots would've held that back. What it has confirmed is that they were out and about both nights and it's possible it was them who disturbed Isobel's killer. We are also left with the possibility that it was them the killer was after last night and that Derek Phelps stepped in.'

'Bollocks,' said Chard. 'Pure bloody guesswork. There's not a shred of evidence . . .'

The phone rang. Chard answered it.

'Yes. Good. I'm coming now.' He replaced the handset. 'The vicar's here. Let's get this bloody fiasco over with.'

Dixon waited until Chard left the room.

'Did you get anywhere with Haskill?' he asked Jane.

'Haskill's in Kuala Lumpur. Malaysian police spoke to him this morning,' she replied.

'And Griffiths?'

'We've got his CV from the agency. Nothing exciting but it confirms he's taught at both schools. CRB check is clear and he's not known to police.'

'He and I need to get better acquainted, then, I think. What about Clive?'

'Clive Cooper. Sacked from St Dunstan's a couple of years before Derek left. Alcohol problems, by all accounts.'

'Where is he now?'

'Don't know yet.'

'And Isobel's father?'

'Bus driver now but used to drive coaches for Woodberrys. They had the contract for . . .'

'. . . St Dunstan's. I remember going on them for away matches.'

'He's divorced from Isobel's mother and married again,' said Jane.

'Interesting.'

'I can't very well speak to him, though, without alerting Chard.'

'True,' said Dixon. 'Leave him for now. What about Isobel's mother?'

'Married again and living in Aberdeen.'

'Who to?'

'I don't know.'

'Find out, will you?'

'OK.'

'Almost ready,' said DI Baldwin, switching on the television. 'DCI Chard's doing this one.'

Dixon nodded. He looked at Jane and rolled his eyes.

DCI Chard was sitting opposite Nigel Lloyd. Next to him was Father Anthony. The dog collar had been replaced by a thick wool pullover, both Sunday services at the school having been cancelled, and he had been going from house to house offering pastoral care to those who needed it, hence the delay in his arrival at the station.

Chard reminded Lloyd that he was not under arrest and then spent the next twenty minutes extracting an almost identical version of events to that given by Simon Gittens. Dixon thought that either they had prepared their stories in advance or both were sensible enough to omit any reference to the gallery in the old convent chapel. Chard pressed him on the noise he heard when he got back to the school.

'It came from the far side of the car park. It was faint but I'm sure I heard something.'

'What could you see?'

'Nothing. We were in the lights at the front of Gardenhurst looking into the dark. Couldn't even see the minibuses in the far corner.'

'What did the noise sound like?'

'I don't know.'

'Was it something moving?'

'It could've been.'

'Large or small?'

'Don't know that either.'

'If you had to make the noise yourself, how would you do it?'

Dixon thought that an interesting question and made a mental note of it for future use. He watched Lloyd mulling it over for several seconds.

'Take your time, Nigel,' said Father Anthony.

'I'd drag my toe in gravel.'

'So it was someone moving on the far side of the car park?' asked Chard.

'Yes, I think so. Or something. I couldn't say it was definitely a person.'

Chard terminated the interview and arranged for a car to take Father Anthony back to the school. Dixon and Jane followed DI Baldwin up to the CID Room on the first floor of Taunton Police Station where Chard was waiting for them.

'Well, that was a waste of time.'

'If you were expecting them to identify the killer, then, yes, it was a waste of time,' replied Dixon. 'But only an idiot would've been expecting that.'

Jane watched the anger flash across Chard's face. His eyes narrowed. He opened his mouth to speak but DI Baldwin spoke first.

'It was useful to the extent that we know the killer was disturbed, surely?'

'And the killer doesn't know that he wasn't seen,' replied Dixon. 'Perhaps he thinks he was, which explains why he killed Isobel down on the playing fields.'

'He must've returned later to get rid of the car too,' said Baldwin. 'Everyone said it was gone the next day.'

'That's right. So he didn't go far, presumably. It also brings us back to the possibility that these lads were the target last night and Phelps got in the way . . .'

'Enough,' said Chard. 'We've got two witnesses who heard something. That's it, so let's not get overexcited. There's certainly no evidence whatsoever that these boys were any sort of target at all. Don't forget, they saw and heard nothing unusual last night.'

'Where are they now?' asked Dixon.

'They've gone back to the school with the vicar.'

'Back? You've sent them back?'

'What else did you have in mind?' asked Chard.

'I'd have sent them home, to be on the safe side. Get Hatton to rusticate them.'

'Rusticate them? What the fuck does that mean?'

'Send them home for the rest of term.'

Chard turned to Baldwin. 'These bloody places even have their own language now.'

'I'd better get back,' said Dixon.

'They're no more in danger than anyone else in that place . . .'

Dixon stared at Chard. 'You'd better hope so. Sir.'

Jane sat in the Land Rover with Dixon while he waited for the windscreen to clear. A can of de-icer had dealt with the outside and the fans would clear the inside. Eventually.

'Did you get the floor plans of the main school?' asked Dixon.

Jane handed him two rolls of paper.

'Here they are. First and second floors.' Jane had to raise her voice to be heard over the noise of the fans and the old diesel engine.

'Thanks.'

'You need to be careful with Chard. If he finds out you've withheld the connection with Fran's disappearance, he'll have you.'

'He's bound to find out about it at some point. It's just a question of when.'

Jane shook her head. 'You're playing a dangerous game.'

'It's not a game. Besides, I haven't found a connection yet, if you think about it. It's still just a . . . well, I don't know what it is, really.'

'Just be careful.'

'I'd better go.'

Dixon arrived back at the school to find a line of girls walking in a crocodile along the main corridor, presumably back from the dining room after supper if the smell wafting from that direction was anything to go by. He didn't recognise any of them, nor did he recognise either of the teachers supervising them. He stepped back into the foyer and watched them troop past. He felt a sudden blast of cold air behind him and turned to see Phillips coming in through the front door.

'It's bloody cold out there,' he said, rubbing his hands together. 'Where've you been?'

'Nipped home for a couple of hours. What's going on?'

'They're coming across one house at a time for supper.'

'What about the police?'

'All finished out the back but there are still some here taking statements. Have they spoken to you?'

'Yes. Is there anything I can do?' asked Dixon.

'Not at the moment. I'll give you a shout if I need you.'

'OK.'

Dixon waited for the line of pupils to pass along the main corridor and then went up to his rooms. Once inside, he made himself a cup of tea and spent the next hour reading Isobel's post mortem report again and examining the floor plans. Then he went down to the dining room for something to eat. He was surprised to find it empty but could see that the kitchen staff were getting ready for the arrival of another house for supper. Dixon helped himself to some food and then sat in the dining room to eat it. He was alone apart from a kitchen porter waiting to collect the dirty plates at the counter in the far corner, where Derek Phelps had been only the day before.

Dixon finished his meal and carried his tray over to the counter.

'Shame about Derek.'

The kitchen porter shrugged his shoulders.

'What's your name?'

'Harry.'

'How long have you been here, Harry?'

'Five years.'

'Did you know Derek?'

'Yes.'

'Was he a friend of yours?'

'Not really.'

'Did he ever mention someone called Clive?'

'Not for a while.' Harry spoke slowly and without looking up.

'He did mention him then?'

'Yes.'

'Why not for a while?'

'Clive's dead.'

'Dead?'

'He killed himself.'

'When was this?'

'A year ago. I dunno.'

'Where . . .' Dixon turned his head to see a long line of schoolboys streaming along the corridor into the serving area behind the dining room. He raised his voice to be heard over the commotion. 'Where was this?'

'Cardiff.'

'Thanks.'

Dixon went back to his rooms, sat on the end of the bed and sent Jane a text message. He waited two minutes and then rang her on the pay as you go number.

'Clive Cooper's dead.'

'How?'

'Committed suicide about a year ago in Cardiff, according to one of the kitchen porters.'

'I'll get the file.'

'Thanks. I need to know why.'

'OK.'

'Soon after Fran disappears he starts drinking, gets sacked from St Dunstan's and ends up killing himself.'

'I'll get it tomorrow. The Cardiff lot may still have their file open.'

'Thanks.'

Dixon set the alarm on his phone for 9 p.m., lay back on the bed and closed his eyes. He still hadn't recovered from the trip back from Cyprus. It wasn't proper jet lag, of course, but it felt like it and he needed a couple of hours' sleep to sharpen his mind. He knew that someone had said something today that had not rung true. It was irritating him but try as he might he could not pin it down. It was either in direct conversation with him or he had overheard it, and all he could say with any degree of certainty was that he had not seen it on a screen, so it was not something that either Gittens or Lloyd had said in interview.

He thought about each conversation in turn. None had been particularly enlightening. Was it something Roger had said, perhaps? Dixon decided he would go to Musgrove Park Hospital for Derek's post mortem in the morning, but Roger had said nothing today to ring any alarm bells, surely? The headmaster, perhaps? Chard? Rowena Weatherly? She knew who he was and why he was there, of that there was no doubt, but she hadn't said anything that might compromise him, nor had she given any indication that she would. The headmaster also knew about Fran but had given Jane no cause for concern. It was also possible that if Rowena Weatherly and the headmaster knew who he was, so did the killer.

Dixon sat up. He wasn't getting anywhere with the investigation, nor was he getting any sleep. It didn't help that he was now in a race against time. If the school governors opted to end the term early, as the headmaster would be recommending, that gave him four days. It would also not be much longer before Chard started looking at previous cases and then Dixon's personal connection would come out.

So far, his only progress had been to identify Gittens and Lloyd as possible witnesses, but neither had seen anything of use. He felt as if he had just had his hair cut and all of the hair down his back was just out of reach. Try as he might, he just couldn't scratch it.

# Chapter Eight

Dixon woke just before midnight. He had a vague recollection of his alarm going off earlier but did not remember switching it off or deciding to have another five minutes' sleep. He was still fully clothed so he got up and stood in the window, looking out into the darkness. He could see two lights on at the far end of the Underwood Building off to his right, and the street lights on the far side of the playing fields were still on, marking the boundary of the school grounds. Otherwise, it was pitch dark.

He stood there for several minutes, listening to the wind and watching the stars disappear behind clouds and then appear again a few seconds later. If he had been at home he might have taken Monty for a walk, but that was not an option tonight.

He began to feel a little shaky so he checked his blood sugar levels. He was getting better at recognising the early signs of a hypo these days and this was confirmed by a blood sugar level of 4.8. Dixon knew it was a bit low for him, particularly at this time of night when it was likely to be dropping still further. He needed something to eat quickly before his level dropped much lower and, whilst he had packets of fruit pastilles, these were for emergency use only. A quick search of the small kitchen revealed a packet of stale biscuits and some cornflakes but no milk, so he decided on a visit to the school kitchens.

He went out onto the landing, locking the door of the flat behind him. All the lights were off, so he waited for his eyes to become accustomed to the darkness rather than switch the lights on. He tiptoed down the stairs and stood in the middle of the main corridor in front of the library. He could see lights on at the far end of the corridor but otherwise the only light this end was coming from under the door of the masters' common room. He tried it and was surprised to find it locked.

He walked down the steps opposite and along the corridor towards the dining room. Light was streaming in through the large windows on his left from the war memorial, which was lit by four lamps set in the ground around it.

He walked past the dining room and down the steps into the kitchens. A light had been left on in the far corner above the ovens, and illuminated green fire exit signs above the doors cast an eerie glow across the stainless steel worktops. Dixon waited until he was satisfied that no one was there and then went in search of food. He guessed that the two large steel doors in the far wall with red and green lights above them were the fridge and freezer but did not risk venturing into either of them. A safer bet was the store room, which had no lock on the door, and he emerged a minute or so later with a piece of fruit cake and a banana.

He was walking back along the corridor towards the masters' common room, brushing crumbs from his jacket, when he heard soft footsteps in the cloisters off to his right. He stopped and waited. The footsteps were running away from him towards the chapel. Then he heard the door of the chapel open and close again with a bang. Dixon sprinted along the corridor and down the two stone steps into the cloisters. He was running on the balls of his feet trying to stop his heels clicking on the tiled floor.

He opened the door to the chapel and listened. Silence. No one would have had the time to run the full length of the aisle and escape through the Lady Chapel at the far end before Dixon opened the door, so they must have gone out through the main double doors at the back of the chapel. He switched on the lights and checked the doors. The left hand door was unbolted. He opened it and looked outside into the darkness, but could see and hear nothing except the wind whipping the tall pine trees on the far side of the lawn to and fro.

He closed the door and bolted it from the inside. Then he turned and looked down the aisle. He could see something on the floor halfway along, so he walked towards it. He stopped when he recognised it was a Ouija board. On the floor next to it was a pad of paper and a white candle that had probably blown out when he opened the back door. Dixon took out his iPhone, switched it to camera mode and took several photographs of the scene. Then he walked up and down the aisle, checking the pews on either side.

When he was satisfied that the chapel was deserted, he went back to the Ouija board and crouched down to have a closer look at it. It had been placed on the stone plinth that marked the site of the old altar, no doubt to add to the drama, the planchette pointing to the words 'GOOD BYE'.

Dixon froze when he looked at the pad of paper. On it was written one word. The writing was faint but he could just about make it out.

FRAN.

Dixon tore the top piece of paper from the pad, folded it in half and put it in his inside jacket pocket. Then he took several more photographs of the scene before leaving the chapel, switching off the lights on his way out. At the door he looked back and smiled. Someone had been trying to spook him, but it hadn't worked.

'You'll have to do better than that,' he muttered, as he walked back down the cloisters.

---

Dixon sat on the end of his bed and took out his iPhone. He deleted the first set of photographs he had taken of the Ouija board showing the writing on the pad of paper. Then he sent Jane a text message.

*How's Monty? x*

He waited a couple of minutes and then dialled Jane's pay as you go number. She answered straight away.

'What's up?'

'Someone just tried to get me off the case.'

'How?'

'They left a Ouija board on the floor in the chapel with Fran's name written on a pad next to it. It would've been found in the morning and then you can bet I'd have faced some awkward questions.'

'A Ouija board?'

'You communicate with the dead. You sit round it with your fingers on a pointer and it spells out words.'

'And it's supposed to have spelt out Fran?'

'That's what we're meant to think. Only I got there first.'

'Someone else knows who you are, then?'

'Looks that way.'

'Are you're sure it wasn't . . . ?'

'Don't tell me you believe that stuff? It takes more than one person, for a start, and I only heard one set of footsteps.'

'No, I meant are you sure it wasn't the headmaster or Rowena Weatherly. They both know who you are.'

'I didn't get a look at 'em, unfortunately. Could've been, I suppose. Check if either of their parents got divorced too, will you?'

'OK.'

'It was pure chance I was there. Otherwise it'd still have been sitting there in the morning.'

'And the chaplain finds it, calls the police, Chard gets Fran's file out and then you're off the case . . .'

'That was the plan, no doubt.'

'But then the connection would've been made, surely?'

'It will be anyway, sooner or later. Or at least it should be. And he'll be banking on getting away with it again. Just like he did last time.'

'So, what happens next?' asked Jane.

'That depends on what you turn up, doesn't it? Otherwise, I'm just sitting here waiting for something to happen.'

'It has already, hasn't it?'

'Phelps?'

'Yes.'

'Not sure that's down to me being here or not. I'm not sure it's the same killer, for a start. I need to have a word with Roger tomorrow.'

'Not the same killer . . . ?' asked Jane.

'No. Think about it. He's armed with a knife and knows how to use it. He cut Isobel's throat, didn't he?'

'Chard hasn't even considered that possibility.'

'Doesn't surprise me. It's just an idea, but Roger'll tell me one way or the other at the post mortem tomorrow. You going to be there?'

'No. I'd better keep digging.'

'Don't forget Clive Cooper.'

'I won't. And you be careful.'

'I will.'

'Monty's missing you,' said Jane.

'Only Monty?'

'No. Now get some sleep.'

Jane rang off, leaving Dixon staring at his phone. He took the piece of paper out of his jacket pocket and looked at the writing. It was in block capitals with any semblance of handwriting style disguised by almost childlike straight lines. No doubt the writer wore gloves too but, either way, it was evidence and might come in useful later. He took the file out from under his mattress, slotted the piece of paper into it and then put the file back.

Dixon set his alarm for 7 a.m. and then closed his eyes. He thought about the Ouija board and remembered rumours of two boys getting caught playing with one at St Dunstan's. Nothing had come of it, of course, except for several lost Saturday afternoons in detention. Then there was the urban myth that every generation told as if it were a true story that happened only last week. The version Dixon knew involved the death of a boy called Rufus at Upham School. He had been experimenting with a Ouija board and legend had it that it spelled out the words 'death to Rufus'. Only a few days later Rufus had been killed in a car accident. Dixon didn't believe in coincidence but on this occasion he could make an exception.

He thought about the other urban myth that used to do the rounds and the vision of an axe murderer banging a severed head on the roof of a car flashed across his mind. Thankfully, he was asleep before the unfortunate victim's wife had to get out of the passenger door.

The staff meeting got under way just after 9 a.m. Dixon had thought it odd that the teachers were required to stand when the headmaster walked into the masters' common room—they were adults after all—but found himself conforming before he had time to question it. Not that he would have done so out loud, of course.

He was sitting on the window seat watching Rowena Weatherly. She was sitting in a leather armchair with her back to him, reading from an exercise book in her lap. From time to time she looked up at the headmaster standing at the front of the room with Robin Phillips. Dixon thought he could recognise most of the teachers now, but there were still some he didn't. They must have had the weekend off. He also noticed that the supply teacher, Griffiths, was not there.

Hatton began by assuring the staff that progress was being made in the police investigation, which came as news to Dixon. Hatton looked away sharply when he saw him looking at him. Hatton had, he said, spoken to the senior investigating officer and been informed that the police would have finished their initial enquiries by lunchtime, after which the school could return to normal. The school would, therefore, spend the morning in private study with lunch, as usual, at 1 p.m. After that, the normal Monday afternoon timetable would take effect and, in the meantime, all housemasters were asked to ensure that their pupils had enough to keep them occupied for the morning. Any coursework due that week could be posted on the intranet so the students could make a start on that if needs be.

'Any questions?' asked Hatton.

A hand went up at the front of the room. The man was wearing army combat trousers, a khaki shirt and green pullover, which told Dixon that he ran the Cadets. At St Dunstan's the CCF had been run by a retired naval chief petty officer.

'Yes, Sarge.'

'We've got the Ten Tors teams doing an orienteering exercise on the Quantocks this afternoon, Sir. Should that go ahead?'

'I don't see why not. What d'you think, Robin?'

'We've not been told it can't, Sir,' replied Phillips.

'Better check with DCI Chard,' said Hatton.

'Yes, Sir.'

'Anything else?' Hatton waited. No hands went up so he continued. 'Right, well, moving on, there's a meeting of the school governors tomorrow afternoon. The proposal is to end the term a week early so the carol service will be Thursday evening and then everyone goes home on Friday morning. Those of you who haven't done so already, give some thought to homework for the holidays and we'd better give them a bit more than usual if they're going to be off for an extra week.'

Dixon was surprised by the mixed reaction amongst the teachers. Some smiled and obviously appreciated the extra week off. Others shook their heads. Rowena Weatherly did neither.

This was not the Rowena Abbot Dixon remembered from St Dunstan's. She had changed her appearance, but there could be any number of reasons for that. She had been a year below them and, apart from playing in the same hockey team as Fran, she had never really had that much to do with them. Then it dawned on him. What had kept him up for hours last night was suddenly all too obvious. Maybe she was just trying to be polite, but Fran was not and never had been 'a good friend'.

'You can manage the carol service this Thursday, Father?' asked Hatton.

'Yes, Sir,' replied Father Anthony. 'The Christmas tree is being delivered on Friday but I'll see if I can bring that forward.'

'Cancel it,' said Hatton. 'I think we can dispense with the tree, in the circumstances.'

Father Anthony nodded.

'Assuming the governors agree, I've arranged for emails to go out straight away and letters in the first class post so all parents should've got the message by the end of Wednesday. No doubt there'll be some complaints, but they know what's been going on and I doubt many will be too surprised.'

'Some'll want a bloody refund. You can bet on that.' The broad Scottish accent gave away William McCulloch sitting at the back.

'Thank you, William. I'm sure the bursar can handle them.'

Hatton turned to Phillips. 'Anything else, Robin?'

'No, Sir.'

'Well, unless anyone has any other questions . . . ?'

'It's our Christmas lunch tomorrow, Sir. Do we go ahead with it?'

Dixon had been watching Rowena Weatherly and did not see who asked the question.

'I don't see why not.'

Dixon had often wondered what possessed people to teach in a boarding school, some of them all their adult lives, and in that moment it came to him. He thought about the character Brooks in *The Shawshank Redemption* who was freed after decades in prison and committed suicide. Dixon made a mental note to look up the definition of 'institutionalised' when he got home. An easier way of putting it, perhaps, was to say that they simply never left school. Dixon smiled. No doubt Jane would tell him that the police was an institution, and she was probably right.

'Right, then, that's it, everyone. Don't tell the students about term ending early until we have a decision from the governors. Mr Dickson, my office, if you will.'

Hatton slammed his office door behind them. 'There's been a distinct lack of progress but I could hardly tell them that, could I?'

Dixon did not respond.

'I gather you found evidence of drug taking in the old chapel?'

'Yes.'

'And you've agreed to keep it quiet?'

'I wouldn't say that.'

'What would you say?'

'I'm here to investigate the murder of Isobel Swan. I'm only interested in drugs if they're relevant. Otherwise, it's an internal matter for the school.'

'Thank you.'

'It may become relevant, of course.'

'Let's hope not.'

'Quite.'

'So, what happens now?' asked Hatton.

'We have various lines of enquiry.' Dixon wondered how many times he had used that exact turn of phrase in the seven years he'd been a police officer.

'You can't tell me, I understand.'

Dixon looked at his watch.

'D'you need to be somewhere?' asked Hatton.

'Derek Phelps' post mortem.'

'Yes, of course. No lessons this afternoon but you're welcome to join me for lunch.'

'Thank you, Sir.'

Dixon's usual tactic in the Met had been to watch post mortems from the comparative safety of the anteroom and listen to the pathologist dictating his notes over the intercom. That had been thwarted of late by Roger Poland, who seemed to take great delight in keeping an eye out for him and inviting him into the lab at the first opportunity. On this occasion, however, Dixon marched straight in.

'What've we got, then?'

Poland looked surprised to see him. 'What're you doing here?'

'Playing truant.'

Derek Phelps was lying face down on the slab revealing the injuries to the back and top of his head. Dixon leaned over for a closer look.

'Still three blows?'

'Yes.'

'Any other injuries apart from the head?'

'No,' replied Poland.

Dixon leaned over and peered at Phelps' hands.

'No defensive injuries either,' said Poland.

Dixon nodded.

'Cause of death?'

'The head injury got him before the cold.'

'Any idea about the weapon?'

'It was blunt. That's about all I can say with any degree of certainty at the moment.'

'Wood, metal, stone?'

'Too early to say. I may have a better idea when I've done some more tests. There are a few fragments of this and that that I've sent to the lab for testing.'

'What about the sequence?'

'The blow to the back of the head came first, then the two on top. You can see where the fractured skull's been compressed again by the later blows.'

'How tall is he?'

Poland picked up a notepad on the side.

'One hundred and eighty-five centimetres.'

'What's that in real money?'

'Six foot one or thereabouts.'

'So his killer's likely to be shorter?'

'Probably. If he was taller then the first blow would've had more of a downward angle to it and been closer to the top of the head.'

'Can you tell for sure?'

'Not really. Not without knowing their relative positions, whether they were both standing on level ground. Phelps could've been bending over when he was hit, for starters. There are too many variables . . .'

'I get the picture.'

'If we had the killer it might be different.'

'We will, Roger. We will.'

Dixon parked in the car park in front of Gardenhurst and walked along the near side of the sports hall, ensuring he would not be overlooked from the Underwood Building. Once at the end he surveyed the scene. The ground fell away steeply to the playing fields below and looked as though it had been built up to provide level foundations for the hall itself. He ducked under the blue tape and walked along the narrow path that ran along the back wall behind several wispy pine trees that had been planted on the bank. Too many cigarette butts to count told him it was a popular spot for a quick smoke.

There was a small patch of dried blood at the base of the wall, perhaps a third of the way along, which was largely obscured from view by one of several supporting buttresses that jutted out. Dixon looked around. The spot was not overlooked by a single window in any of the buildings in the vicinity. Perfect for a smoke and perfect for a murder. It also occurred to him that Phelps could not have been keeping a look out for someone when he was killed. If he had been then surely he would have been at one corner of the hall and not a third of the way along the back wall. No, he had come to meet someone and that someone had killed him.

Without knowing whether the killer had been standing on the narrow path running behind the trees or further down the steep bank, it was impossible to get a clear idea of the killer's height from the injuries to Phelps. It was reasonable to assume he was on the path, perhaps, because that would be the only way of guaranteeing a sure footing when swinging the murder weapon and, on that basis, the killer could well be shorter than Phelps. Six foot one. That ruled out no one except Griffiths, the supply teacher, who was well over six feet tall. Dixon wondered how tall Isobel's father was. And her driving instructor.

It was just after 11.30 a.m. by the time Dixon got back to the masters' common room. There was a note pinned to the door.

'In my lab. Room 31. Down corridor opposite. Robin.'

Dixon walked down the steps and along the corridor. The door to room 31 was open so he walked in and looked around. There were four long workbenches, each with a small sink at either end and another in the middle. Gas taps were spaced out at regular intervals along the bench, bringing back unpleasant memories of Bunsen burners and the various practical jokes that went with them. He winced at the memory of red hot ten pence pieces flicked along the desk. Mercifully, he hadn't fallen for that one. Dixon had hated chemistry almost as much as he hated physics, but he wouldn't tell Phillips that.

'Is that you?' The voice came from a small office at the back of the room, hidden behind the whiteboard.

'Yes,' replied Dixon, peering around the door.

Phillips was sitting at his computer with his back to him. 'The orienteering exercise is on this afternoon and the head thought you might like to go.'

'On?'

'Yes. DCI Chard said it'd be OK.'

'Did he.' Dixon took a deep breath, closed his eyes and counted to ten.

'The twerps responsible for your find in the old chapel are going,' continued Phillips, turning around, 'and the old man thinks it might be an idea if someone kept an eye on them.'

'Who are they?'

'Gittens and Lloyd.'

Dixon smiled.

'D'you know them?' asked Phillips.

'They turned up at breakfast yesterday morning looking like they'd had a heavy night of it.'

'They probably had. Anyway, you're young, fit and available.'

'I'll go, yes, that's fine with me.'

'I can lend you my golf trousers and a waterproof top. I'm sure we can find a rucksack somewhere too.'

'I'll need a pair of trainers.'

'Size?'

'Ten.'

'We'll have a rummage in the lost property,' replied Phillips.

# Chapter Nine

Dixon was sitting in the front passenger seat of the largest of the four school minibuses as Sarge drove north-west out of Taunton on the A358, past the Royal Marine base at Norton Fitzwarren and on towards Bishops Lydeard. He had been introduced to Regimental Sergeant Major Brian Tuckett, Royal Artillery Retired, to give him his correct title, an hour or so before, and had since been kitted out in a pair of army combat trousers, a Brunel rugby shirt and a green Berghaus jacket with fleece liner that smelt as if it had spent far too long in the bottom of the lost property box. He had also borrowed a pair of trainers, gloves and a small blue rucksack that was on the floor of the minibus between his feet. It contained a fruit cake, a bottle of water, a spare map and a woolly hat. Dixon was travelling light.

He thought about his last visit to the Quantocks, which had not ended well, and wondered where Westbrook Warrior was now that half the syndicate that had owned him was either dead or in prison. Dixon hoped it was not in a tin of dog food. The Warrior had won his last race in some style and deserved better.

He checked his pockets for his phone and sent Jane a text message.

*Orienteering exercise on Qtocks babysitting Gittens & Lloyd at least it's not raining x*

Dixon looked up at the Quantocks on the skyline ahead and could make out a light dusting of snow on the tops. They had not yet been given the route but he hoped it would not take more than a couple of hours. He had better things he could and should be doing and, whilst Sarge had been at pains to impress on him that he shouldn't interfere with the map reading, Dixon had no intention of walking miles in the wrong direction.

He looked over his shoulder at the pupils in the seats behind him. There were three teams of six. Twelve boys and six girls, all entered into Ten Tors on Dartmoor the following May. The girls and one team of boys would be doing thirty-five miles and the other team of older boys, including Gittens and Lloyd, would be doing forty-five miles. Dixon hoped that neither Gittens nor Lloyd would be doing the map reading.

Dixon frowned. He thought it odd that no mention had been made of the Ouija board, either during the staff meeting or afterwards by Phillips. It must have been found this morning by someone, most likely by Father Anthony or possibly the cleaner, and the only conclusion Dixon could draw was that it had been treated as a childish prank and ignored. Either that or Phillips had simply not mentioned it. After all, he still didn't know that Dixon was a police officer. What remained, of course, was that someone had made an attempt, albeit feeble, to have Dixon taken off the case. Someone close enough to the school to be wandering around at that time in the morning. Dixon hadn't heard a car. He wondered whether he could rule out the driving instructor and Isobel's father on that basis.

The minibus turned right just after Bishops Lydeard and headed north up onto the Quantocks. Dixon could see Great Wood off to his left and ominous rain clouds in the sky behind it away to the west. He checked his phone to find that he only had one bar. Still, a weak signal was better than no signal at all. He listened to the light hearted banter coming from the back of the minibus. Whether the girls liked it or not, they were in a race with the boys and the social standing of an entire gender depended on the outcome.

Sarge looked at Dixon and rolled his eyes. 'It's not a race,' he shouted.

Dixon spotted a large green sign for Quantock Lodge Leisure as Sarge turned into the entrance. The sign gave the usual information, including address, telephone number, activities, opening hours and such like. Non-members were welcome, apparently. Dixon took out his phone and sent Jane another text message.

*Starting TA5 1HE x*

He watched the screen nervously to check that the message had gone. The mobile signal came and went so he held his phone above his head and moved it left and right until he got the 'message sent' confirmation that he was waiting for. Next he opened Google Maps, selected Hybrid view, tapped the '3D' button and then entered the postcode in the search field at the top of the screen. He was now looking at a three dimensional satellite image of the Quantock Hills with white lines marking the main roads. He watched a red pin drop onto his current location. At least he knew where he was. For now.

Sarge parked in the far corner of the car park, opposite the swimming pool. It looked far more inviting than the cold and dark woods behind it.

'Everybody out.'

Dixon got out of the minibus and slid open the side door while Sarge opened the double doors at the back. Pupils began climbing out, some more reluctantly than others, and it came as no surprise that Gittens and Lloyd were last out.

'Right, into your teams, everyone,' shouted Sarge. 'A simple exercise today, so don't get lost.' He handed a map and compass to each team leader. The maps were folded open at the correct location and sealed in waterproof wallets. 'We're at grid reference ST 18638 37602.' Sarge sighed loudly. 'You're not writing this down, are you?'

Most of the pupils took a pencil and paper out of their pockets. Gittens and Lloyd took out their phones.

'Phones in an emergency only. Idiots. This is about learning to use a map and compass, not sat nav. What happens if you can't get a signal?'

'Yes, Sarge.'

'I'll be enjoying the hospitality in the Windmill Inn at West Quantoxhead. Grid reference ST 11223 41809. And don't take too long about it or Mr Dickson here will have to drive us home.'

'Yes, Sarge.'

'Mr Dickson will be going with your team, Martin. He fancied an afternoon stroll.'

'Yes, Sarge.'

'My mobile number is in the top right corner of each map. Right, then, off you go, and I'll give you a clue,' said Sarge, pointing to a wooden five bar gate to his right. 'It's that way.'

Dixon watched the team of younger boys dash off towards the gate and was relieved that his own team began by studying the map, as did the girls. He knew that the Windmill was on the A39 to the north-west of his current location and, on that basis, the exercise was quite straightforward. Up through Great Wood and then along the top to West Quantoxhead. Monty would be upset if he knew what he was missing.

'Are you ready, Sir?' asked Martin.

'Yes, don't mind me, I'll just tag along,' replied Dixon.

He followed the group through the gate and along the forest track. The trees either side gave way to fields, telling Dixon that they were not yet into Great Wood itself, but the trail became very much darker up ahead, the team of younger boys having already disappeared into the gloom. Dixon hoped he would not need a torch. It was the one thing he had forgotten, but he could always use the light from his phone if he had to.

He watched the team of boys walking ahead of him. They looked very much like he and his teammates had done when they had done Ten Tors. Dressed head to toe in waterproofs, it was difficult to tell them apart, although Gittens and Lloyd were the only ones wearing blue. All carried small rucksacks but Dixon thought it best not to ask what was in them. Ten Tors would be a very different proposition, of course; forty-five miles across the open moor carrying a tent, sleeping bag, a cooker and food.

The forest trail consisted of a dirt track, wide enough for one vehicle, with deep drainage ditches either side. It was hard underfoot but occasional softer patches revealed heavy tyre tracks and hoof prints. The path soon began climbing steeply up into the woods and Dixon could feel his breathing becoming more laboured. He was not as fit as he should be, but then a week of eating and drinking in Cyprus was probably to blame for that. The trees either side were becoming thicker too and the path darker. Dixon recognised chestnut trees to the left of the path and on the right, above the path on a steep bank, were pine trees. Various deer tracks wound their way up the bank and through the trees, although any deer had long since been scared off by the noise of the younger boys ahead.

Dixon felt his jacket for a hood and was relieved to find one folded away inside the collar. He ripped open the Velcro and pulled the hood over his head. Then he took off his rucksack, retrieved his gloves and put them on as he walked along. A cold walk in the woods was fine. A cold and wet one was not.

He watched Gittens and Lloyd shuffling along at the back of the group and wondered what on earth had made them volunteer for Ten Tors. Perhaps they saw it as an opportunity to get out of school for a while, or even as a chance to have a smoke or two. If so, Dixon had well and truly ruined that.

The group stopped at a fork in the track and Dixon listened to them discussing the options. Clearly, Martin was a democratic team leader.

'If we drop down here, we can cut across Quantock Combe, follow this path here, and then come out on the top at Crowcombe Park Gate. It cuts off miles.'

The words 'drop down' didn't inspire much confidence in Dixon. Having gained height it seemed a shame to lose it but he resisted the temptation to intervene. He took out his phone to check Google Maps and was disappointed to see that he had no signal. The map still opened though, despite the warning 'Cannot Determine Location', and he was able to see the fork in the path. Martin was right about the path to Crowcombe Park Gate. It was just the loss of height and then having to gain it again that concerned Dixon. Still, they had to learn. Oddly enough, it was Gittens who sounded a note of caution, but he was overruled and the group took the right fork, heading down into Quantock Combe.

It was impossible to tell whether the younger boys had come this way. They were now well out of sight and the only thing Dixon could say for sure was that the girls' team behind them did not follow. He looked back to see them pause at the fork in the path and then continue straight on. Very wise.

The path down into the combe descended diagonally across the side of the hill and then took a sharp right turn almost back on itself at the bottom. Pine trees had been planted on both sides, above the path on the left and below it on the right. The path below was visible down through the trees. It was muddier than the path they had been following and, judging by the tyre tracks and large piles of logs, a number of lorries or tractors had been going up and down it in recent days. Dixon checked his phone. Still no signal, and it was becoming less likely that he could get one now that they were descending into the combe.

He followed the group to the bottom of the path and then around to the right. He could see several deer watching them from above, their heads silhouetted against the sky that was visible behind them through the pine trees. There was a large turning area for the lorries at the bottom of the combe and yet more piles of logs waiting to be removed.

A small wooden footbridge took the group over a stream and then they began the climb up the far side on a narrower and altogether more unpleasant path that was certainly not suitable for vehicles. Dixon followed a line of deer prints in the soft mud and soon found himself negotiating muddy puddles, fallen trees and bushes that encroached on either side.

He listened to the complaints that were becoming more and more vocal from the team ahead of him. Several swear words were directed at Martin and Dixon had to admit that he had a good deal of sympathy with the complainants.

'What the fuck was that?'

The shout came from Martin, whose instinctive reaction had been to duck.

'What?'

'It sounded like a bee or a wasp.'

'At this time of year?'

Dixon knew what it was. He ran forward.

'There's another one!' said Lloyd, ducking and turning away.

'Get down!' shouted Dixon. He dived on Gittens and Lloyd, knocking them off the path and into the undergrowth on the slope below. Then he reached up, took hold of Martin by the coat and pulled him over. 'Get down, all of you.' The others in the team all threw themselves on the ground.

'Which direction did it come from?' asked Dixon.

'Above us,' said Martin. 'What is it?'

'Bullets.'

'Oh, shit.'

Dixon was lying flat on his back so he turned his head to survey the immediate vicinity. There were several large pine trees within reach as well as a tree trunk lying on the ground.

'Get off the path. Behind a tree, if you can, but stay down. Crawl.'

The boys began crawling towards the tree nearest to them. Gittens was too frightened to move and stayed where he was, lying face down in the mud. Dixon rolled onto his front and crawled towards the tree trunk on the ground.

'Martin.'

'Yes, Sir.'

'Above left or right?'

'I don't know.'

'You heard something fly past you, right?'

'Yes.'

'Was it going left to right or right to left?'

'Right to left, I think.'

Above us and to the right, thought Dixon. He craned his neck to peer over the tree trunk that he was hiding behind but dived down when a bullet hit the tree behind him. He looked at the hole it had made, which was smaller than he had expected. He took his rucksack off and held it up, just above the tree trunk. A bullet slammed into it.

Dixon examined the small hole the bullet had made in the top pocket of his rucksack.

*I know who you are.*

He took out his phone. Still no signal. Google Maps told him that there was a road above them, leading up to Crowcombe Park Gate and then down to Crowcombe itself. It was a dead end in the other direction. He could see two lay-bys on the satellite picture that would accommodate a car. Then he zoomed in on the gate itself, looked at the picture and nodded. If he could get up to the gate ahead of the car, he might have a chance.

'Anyone got a signal?'

'No, Sir,' replied Martin.

'Anyone else?' asked Dixon.

'Simon had one, Sir. Not sure if he's still got it,' said Lloyd.

'I need your phone, Simon.'

No response.

'Can you get off the path?'

Dixon crawled over to him. Gittens was still lying face down in the mud, shaking and crying. Dixon whispered in his ear.

'Simon, I need your phone.'

No response.

'Now is not the time, old son. Where's your phone?'

Gittens reached under his chest into his inside jacket pocket and then handed Dixon his phone.

'Good lad. Now, stay where you are and don't move.'

Gittens nodded.

Dixon crawled back to his tree trunk and tapped the screen on Gittens' brand new Samsung Galaxy S5.

'What's your passcode, Simon?' asked Dixon.

'It's his birthday, Sir. 0206, I think,' said Lloyd.

Dixon tried it and the home screen appeared. He rang Jane, dialling her number from memory.

'Detective Constable Winter.'

'Jane, it's me. Listen very carefully. We're in the woods south east of Crowcombe Park Gate. Someone's shooting at us . . .'

'Shooting at you?'

'Yes. We need armed response and the helicopter. I've got six boys with me and we can't move.'

'Is everyone OK?'

'So far.'

'They're after Gittens and Lloyd?'

'No.'

'Who, then?'

'Me.'

'Oh, shit. D'you know who it is?'

'Rowena Weatherly.'

'Are you sure?'

'Yes. She qualified for Bisley at the age of sixteen. She left the Ouija board and she and Fran were not friends at all, let alone good friends.'

'What's Bisley?'

'The Imperial Meeting. Rifle shooting.'

'Why, though?'

'Do you mind if we worry about that later. We need some help. And call an ambulance too, just in case.'

'OK. You be caref . . .'

Dixon had already rung off.

'What do we do now, Sir?' asked Martin.

'Give me a minute,' replied Dixon.

He crawled along the tree trunk, holding the rucksack above his head, and had gone no more than a yard when another bullet slammed into it, puncturing the water bottle inside. He continued crawling and counted to twelve before another bullet hit it. He lay back in the mud, breathing heavily and feeling the first signs of dizziness that signalled his blood sugar was getting dangerously low. He reached into the rucksack for the fruit cake. It had been a strenuous business, but it had confirmed what he needed to know.

Firstly, he was the target and, secondly, Rowena was using a single shot .22 calibre target shooting rifle, either her own or taken from the range at the school. No doubt she had a key.

Dixon spoke through a mouthful of cake.

'Right, we're gonna make a run for it. Next time she fires, I want everyone to get up and run down the hill to the bottom of the combe. Don't stop for anything. Is that clear?'

'Yes, Sir.'

'This includes you, Simon.'

'Yes, Sir.'

'When you get to the bottom, turn left and don't stop until you get clear. You should come out at Adscombe. There are some houses there so bang on doors until someone lets you in. OK?'

'Yes, Sir.'

'Anyone wearing a blue rucksack, leave it behind. In fact, all of you dump your rucksacks, they'll only slow you down.'

'What about you, Sir?' asked Martin.

'Don't worry about me, you just get clear,' replied Dixon.

Dixon lay back down and closed his eyes. Shit happens, he thought. Then he sat up behind the tree trunk.

'Everybody ready?'

'Yes, Sir.'

'When you hear the gunshot, get up and run like hell. Right, on the count of three. One, two, three . . .'

Dixon held up his blue rucksack and it was immediately hit by a bullet. All six boys got up as one and ran down the slope, crashing through the undergrowth. Dixon jumped up and began running diagonally up the slope to his left. He was carrying his rucksack in his right hand, trying to hold it out behind him as far as he could. On the count of ten, he dropped it behind him and then dived on the ground. The rucksack was thrown into the air as another bullet tore into it. Then Dixon was on his feet and running again up the slope. The cold, still air rasped the back of his throat and his lungs were burning but he kept going, lunging up through the bushes. On the count of eleven he dived on the ground, just as another bullet ripped through the collar of his jacket.

He could see the trees thinning near the edge of the wood so he knew he was getting close to an area of open ground below the road. He crawled upwards towards the light for several yards before getting up and then immediately diving on the ground. His face was peppered with splinters as another bullet glanced off the tree behind him. Then he was up and running again. He could see a figure running back through the trees off to his right, a hundred yards or so away. The race was on.

The undergrowth was clawing at his face as he ran. He tried to shield himself from the brambles, buckthorn and pine tree branches as best he could but he had to watch the ground ahead of him as he ran. Stopping was not an option either.

Finally, he broke clear of the wood and out into the open. The first lay-by was empty but trees screened the second. Dixon could hear a car engine starting up. He looked to his left towards the gate. Just before the junction, the road narrowed and fences came in on either side, meeting at a small forest cattle grid.

Dixon jumped the drainage ditch and ran along the road. He took his woolly hat off as he ran and threw it on the ground. Then he jumped the cattle grid and turned to look back up the road.

Rowena Weatherly was driving straight at him in a dark blue VW Beetle. She was accelerating hard and Dixon could hear the engine screaming in protest. She was hunched over the steering wheel but was too far away for him to pick out her facial features.

He squatted down and took hold of the first tubular steel bar of the cattle grid in both hands. Then he braced both feet against the edge of the frame and heaved. It took all the strength in his legs and arms but he was able to lift the grid a few inches and then drag it clear of the pit underneath. He was only able to drag it a few feet but that would be enough. Then he stood back to watch.

Rowena realised too late that Dixon had moved the cattle grid. She stamped on the brakes, locking her wheels, but still slid into the pit at over forty miles an hour. The front wheels of her car dropped into the pit with a bang and the cattle grid flicked up, landing on the bonnet.

Dixon saw the airbags deploy in the front of the car but it was only when the smoke and dust cleared that he realised Rowena had not been wearing her seatbelt. Blood was trickling down the left side of her forehead. She was swaying backwards and forwards in the front seat, at best groggy and at worst unconscious. Dixon didn't know which but, either way, she wasn't going anywhere.

He ran round to the passenger door, opened it and took out the rifle, which was lying in the passenger foot well, and then sat down on a grass mound adjacent to the driver's side door of the car. He was shaking but this time it wasn't low blood sugar that was causing it.

# Chapter Ten

Dixon sat watching Rowena and listening to the sirens in the distance gradually getting louder. He could hear at least two, but they were still some way off. He took out his phone to find that he had a signal now that he was clear of the trees and on the top of the hill, so he rang Sarge.

'We've had a bit of an incident, Sarge. I sent the boys back down Quantock Combe so they should come out at Adscombe.'

'What happened?'

'A road traffic accident, I'm afraid, but the boys are all fine. The police are on the way so I'll send some of them over there to find them. OK?'

'What should I do?'

'Wait where you are for the other teams. Just keep your phone on.'

'But everyone's all right?'

Dixon looked at Rowena still slumped unconscious in the driver's seat of her car.

'Everyone who needs to be.'

Dixon rang off. No sooner had he done so than his phone started ringing. 'Oh, thank God for that. Are you all right?' said Jane, when he picked up.

'Yes, fine.'

'Where is she?'

'In her car. Did you call an ambulance?'

'Yes, it's on the way. Helicopter's up too.'

'See if you can get a car over to Adscombe to find the boys. There are six of them in walking gear, probably knocking on doors . . .'

'There's been a call from someone there. They're fine.'

'Good. You can stand down armed response. Get the helicopter to check the rest of the woods with its thermal imaging camera.'

'Will do,' replied Jane. 'Where's Rowena's car, then, if she's in it?'

'In the cattle grid.'

'In it?'

'You'll see it when you get here. We're on the top at Crowcombe Park Gate.'

'Where's the gun?'

'I've got it.'

'And what's she doing?'

'Sleeping it off,' replied Dixon.

He rang off and listened to the sirens. There were several but two were much nearer now, the nearest down in Crowcombe at the bottom of the hill. One in the far distance suddenly went quiet and Dixon thought it was probably the armed response unit turning for home.

He looked along the top of the hill and spotted the two remaining teams in the orienteering exercise coming towards him. The team of younger boys was in front, with the girls following not far behind. Both teams were still a hundred yards or so away when a police car sped around the corner and up towards the gate. It skidded to a halt when the occupants saw Dixon holding the rifle, so he put it on the ground and waved them on.

The car pulled onto the grass in front of the cattle grid and a uniformed WPC got out of the driver's seat. The blue shirt under his uniform told Dixon that her passenger was a police community support officer.

'Inspector Dixon?'

'Yes.'

'WPC Harden, Sir, and this is PCSO Stevens. We were in Bishops Lydeard when we got the shout.'

'That is Rowena Weatherly, the suspect in a multiple murder investigation. She was shooting at me with this.' Dixon held up the rifle by the barrel. 'Lock it in the boot of your car, will you?'

'Yes, Sir. Is she . . . ?'

'She's unconscious, that's all.'

'An ambulance will be here in fifteen minutes, Sir,' said PCSO Stevens. He put the rifle in the boot of the patrol car and took out a first aid kit, which he carried over to Rowena's car.

Dixon turned to WPC Harden.

'You know that I'm undercover?'

'Yes, Sir.'

'Good.'

Dixon heard footsteps behind him and turned to find himself being surrounded by the two orienteering teams.

'What's happened, Sir?'

'Isn't that Miss Weatherly, Sir?'

'It is,' replied Dixon. 'She's had an accident but the police are here and an ambulance is on the way.'

'Is she dead?' asked one of the girls.

'No. She's unconscious but we can't move her until the paramedics get here.'

'What do we do, then, Sir?'

'We wait. I'll ring Sarge. He can come and pick you up. Wait over there,' said Dixon, pointing to a small car park below the gate.

He was on the phone to Sarge when the helicopter appeared overhead, the down draft from the rotor blades sending the thin dusting of snow that was lying on the ground high into the air. Dixon turned away and pulled his collar up. Then he walked over to WPC Harden.

'Their teacher's on the way to fetch them.'

'Yes, Sir.'

'Get the helicopter to search the woods south and east of us with its thermal imaging camera, just to be on the safe side.'

Dixon watched WPC Harden shouting into her radio and was relieved when the helicopter turned away to search the woods.

'Check someone is on the way over to Adscombe to collect the boys I was with as well, will you?'

'Yes, Sir.'

Dixon walked over to the pupils milling about in the small car park.

'Sarge is on his way to collect you. He'll be ten minutes or so. OK?'

'Where are the others, Sir?'

'I sent them back the way we came. The police'll pick them up at the other end, don't worry. Try to keep moving then you won't get cold.'

Dixon walked over to Rowena's car and watched PCSO Stevens putting her neck in a brace. She had tried to kill him. Why? He needed some time to think. Some peace and quiet. But standing there listening to the helicopter hovering over the woods and the sirens getting ever closer, all he knew for sure was that this was one walk Monty would not mind having missed.

Rowena had regained consciousness and was under guard in the back of an ambulance by the time Jane arrived. Two other police cars were also on the scene and the helicopter was still hovering over Great Wood off to the south-east, its lights just visible in the gloom.

Dixon watched Jane pull in to allow the school minibus to turn out of the small car park with the two orienteering teams safely on board. Sarge was on his way back to the school, having been assured that the other team had been picked up by the police and would be dropped back to the school later. He had taken some convincing that it had been a simple car accident, but he'd very quickly realised that was the only explanation he was going to get and so left it at that.

'Are you all right?' shouted Jane, jumping out of her car and hurrying over to Dixon.

'Fine, really,' replied Dixon.

She took hold of his elbow and turned him first to the left then to the right.

'Your face is cut to ribbons.'

Dixon rubbed his cheeks and chin with both hands and then looked at his palms. Both were smeared with thin streaks of blood.

'It's just scratches.'

'And there's a bullet hole in your collar.'

'Is there?' replied Dixon, pretending he hadn't noticed.

'Has she been arrested?'

'WPC Harden here did the honours when she came round. Attempted murder.'

'Who of?'

'Me.'

'Did she say anything?'

'Apparently not.'

'Chard and Baldwin are on the way.'

Dixon nodded.

'And DCI Lewis has been on the phone too,' said Jane.

A paramedic walked over and spoke to Dixon.

'She's fine. A bit groggy, perhaps, but that's it. We'll take her to Musgrove Park. They may keep her in overnight for observation. Then you can have her.'

'Thanks,' replied Dixon.

'Let me have a look at your face,' said the paramedic, peering at Dixon. 'Superficial scratches. You'll live. Here, wipe your face with this.' He handed Dixon a paper sachet. He tore it open and pulled out a medicated paper towel, which he used to wipe his face.

'Bloody hell.'

'What?' asked Jane.

'It stings like bug . . .'

'We'll be off, then,' said the paramedic.

Two officers accompanied Rowena Weatherly in the ambulance and two more followed in a patrol car. Dixon and Jane watched them leave.

'What about the car?' asked Jane.

'A tractor is coming to pull it out.'

'You lifted the cattle grid?'

'Just enough to drag it a few feet.'

'Was it heavy?'

'You could say that,' replied Dixon. 'It's a bloody good job it was a small one.'

Jane smiled.

'Tell me what happened, then.'

'She just started shooting at us.'

'Us?'

'Me. So I sent the lads off in the other direction and made a run for the road. Got here first, as you can see.'

'Any idea why?'

'Yes.'

'Well?'

'I want to watch her interviewed first. And I want to be there when they search her rooms.'

A dark blue Vauxhall Vectra pulled into the car park behind them. Dixon watched DCI Chard and DI Baldwin getting out.

Chard turned up his collar and then rubbed his hands together before thrusting them deep into his coat pockets.

'You look like you've been dragged through a hedge backwards.'

'Funny you should say that,' replied Dixon.

'Where is she?'

'On her way to Musgrove Park.'

'Under arrest?'

'Yes.'

'What about the rifle?'

'In the boot of WPC Harden's car. It's a .22, probably from the school range but the headmaster can confirm if one's missing.'

'And no one was hit?'

'No, Sir.'

'Well done.'

'Thank you, Sir.'

'We'll interview her as soon as we can.'

'The paramedics said they might keep her in overnight for observation,' said Jane.

'I'll check with the hospital,' said Baldwin.

'What about the boys in the orienteering team?' asked Dixon.

'On the way to the station. We'll get statements from them and then drop them back later.'

'To the school?'

'Yes. Is there a problem?'

'They're the only ones who know what happened here. The rest think it was an accident. Send 'em back to the school and my cover's blown.'

Chard looked at Baldwin and then turned back to Dixon. 'Seems to me we don't need you anymore. Your job is done. After all, we've got her now, haven't we?'

'If you assume Rowena Weatherly killed Isobel Swan, then yes. But she didn't.'

'And you know that for sure?'

'No more than you know for sure that she did.'

'Point taken.'

'Shall I get on to the headmaster?' asked Baldwin.

'Better had,' replied Chard. 'Tell him to ring their parents. They'll need to go home when we've finished with them. No phones and no Internet either.'

'Yes, Sir.'

'Do you need a lift back, Dixon?' asked Chard.

'No, thank you, Sir. I'll go with Constable Winter.'

Dixon watched the tractor pulling the VW Beetle out of the cattle grid, two large planks being used as a makeshift ramp. The car was then winched onto the flatbed lorry. The tubular steel grid itself had buckled and so it too was dragged clear before the road was closed off with police tape and traffic cones.

'Highways are on their way with Road Closed signs now, Sir,' said WPC Harden.

'Good.'

'We'll wait for them to get here and then drop the gun down to Taunton. And we'll be back tomorrow morning with a dog team to look for any cartridge cases.'

'Better tell the helicopter they can go too. I'm assuming they've not found anything?'

'Nothing, Sir.'

'Let 'em go, then.'

'C'mon, let's get out of here,' said Jane. 'You must be freezing.'

'I am.'

They followed the flatbed lorry down through Crowcombe and, once out onto the main road, Jane overtook it and accelerated towards Taunton.

Dixon was fiddling with the heater. 'Did you get Clive Cooper's inquest file?' he asked.

'It's on the back seat.'

'Well?'

'It was an open verdict. Not suicide. He was found in the River Taff by the Millennium Stadium. Injury to the back of his head but no real evidence of foul play.'

'I bet there wasn't.'

It was just after 7 p.m. when Dixon stepped out of the shower, wrapped a towel around his waist and looked in the mirror. His face and neck were covered in scratches, some of them deep, and it would be a few days before he could shave again. Every cloud, he thought. He hated shaving.

He walked into the living room to find Jane sitting on the arm of the sofa reading the *Iliad*. She looked up.

'It's all Greek to me.'

'It is Greek,' said Dixon.

'I know that, idiot. And these rooms are so dark and miserable. Haskill must be a bit . . .'

'He does teach ancient history.'

'That explains it,' said Jane, shaking her head. She looked at her watch.

'Baldwin rang. Rowena's staying in hospital overnight. Chard will interview her in the morning. They're going into her rooms here in ten minutes.'

'Let's get over there, then.'

'She's got a flat down by the river too, one of the new ones at Firepool Lock.'

The headmaster was letting DI Baldwin and a team of scientific services officers into Rowena's rooms on the first floor of Gardenhurst when Dixon and Jane arrived. Hatton stepped back to allow the others past and then held out his hand to Dixon. They shook hands.

'I gather I have you to thank that I'm not explaining to more parents that their child is dead.'

'They were never the target.'

'Who was?'

'Me.'

'Why?'

'That remains to be seen.'

'Well, at least you're all right. I've explained to DI Baldwin that we've got a rifle missing from the range. Miss Weatherly had a key.'

Dixon nodded. The information came as no surprise.

'Anyway, I'll leave you to it,' said Hatton. 'I'm sure you've got better things to do than stand around chatting.'

'We do,' replied Dixon.

He followed Jane into Rowena's room. It was a large bedsit, with the kitchen along the wall to the left of the door, a small dining table, a lounge area and then the bed along the far wall. A door led into a small en suite shower room.

'There's similar teachers' accommodation on each floor so they can keep an eye on the students, apparently,' said Baldwin. She turned to the scientific services team. 'Right, get to it.'

Dixon noticed a hockey stick bag hanging over the back of a dining chair.

'Bag up that hockey stick, will you?'

'Why?' asked Baldwin.

'Possible murder weapon,' replied Dixon. 'Derek Phelps.'

An officer wearing disposable paper overalls picked it up.

'It's empty, Sir.'

'Bloody thing could be anywhere,' said Baldwin.

Dixon looked at the piles of exercise books on the dining table, before putting on a pair of disposable rubber gloves and flicking through them. Essays on Mussolini, the rise of Adolf Hitler and the causes of World War One. Someone's homework wasn't going to get marked for a while.

'Jane, check the bedside table, will you?'

'What am I looking for?'

'Dunno. But you'll know it when you see it.'

Jane shrugged her shoulders and began opening the drawers. Dixon turned his attention to a bookshelf, flicking through each book in turn.

'Anything?' he asked.

'No,' replied Jane.

'Nothing in the bathroom either,' said Baldwin, squeezing past a scientific services officer in the doorway.

'No jewellery even?'

'Nothing.'

'Let's try her flat, then,' said Dixon.

A scientific services team was already at work in Rowena's ground floor flat at Firepool Lock by the time Dixon and Jane arrived. Overlooking Firepool Weir on the River Tone, it was a new purpose built block of flats rendered and painted white with wood cladding and large windows. The flat itself was immaculate. Polished oak flooring throughout the open plan living area, white leather furniture and glass tables with matching dining suite and kitchen units gave

Dixon the distinct impression that Rowena had bought the show flat. He picked up a copy of *House Beautiful* magazine from the coffee table and looked at the date.

'This is last May's.'

'D'you think she's ever stayed here?' asked Jane.

'SOCO will soon tell us,' said Dixon. 'You check the wardrobes, I'll start in the kitchen.'

The kitchen cupboards contained tins of beans, chopped tomatoes and a bag of spaghetti. Otherwise nothing. The fridge was empty, switched off and the door ajar. Not surprising of itself perhaps, given that she would be living in the school during term time.

'There are some clothes in the wardrobe,' shouted Jane.

Dixon walked through into the bedroom to find Jane sliding clothes along on their hangers in a large built in wardrobe. He noticed a suitcase on the top shelf.

'All women's,' said Jane. 'The bedside tables are empty too.'

Dixon looked at the bed. The duvet hardly had a crease in it and he wondered if it had ever been slept in. It was a divan bed, with a large drawer in the base, so he knelt down and opened it. He reached in underneath the piles of clean bedding and felt around, more in hope than expectation. Then he pulled the clean bedding to the front of the drawer and felt around at the back. He stopped when his fingers closed around a small box, black leather with a large gold lock.

'It's a jewellery box,' said Jane, looking over his shoulder. 'There's nothing in the bathroom either except a few towels and a bottle of shampoo.'

Dixon flicked the clasp with his finger and it opened to reveal a gold locket and chain with small diamonds set into the front in the shape of a star. He held it up by the chain and could see that the back was blank, possibly to accommodate an inscription.

'Open it,' said Jane.

Dixon tried to pull it open but found it impossible wearing disposable rubber gloves.

'You got a pen?'

Jane fumbled in her handbag and produced a black BIC biro.

'Perfect.' Dixon took the top off and then pushed the sharp end of the lid gently into the small indentation along the leading edge of the locket. It was designed for a fingernail, but he could not risk leaving prints and so the pen would have to do. It opened. Just a crack but that was enough and he was then able to prise it apart. Inside he found a lock of blonde hair and a tiny black and white photograph of a woman holding a baby. The picture was faded and had been cut to fit into the locket. He froze.

'What is it?' asked Jane.

Dixon handed her the locket.

'It looks like Isobel Swan,' she said, staring at the photograph.

'Or Fran.'

'Yes, it could be Fran.'

'It's neither of them, though, is it?'

'Who is it, then?' asked Jane, closing the locket. She dropped it into an evidence bag and then put it in her handbag.

'Rowena's mother,' said Dixon. 'And the baby is Rowena.'

'How d'you . . . ?'

'A hunch. Think about it. The photo is the right age and who else is the lock of hair going to belong to?'

'It could . . .'

'Of course it could. But a DNA test will soon tell us, won't it?'

'It will.'

'And what colour do you think Rowena's hair is underneath all that black dye?'

'You still haven't told me why Rowena tried to kill you,' said Jane.

They had arrived at the Greyhound at Staple Fitzpaine with seconds to spare before the pub stopped serving food and were now sitting by the fire waiting for their fish and chips to arrive.

'I'm the only one making the connection with Fran's disappearance. At least that's what she thinks.'

'It'll be interesting to see what she says tomorrow.'

'It will,' replied Dixon, looking at his watch. 'I'm glad you left Monty with your parents. Poor bugger'd be starving by now.'

'I'm picking him up in the morning. They're off to my aunt's for the week.'

'Bring him with you.'

'OK.'

Dixon took a large swig of beer.

'What's it like being shot at, then?' asked Jane.

'Didn't really have to time to think about it. One of the boys heard a bee buzz past him and then we were into it.'

'A bee?'

'That's what it sounds like if you're on the receiving end. The bullet whizzes past you, then you hear the shot. Speed of sound and all that.'

'How'd you know that?'

'Haven't you ever seen *Saving Private Ryan*?' asked Dixon.

'No.'

'You have got a treat in store.'

'You and your bloody films,' said Jane, shaking her head.

Jane dropped Dixon outside the front entrance of the school just before 11 p.m. He leaned across and kissed her.

'Can I . . . ?'

'Better not. You'll get me expelled. Text me when you get home.'

'OK. And be careful.'

He got out of her car, ran across to the shelter of the doorway and turned just in time to watch her tail lights disappear down the drive. He hoped Jane understood. It was Fran's time now. Find her killer and then he could move on. Perhaps.

He tried the front door. It was locked, so he walked around the headmaster's house and in through the back door of the school. He tiptoed along the main corridor, keeping his heels off the tiled floor, and up the stairs to his rooms. He opened the front door to find a folded piece of paper that had been pushed under the door.

'Masters' Christmas lunch. Small dining room (opposite big one). 12.30 for 1 p.m. Robin.'

He made himself a coffee and sat on the small sofa to read Clive Cooper's inquest file. The cause of death was given as 1(a) drowning, although the pathologist was unable to confirm whether his head injury occurred before or after he entered the water. Nor was there any evidence of where or how he entered the water, hence the open verdict. Dixon noticed that the coroner had released the body for cremation after the inquest, so exhumation for further examination by Roger was not an option. He wondered whether it would be worth Roger looking at the pathologist's notes and photographs to see if there was any similarity with the injuries to Derek Phelps. Dixon would be speaking to him in the morning about his hockey stick theory anyway.

Of the witness statements, the only one of interest came from Clive Cooper's elderly mother, Edna. She lived in Wiveliscombe and gave a detailed and tragic account of her son's descent into alcoholism, which had begun fifteen years ago. Dixon frowned. No mention was made at all of her son's longstanding friendship with Derek Phelps, nor was any reason given for his drinking.

She had last seen her son the Christmas before he died, when he was living in a hostel in Cardiff. She had sent him a train ticket home but he had stayed only a few days before he disappeared, along with the contents of her purse. She heard nothing further from or about him until a knock on the door from the police three months later.

Her closing remarks dealt with what she understood to be her son's state of mind the last time she saw him. He had been brought up a strict Catholic and was, as far as she was aware, not the type to commit suicide, nor had he ever demonstrated any suicidal tendencies. It was an odd phrase for an elderly woman to use about her son and Dixon suspected she had been led in this evidence by the officer taking the statement. Nevertheless, her statement was clear as far as it went. He closed the file and hid it under the mattress with Isobel's file.

It had been a long and interesting day. He had been involved in firearms incidents before but had never experienced anyone shooting at him with intent to kill. Best not to dwell on it. There would be plenty of time for that later.

He set the alarm on his phone for 7 a.m. and went to sleep with the bedside light on.

# Chapter Eleven

Rowena Weatherly had been rearrested on arrival at Taunton Police Station the following morning on suspicion of the murders of Isobel Swan and Derek Phelps and was now in a private conference with her lawyer, Stephen Dunn. DCI Chard was pacing up and down in the CID Room waiting for Dixon to finish with the coffee machine.

'I've got a good feeling about this, Dixon,' said Chard.

'I shall watch the interview with interest, Sir,' replied Dixon, turning around with a plastic cup in each hand. He walked over to Jane's desk in the far corner of the CID Room and handed her one of the cups.

'What'd he say?'

'He says he's got a touch of wind this morning.'

Jane coughed and spluttered, spraying coffee across her keyboard. Tears of suppressed laughter began streaming down her cheeks.

'Come now, Constable, get a grip,' said Dixon, patting her on the back.

Jane began mopping up the coffee on her desk with a tissue.

'Did you see Monty?' she asked.

'He was asleep on the parcel shelf when I got here so I didn't wake him up.'

'He's fine.'

'Do me a favour, will you?' asked Dixon.

'What?'

'Ring Clive Cooper's mother in Wiveliscombe and make us an appointment to go and see her this afternoon. Threeish. I've got the masters' Christmas lunch so you could pick me up at 2.30 p.m.?'

'Fine. Leave it with me.' Jane knew better than to ask why.

'Was there anything interesting in Derek Phelps' stuff?'

'There's a box down in the store. Nothing that springs to mind though.'

'How long till the interview starts?'

'Half an hour or so. Her lawyer's only been in with her twenty minutes.'

'Let's have a look in this box, then,' replied Dixon.

'I'll go and get it.'

While Jane went down to the store Dixon logged in to her computer, and had just about finished deleting all his emails when she dumped the box on the corner of the desk next to him.

'It's the personal items from his room at the school.'

'Did he live anywhere else?'

'No. Not that we've been able to find, anyway.'

'So, this is it?'

'Apart from a CD player, clothes and books, that sort of stuff. The school are waiting for the nod from us before they dispose of it.'

'Where is it?'

'Still in his room.'

'Gloves?'

'There are some in the drawer,' replied Jane.

Dixon put on a pair of disposable rubber gloves and began rummaging in the box. He pulled out a brown leather wallet in a small clear plastic bag and held it up in front of Jane.

'Nothing of interest,' she said.

'Bank cards?'

'There's a Barclays current account. We're waiting for the statements to arrive.'

'How far back?'

'Twelve months.'

'Get onto the bank and ask for statements going back as far as they can.'

'As far as they can?'

'At least ten years. Twelve would be better if they can do it.'

Dixon put the wallet on the desk and then turned his attention back to the contents of the box. He placed an iPod, no doubt loaded with Beatles songs, several pairs of spectacles and a small leather bound pocket Bible on the desk before pulling out a set of keys.

'Door keys, a bike lock and his locker in the staff room.'

Next came various boxes of prescription medication, all bagged up.

'They all check out. We've spoken to his doctor.'

Dixon nodded. 'You were right, then,' he said.

'What?'

'Nothing of interest.'

---

The interview with Rowena Weatherly began just before 10 a.m. DCI Chard introduced those present for the tape and then reminded Rowena that she was under caution. Dixon and Jane were watching on a television screen in an adjacent room. They could see both

DI Baldwin and Rowena's lawyer, Stephen Dunn, making notes. Rowena herself sat impassively, staring at the table in front of her.

'Right, then, Rowena, let's talk about yesterday. What was that all about?' asked Chard.

'No comment,' said Dixon. Jane rolled her eyes.

To everyone's surprise, Stephen Dunn spoke first.

'My client wishes to read a prepared statement for the tape, after which she will answer 'no comment' to each and every question asked of her.'

DCI Chard looked at DI Baldwin and then back to Rowena. 'Go ahead.'

Rowena took a folded piece of paper out of her pocket and, without looking up, began reading aloud.

'I was in love with Isobel.'

Dixon sat back and folded his arms.

'I asked her to marry me but she said that she hated me and threatened to expose me to the school,' continued Rowena. Tears were streaming down her face. 'I couldn't allow that. So I killed her. I cut off her ring finger so that no one else could have her. Derek Phelps was blackmailing me so I agreed to meet him behind the sports hall and killed him. I was not trying to kill Nick Dixon. I believed that Gittens and Lloyd could identify me and I was trying to kill them. Tell Nick I'm sorry he got in the way.'

Rowena folded the piece of paper and passed it to Dunn.

'Is that it?' asked Chard.

'No comment.'

'You're gonna have to do better than that, Rowena. We need to verify . . .'

'No comment.'

'From where I'm sitting it looks like a pack of lies. If you want us to believe you then we need more details. Proof.'

'No comment.'

DCI Chard turned to Dunn. 'I suggest you explain to your client that we need her to prove what she's said. Otherwise she's just wasting everyone's time.'

Dunn leaned across and whispered in Rowena's right ear. She listened and then nodded.

'Go ahead,' said Dunn.

'This is gonna be good,' said Dixon.

'How did you kill Isobel?' asked Chard.

'She came to my room for a glass of wine. I told her I wanted to apologise for my behaviour. I drugged her with ketamine, cut off her ring finger and then tried to get her in the car. That's when Gittens and Lloyd saw me. Or at least I thought they saw me.'

'Where did you get the ketamine?'

'No comment.'

'What happened then?'

'I hid down on the playing fields. Cut her throat and left her body in the stream. Then I disposed of the car.'

'Tell me about this car.'

'It was an old Ford Focus with a boot. Not the hatchback. I paid cash for it.'

'Where is it now?'

'I dumped it.'

'Where?'

'Bristol. Then I caught the train back.'

'When?'

'A few days later. I don't remember.'

'What about Phelps, then? How'd you kill him?'

'I hit him with my hockey stick. Three times on the back of the head.'

'Where's the stick now?'

'I left it in the girls' changing rooms.'

'Describe it for me.'

'It's a Grays. Pink and white with a black handle.'

'Hidden in plain sight. Very clever,' said Dixon.

'You believe her?' asked Jane.

'About the murder of Phelps, yes. The rest is bollocks.'

'So, what about yesterday, then?' asked Chard.

'I took the gun from the range and followed the minibus. I knew they'd be coming past Crowcombe Park Gate one way or the other so I waited for them.'

'And you were after Gittens and Lloyd?'

'Yes.'

'Have you met Nick Dixon before?'

'No comment.'

'You knew he was a police officer?'

'No comment.'

'That's enough for now I think, Inspector,' said Dunn. 'My client has clarified her statement, as you requested.'

Chard terminated the interview and Rowena was taken back to the cells. Dixon listened to the voices outside in the corridor.

'Get the superintendent to extend the time we can hold her while we see what else we can find,' said Chard. 'First things first, though. Let's go to the Vivary Arms for a celebratory beer.'

Dixon shook his head. 'He'd believe her if she confessed to shooting JFK . . .'

The door opened and Chard walked in, followed by DI Baldwin.

'A good result all round, I think,' said Chard.

'If you assume she's telling the truth,' replied Dixon.

'And you don't think she is, I suppose.'

'About the murder of Phelps, yes. She killed him to protect whoever killed Isobel Swan. And there is no way on God's clean earth that she was shooting at Gittens and Lloyd yesterday. I know. I was on the receiving end of it.'

'Well, you're in a minority of one,' said Chard.

'Two.'

Dixon looked at Jane and smiled. Then he turned to Chard.

'You enjoy your beer, Sir. Jane and I have got a murder to investigate.'

Dixon left Jane tracking down CCTV coverage of Bristol Temple Meads railway station for the three days after Isobel Swan's murder. If Rowena was telling the truth about dumping the car then she would appear on camera travelling back to Taunton. It was a good place to dump a car, of course, provided she chose her spot carefully. With the keys left in it, it would pretty soon be taken for a spin and then left burnt out in a field somewhere with entirely unrelated fingerprints all over it. Dixon had to admire her ingenuity. Talk about getting someone else to do your dirty work for you. Dixon nodded. That was exactly what Rowena was doing. Someone else's dirty work. Cleaning up the mess. Or trying to. And now taking the fall for it.

He walked around the corner into Vivary Park and let Monty off the lead. Watching him tear off across the grass had never failed to raise a smile from Dixon. Until today. He was remembering walking through Vivary Park on a summer's evening many years ago, hand in hand with Fran, after a meal in the wine bar at the top of the High Street. La Bonne Vie. And it had been a good life. It was going to be an even better life too.

Dixon looked across at the bandstand. It was in need of a fresh coat of paint but it was still the same bandstand where they had sheltered from the rain and sat talking for hours without noticing it had stopped. He could picture her face there in front of him even now. It had been that night he had told her he loved her and that he would never let her down.

He was brought back to the present by a stick dropping onto his shoes. Monty was sitting at his feet looking up at him.

'C'mon you, best get back.'

Dixon threw the stick in the direction of the exit and followed Monty as he tore off after it. He stopped at the gate to put his lead on and looked back at the bandstand. He knew then that he still loved Fran and, no, he wouldn't let her down.

Dixon looked at his watch. It was just after midday.

'I'm off back to the school, otherwise I'll be late for that bloody lunch. Here are your keys,' he said, dropping Jane's car keys onto her desk.

'OK. I'll pick you up at 2.30 p.m.'

'How far have you got?'

'British Transport Police are getting the CCTV for us,' replied Jane.

'Good.'

'And I've sent two WPCs to search the girls' changing rooms for Rowena's hockey stick.'

'Check whether she's got any brothers, will you?'

'How?'

'They'd have gone to St Dunstan's too, I expect. Check there first. If they were older they'd have been there before her and . . .'

'I get the idea.'

'And I want Rowena's birth certificate. Plus anything else you can find on her family. Marriage certificate, decree absolute, anything. See if Louise Willmott can give you a hand.'

'What I still don't understand is how you can be so sure that Rowena didn't kill Fran,' said Jane.

'Do you remember the hockey tour I told you about? The one Fran was supposed to have been on when she disappeared.'

'Yes.'

'The one her parents stopped her going on because it was too close to her exams.'

'Yes, I remember.'

'Well, Rowena went on it,' said Dixon.

'So she was . . .'

'. . . Playing hockey in Holland when Fran disappeared. That's right.'

'Ah, there you are,' said Phillips. 'Come and sit over here.'

'Sorry I'm late,' said Dixon.

'You've not missed anything. Don't worry about it. Father Anthony will be saying grace in a min . . . here we go.'

Father Anthony was sitting at the next table and had his back to Dixon when he stood up.

'For what we are about to receive may the Lord make us truly thankful.'

'Here, have some wine,' said Phillips, filling up Dixon's glass. 'We've dispensed with the silly hats this year but we can still have a glass or two of plonk, can't we?'

'I suppose we can.'

'I gather you were the hero of the hour yesterday?'

'What?'

'Rowena's car accident. Silly arse didn't notice the cattle grid wasn't there or something. Or so rumour has it.'

'Yes.'

'Can't think what she was doing up there, though.'

'I just assumed she was looking out for the girls' team,' replied Dixon.

'That might be it. Oh well, chin, chin.' Phillips took a large swig of wine and then topped up his glass.

'No sign of the headmaster,' said Dixon, looking around the room.

'He never comes to these things,' replied Phillips. 'And he'll be lunching with the governors today, I should imagine.'

'Or Mr Griffiths?'

'Don't know where he is. He was invited but then he is just a supply teacher.'

'As opposed to a trainee teacher.'

'Quite,' said Phillips. 'You can't afford to miss out on a free lunch.'

Dixon smiled. He took a sip of wine and tried to listen to the various conversations going on around him. There were three long dining tables with bench seating on either side, smaller versions of the seating in the main dining room. To his left the conversation seemed to be about the governors' meeting that afternoon and the possible cancellation of Saturday's rugby match with Sherborne that might result. On his right, Phillips was involved in an animated discussion about the competence of the local police. Dixon resolved to keep out of that particular conversation and tried to focus on the next table, the third being out of earshot above the general hubbub. Father Anthony was surrounded by ladies and seemed to be fending off suggestions that he should play tennis again. A dodgy knee was his excuse, apparently.

Dixon marvelled at their ability to ignore the fact that a member of staff and a pupil at the school had been murdered. Still, the show must go on. No doubt that would be their excuse.

'What d'you think of life in a boarding school, then?' The question came from the teacher sitting opposite Dixon. 'Clarke. French,' he said, holding out his hand.

'Eventful,' said Dixon, shaking Clarke's hand.

'It's not usually like this. Pretty dull most of the time.'

'You talking shop?' asked Phillips.

'I was just asking him if he was enjoying it here.'

'Of course he is. Aren't you, Nick?'

'Very much so,' replied Dixon, through a mouthful of roast potato.

Suddenly, he felt a hand on his shoulder. 'Excuse me, Sir. The headmaster's asking to see you.' It was Gabriel White, the head boy, given away by the badge on the collar of his jacket.

'Better go,' said Phillips. 'I'll make sure they don't clear your plate away.'

'Thanks.'

'He's in his office, Sir,' said White.

'Thank you.'

Dixon's phone was ringing in his pocket as he walked along the main corridor.

'We've got the hockey stick,' said Jane when he answered.

'Where is it?'

'On the way to the lab.'

'Ring Roger. Ask him whether a hockey stick caused the injuries to Derek Phelps. Email him a copy of Clive Cooper's post mortem report and get him to liaise with the pathologist in Cardiff. Ask him if the pattern of injuries is the same or similar. And I want to know if a hockey stick could've caused Cooper's injuries.'

'You think she killed Clive Cooper as well?'

'I do.'

'Bloody hell.'

Dixon was standing outside the headmaster's office. 'Gotta go,' he said, ringing off. Then he knocked on the door.

'Come in.'

'Ah, Dixon, sorry to tear you away from your lunch but I'm meeting the governors in half an hour and Chard's telling me Rowena Weatherly's been charged?'

'Not yet, no. Not as far as I know, anyway.'

'What the . . . ?'

'There's a news blackout on it at the moment but she's confessed to the murders of Isobel Swan and Derek Phelps and the attempted murders of Gittens and Lloyd.'

'So, that's it, then, surely?'

Dixon hesitated.

'Come on, off the record. I have to know. More lives might be at stake.'

'That's not it, no.'

'Why?'

'You and I both know the answer to that question. Fran Sawyer. St Dunstan's, seventeen years ago. Rowena's protecting someone and doesn't want the connection made.'

'Who?'

'That remains to be seen. Her father. Brother, possibly.'

Dixon looked for the slightest flicker of a reaction in the headmaster's eyes but saw none.

'So we should still go ahead and end the term early?'

'Yes, you should.'

Dixon watched Hatton sucking his teeth.

'Thank you. This conversation won't go any further.'

Dixon nodded and then left the room. He stood in the main entrance hall and looked up at the clock above the corridor. There was just enough time to get back to the dining room for his Christmas pudding before Jane arrived at 2.30 p.m. He had done his insulin injection before lunch and needed the sugar.

Dixon was standing outside the main entrance of the school, with his back to the front door, watching the sleet melt as soon as it hit the ground and listening to his stomach grumbling. Phillips had done as he had promised, although all that was left on Dixon's plate when he got back to the dining room had been one roast potato and several Brussels sprouts sitting in a puddle of congealed gravy. All of it stone cold. The Christmas pudding had not made up for it either.

He was thinking about the Ouija board and Rowena's feeble attempt to have him taken off the case. That was assuming it had been Rowena, of course. The board had disappeared, so dusting for fingerprints was not an option now and the handwriting on the note he had kept was deliberately disguised. Were there prints on it, perhaps? Unlikely. Whoever wrote it would have worn gloves. Particularly if it hadn't been Rowena. Whoever she was protecting was smart enough to have got away with killing Fran and would be unlikely to make such a simple mistake now. Anyway, he could hardly reveal the connection himself. All in good time, perhaps, but not yet.

The sleet had turned to rain by the time Jane pulled into the car park. She saw Dixon sheltering in the doorway and parked across the entrance with her passenger door facing him.

'Thank you,' he said, getting in.

'My pleasure.'

Jane waited until Dixon had put his seatbelt on before turning out of the car park and heading west out of Taunton towards Wiveliscombe.

'Tell me about Edna Cooper, then.'

'She lives at 91c Stile Road, Wiveliscombe. It's a small housing association flat. Has an ancient conviction for shoplifting. A widow. Husband died in 1989.'

'Long time to be a widow,' said Dixon.

'It is.'

'What'd she get for the shoplifting?'

'Conditional discharge.'

'Does she have any other children?'

'No.'

'Lost her husband and her son,' said Dixon, shaking his head.

Dixon unzipped his jacket, reached in and pulled out Clive Cooper's inquest file. He took out Mrs Cooper's witness statement and then threw the file onto the back seat. He had read the statement three times before Jane spoke.

'I didn't think it was that interesting.'

'It's interesting for what it doesn't say more than what it does,' replied Dixon, without looking up.

Jane shook her head and carried on driving.

Stile Road was to the north of Wiveliscombe and they had driven up and down it several times before they spotted number 91. It was a small block of four flats, built of red brick, with a central entrance hall and stairs leading up to a balcony on the first floor. Each flat had its own front door, the ground floor flats at the side and the upstairs flats on the balcony. 91c turned out to be up the stairs.

'No lift,' said Dixon.

'You don't need a lift.'

'I don't but Mrs Cooper might. One day.'

'True,' replied Jane. 'They'd move her into a home, I suppose. Or a warden controlled block.'

'There's a cheerful thought.'

Dixon knocked on the pane of frosted glass in the door and then began rummaging in his pockets.

'Here,' said Jane, handing him his warrant card just as a figure appeared behind the door.

'I owe you one.'

'One more.'

'Quite.'

Mrs Edna Cooper looked them up and down. 'Police?'

'Yes. Detective Inspector Dixon and Detective Constable Winter.'

'You'd better come in.'

Dixon and Jane followed her into a small living room at the back of the flat. It overlooked the garden, although 'area of wasteland' was a more accurate description.

'They keep threatening to come and sort it out but never do. Cuts,' said Mrs Cooper, shrugging her shoulders. 'Sit down.'

Dixon looked at the sofa. It was old, covered in cat hair and turned out to be just as uncomfortable as he had feared. Jane pulled a chair out from under the small table in the window, took out her notebook and sat down.

'I need something to lean on, if that's OK?'

'Fine.'

'We wanted to talk to you about your son,' said Dixon.

'What d'you want to know?'

'Tell me about his relationship with Derek Phelps.'

'They were friends. It wasn't a relationship in that sense.'

'Did you ever meet him?'

'Yes, a couple of times.'

'How did they meet?'

'At work. They were both kitchen porters at St Dunstan's. Worked together there for years, they did. Until Clive got the sack.'

'Why was that?'

'Drinking. He was supposed to have hit someone as well but it never went any further. It was the finish of him. He was never going to get a job anywhere else.'

'Why not?'

'He'd only got that thanks to a local charity. He wasn't quite . . . well, he couldn't read or write, you see. Neither of them could.'

'I understand,' replied Dixon. 'D'you have a photo of him?'

Mrs Cooper reached into her handbag on the floor and took out her purse. She opened it and passed it to Dixon, jabbing her finger at a Perspex window on one side.

'That's him. Taken twenty years ago. The other one's my husband.'

Dixon looked at the photograph. He recognised Clive from St Dunstan's and remembered an intimidating man who often muttered to himself under his breath. He had quite a reputation, did Clive.

'What sort of things did they do together?'

'Who?'

'Clive and Derek.'

'Drink, mainly. They went to rock concerts sometimes.'

'Who was the dominant one?'

'Derek was the boss.'

'So, Clive would do what Derek said?'

'Yes.'

'Always?'

'Yes, I think so.'

'When did his drinking become a problem?'

'Oh, I don't know. A couple of years before he left St Dunstan's? Maybe. More, perhaps. It was amazing they put up with him so long.'

'What was his relationship with Derek like around this time?'

'It fell apart. They were always fighting. It was Derek he hit when he got the sack. I'm sure of it.'

'Did he ever explain to you why he was drinking heavily?'

'No.'

'Did he get help for it?'

'What, Alcoholics Anonymous or something?'

'Yes.'

'No, he never did that. Never accepted he had a problem.'

'Did you discuss it with him?'

'No. Never. He wasn't that sort of person and we didn't have that sort of relationship.'

'Did he say anything about Derek? Explain why they'd fallen out?'

'He said he didn't want anything more to do with him. Couldn't go along with it anymore.'

'It?'

'Those were his words. I asked him what he meant but he refused to explain.'

Dixon looked at the wall next to Mrs Cooper's chair. There was a picture of Jesus Christ in an ornate gold frame with rosary beads draped around it. She was wearing a crucifix too.

'What about his religion?'

'He was brought up a strict Catholic and stayed that way until the end.' She pointed at the picture on the wall. 'Those are his rosary beads. They found them in his pocket when they pulled him out the river.'

'What about the rest of his stuff?'

'His clothes went to the tip. That's all they were fit for.'

'You mention a rucksack in your statement?'

'It's in the wardrobe in the spare room. I couldn't bear to touch it.'

'Can we see it?'

'Just take it.'

Dixon looked at Jane and nodded. She got up and went to get the rucksack.

'It's the door on the left, dear,' said Mrs Cooper.

'One last question,' said Dixon, 'what d'you think happened to him?'

'I don't know and, to be honest, I really don't care anymore.'

'What d'you make of that?' asked Jane, as they sped east on the B3227 towards Taunton.

'Clive started drinking a couple of years or perhaps longer before he got sacked from St Dunstan's. That's what she said. That was before Phelps left ten years ago.'

'Which was not long after Fran disappeared,' said Jane.

'It's not. And he fell out with Derek at the same time because he couldn't go along with "it" anymore.'

'I'd love to know what the "it" is.'

'It's going to be one of two things. Either Derek killed Fran or he was blackmailing whoever did.'

'D'you think he killed Fran?'

'Not a chance. He'd never've got away with it.'

'So, he was blackmailing someone?'

'He was.'

'Who?'

'I dunno. But it sure as bloody hell wasn't Rowena Weatherly.'

Dixon's phone rang just as Jane was parking her car behind Taunton Police Station. It was Roger Poland.

'It's a hockey stick, all right. Let me rephrase that. The injuries are consistent with being hit by a hockey stick.'

'Phelps?'

'Both. The pathologist in Cardiff emailed over her photos.'

'Thanks, Roger.'

'How're you getting on?'

'Close. Just need to be a bit closer.'

'You'll get there.'

'I will.'

'And don't do anything stupid when you do.'

'I won't.'

Dixon rang off. Jane had parked the car and was walking out of the car park with Monty on a lead. No doubt she would be back in five or ten minutes, so he opened the glove box and pulled a pair of disposable rubber gloves out of the box that was wedged in alongside the service booklet, a torch and a pair of sunglasses. Dixon also spotted a packet of fruit pastilles. He smiled. She must have put them there just for him.

He reached over his shoulder and dragged Clive Cooper's rucksack between the seats into the front of the car, dumping it on the driver's seat. Then he opened it. The top flap felt heavy, so he unzipped the pocket and looked in. There was a penknife, a half empty tube of toothpaste and a roll of toilet paper in a plastic bag, presumably to keep it dry. There was also a blue plastic cigarette lighter.

He zipped the pocket back up and allowed the flap to fall behind the rucksack. Then he peered into the main compartment. He had no intention of emptying out the contents in Jane's car and was really just killing time until she got back with Monty. Her calming influence might be useful if he bumped into DCI Chard in the station.

He reached in and began feeling around inside the main compartment. There was some light coming from the police station windows and the outside light above the back door but not nearly enough for him to see what he was doing. It felt a bit like a lucky dip.

Then his fingers closed around a small book. It felt soft to the touch, even through rubber gloves. He flicked it open and felt the paper. It was thin. Pocket Bible thin.

Jane arrived back with Monty ten minutes later to find Dixon waiting by the back of her car. She noticed that he was wearing gloves and carrying Clive Cooper's rucksack.

'What's up?'

'Not sure yet. Can you get Phelps' stuff out of store?'

'Again?'

'Yes, again.'

'OK, if you say so.'

Dixon followed Jane to the store and waited while she fetched the box. They were on their way up the stairs when Chard appeared on the landing above them.

'Where have you two been?'

'Doing your j . . .'

'To interview Clive Cooper's mother. We'll fill you in later, Sir,' said Jane.

'Who's Clive Cooper?'

'A friend of Derek Phelps.'

'Don't know why you're bothering. The lab's confirmed blood on the hockey stick and we're gonna charge her in the morning.'

'For Isobel Swan and Phelps?' asked Dixon.

'Yes.'

'But she didn't kill Isobel Swan.'

'And you can prove that, I suppose?'

'Can you prove she did?'

'She's confessed. And she knows all sorts of stuff that's not been made public.'

Dixon sighed.

'Just don't go mucking it up,' said Chard.

'You don't need my hel . . .'

'We won't, Sir,' said Jane.

Once in the comparative safety of a vacant office off the CID Room, Dixon took the small Bible out of the box of Derek Phelps' belongings and put it on the table. It was bound in soft black leather with gold lettering on the front. *New World Translation of the Holy Scriptures*. Then he reached into Cooper's rucksack and felt around for the book that he knew was in there. His fingers closed around it and he pulled it out of the rucksack, placing it on the table next to Derek's. It too was bound in black leather with identical gold lettering on the front.

'Holy shit,' said Jane.

Dixon frowned at her.

'Pardon the pun,' she said. 'What's the *New World Translation*?'

'Jehovah's Witnesses,' replied Dixon.

Jane nodded.

Dixon picked up Cooper's Bible and opened it. On the flyleaf, written in faded black ink that had turned brown with the passage of time, was the reference 'Colossians 3:25'. The handwriting was old fashioned, classical even, and he was sure a fountain pen had been used.

'What does it say on the flyleaf of that one?' asked Dixon.

Jane picked up Derek's Bible, opened it and read aloud. 'Colossians 3:25.'

'It's from the New Testament.' Dixon turned to the back of the Bible and began flicking through the pages. 'Here we are. "Certainly the one that is doing wrong will receive back what he wrongly did, and there is no partiality".'

'What does it mean?'

'Do wrong and you'll get it back. No exceptions. Otherwise known as revenge. Do we know any Jehovah's Witnesses?'

'Arnold Davies.'

'The driving instructor,' said Dixon, nodding. 'I think we need to have a word with Mr Davies, don't you?'

# Chapter Twelve

Cotford St Luke was a maze of new houses built on the site of the old Tone Vale Hospital. It was described as a 'new village' on Wikipedia and had been built almost entirely from scratch in the years since Dixon had left St Dunstan's. He switched to Google Maps and looked for Burge Avenue, which was at the western end of the village. He sighed.

'What's up?'

'It's all communal car parks and allocated parking. I was hoping for a car with "L" plates on it parked in a drive.'

'Lazy bugger. Enter the full address and it'll drop a pin on it.'

Dixon typed 37 Burge Avenue into the search field, hit 'Enter' and watched a red pin drop onto the grey tiled roof of a house at the furthest end of the avenue, backing onto open fields. He zoomed in.

'There is a drive so we'll soon see if he's in.'

'Good.'

Dixon took Arnold Davies' witness statement out of the file, switched the internal light on in the car and tried to read it again.

'Try not to swing the car about, will you? I'm gonna throw up in a minute.'

'What'd you expect, reading in a car?' replied Jane. 'You must've read it five times already.'

She turned into Cotford St Luke and slowed down.

'Which way?'

'Straight over the first roundabout, left at the next and then just keep going. Burge Avenue is a dead end.'

Jane crept along Burge Avenue looking for the house numbers on the right while Dixon peered at the houses on the left. Few had their outside lights on and spotting the numbers was far from easy in the streetlights.

'There it is,' said Jane.

Parked in the drive of a house at the far end of Burge Avenue, directly under a street lamp, was a light green Nissan Micra. It had a large white sign on the roof announcing 'Arnold's Driving School', the 'L' of Arnold being large and bright red, just like an 'L' plate.

'Why do driving instructors have to do that?' asked Dixon.

'What?'

'I was taught to drive by a bloke called Nigel and his "L" was . . .'

'I get it,' said Jane.

She parked across the drive of number 37 and turned to Dixon.

'Well?'

'Let's go and speak to him. Just checking the detail in his statement at this stage. All right?'

Jane nodded and got out of the car. She put her hand on the bonnet of the Nissan Micra.

'Still warm.'

Dixon looked at his watch. It was just after 5 p.m. 'You'd have thought he'd be out on the road now, wouldn't you?'

'I suppose you would,' said Jane, ringing the doorbell.

Dixon peered through the frosted glass window. A light came on in the hall and he watched a figure walking towards the door.

Blue trousers and a red top of some sort. At least there was no dog barking to set Monty off in the back of Jane's car.

'Yes.'

'We're looking for Arnold Davies.'

'And who are you?'

'Police, Sir.'

Davies didn't wait to see their warrant cards. He stepped forward onto the front step, closing the door behind him. Dixon thought him to be in his early sixties perhaps. A pair of reading glasses was sitting on top of a thick head of greying hair.

'Can we do this somewhere else? My wife's . . .' his voice tailed off and he looked nervously over his shoulder.

'Down at the station, Mr Davies? asked Dixon.

'Yes, yes. Anywhere.'

'Station it is, then.'

'How long will we be?'

'That depends on you, really,' replied Dixon. 'Say, a couple of hours.'

Davies opened the front door and shouted. 'Got a couple of lessons, dear. Back about sevenish.'

'OK,' came the reply.

Dixon looked at Jane and shrugged his shoulders. Then he turned to Davies.

'Constable Winter can drive your car, Sir, otherwise Mrs Davies will wonder what it's still doing there, won't she?'

'What did you make of that?' asked Jane.

Arnold Davies was waiting in an interview room at Taunton Police Station, drinking a cup of tea.

'Buggered if I know what he's up to,' replied Dixon.

'I was half expecting a chase across the fields at the back, but that . . .'

'It was odd, I'll give him that. Anything from Louise?'

'Not yet.'

'Let's go and see what Davies has got to say for himself, then.'

Dixon and Jane sat down opposite Arnold Davies. Dixon switched on the tape, introduced everyone for the record and then reminded Davies that he was not under arrest. He nodded.

'I need you to acknowledge, for the tape.'

'Oh, yes, sorry.'

'You've declined a solicitor?'

'Yes.'

'We wanted to clarify certain issues arising from your statement . . .'

'I've not made a statement yet.'

'Yes, you have.' Dixon opened a file on the desk in front of him and took out a copy of a handwritten witness statement. He looked at the names at the top. 'You gave this statement to WPC Hamzij on 27th November, it says here.'

'That was about the dead girl.'

'Yes.'

'So, this isn't about . . . oh, thank God.' Davies closed his eyes and began muttering under his breath.

'About what, Mr Davies?' asked Dixon.

'I've had a girl complaining about me, making threats to report me for touching her. It's all lies. She failed her test, that's all, and wants her money back.'

Dixon looked at Jane. She shook her head.

'No complaint has been made to police, Mr Davies, and that is not why you're here.'

'Thank you.'

'What does Colossians 3:25 mean to you?'

'Certainly the one who does wrong will be repaid for the wrong he has done, and there is no partiality.'

'You know it by heart?'

'Bible study is part of being a Jehovah's Witness, Inspector. I would expect every Witness to know that quotation.'

'That's a modern version?'

'The 2013 Revision. The 1984 version is "Certainly the one that is doing wrong will receive back what he wrongly did, and there is no partiality".'

'And what do you understand it to mean?' asked Dixon.

'Do wrong and you'll receive it back. No exceptions.'

'Revenge?'

'Revenge, retribution, vengeance, call it what you will.'

'What happened to turning the other cheek?'

'It's all in the context. You can twist the words any way you want when you take them out of context.'

'Have you ever given a Bible to anyone?'

'I give Bibles to people all the time. It's what we do.'

'How about one with Colossians 3:25 written on the flyleaf?'

'No.'

'Tell me about your relationship with Isobel Swan.'

'The word "relationship" worries me. I didn't have a relationship with Isobel. I teach people to drive and she was learning.'

'So, it was a teacher and pupil relationship?'

'I suppose it was, seeing as you put it like that.'

'How well did you know her?'

'Not well at all. She had a lesson once a week. She'd started at the beginning of term so what's that, ten lessons, perhaps?'

'Do you keep records?'

'My appointment diaries.'

'Going back how far?'

'Since I started. Thirty-two years.'

'Have you ever taught pupils from St Dunstan's?'

'Yes.'

'Did Isobel say anything during her lesson that day that gave you any cause for concern?'

'Nothing. It was just an ordinary lesson. We did some parallel parking, I think, then I dropped her back at about six o'clock.'

'How did she seem?'

'Like her usual self.'

'Does the name Rowena Weatherly mean anything to you?'

'No.'

'What about Fran Sawyer?'

'No.' Davies shook his head.

'She was a pupil at St Dunstan's. You taught her to drive seventeen years ago.'

'Doesn't mean anything to me.'

*It does to me.*

'Let's try again. She disappeared the day she passed her test . . .'

'That was her name? I do remember that, yes. Tragic. I'm sorry, I couldn't recall the name.'

'What can you remember about that day?'

'She took her test. Passed it. And then I dropped her back to the school. I remember her boyfriend was waiting for her with a bunch of flowers.'

'Is that it?'

'It was a long time ago. I gave a more detailed statement at the time. Two, I think, from memory.'

'The night Isobel was murdered, where were you?'

'I led a Bible study group at the Kingdom Hall in Staplegrove. I was home by 10 p.m. and went to bed. My wife has confirmed all this.'

'Do you share a bedroom?'

'That's a very personal question, Inspector.'

'It is.'

'Do I have to answer it?'

'You do.'

'No, we don't. We haven't done for years.'

'So, you could have gone out again later and Mrs Davies might not have heard you?'

'I didn't.'

'But you could've done?'

'You don't honestly think I . . .'

'I have to keep an open mind, Mr Davies.'

'Am I under arrest?'

'No.'

'Then I can go?'

'You can,' said Dixon.

He terminated the interview and Jane showed Mr Davies out of the station. Dixon was still sitting in the interview room when Jane got back.

'Well?'

'He's still a possible, but I believe him, oddly enough,' replied Dixon, shaking his head.

'So do I. What now, then?'

'We have a closer look at Griffiths. The headmaster too. And I think the time has come to rattle Rowena's cage.'

'Have a look at this,' said Jane, leaning across to the printer next to her desk.

'What is it?' asked Dixon, turning around from the coffee machine with a cup in each hand.

'Rowena's birth certificate,' replied Jane. She waited until Dixon put the coffees down before handing him the piece of paper. 'Louise just emailed it over.'

'Anything else?'

'"Hi Jane, Rowena's birth certificate attached. It was found in her flat at Firepool Lock",' Jane read from Louise's email. '"Both parents disappear off the radar after that. No trace of any siblings either. Sorry. PS I've also attached her divorce papers".'

'Print them off, will you?'

Dixon looked at the birth certificate. Rowena had been born on 2nd July 1979 in the County of Fife, Registration District Dunfermline. Rowena Judith Sampson. Her father's name was Gordon Patrick Lee and he was a student.

'Not worth the paper it's written on,' said Dixon.

'Eh?'

'How do we know it's hers, for a start. And if her father's been changing his identity, he's gonna change his daughter's too, isn't he?'

'It could be the real thing, though. There's no maiden name for the mother,' said Jane. 'And the first name is Rowena.'

'All that tells us is that the parents weren't married,' replied Dixon.

The mother's name was given as Charlotte Rebecca Sampson.

'I wonder what happened to her.'

'Let's have a look at that decree absolute,' said Dixon. 'It's gonna be more recent.'

Jane reached over and took several pieces of paper from the printer, before passing them to Dixon.

'This is a nullity petition.'

'What does that mean?' asked Jane.

'Her marriage was annulled.'

'Is there a difference?'

'A big difference,' said Dixon, flicking through the pages. 'The petitioner was her husband, Peter John Taylor. Here we go, the Facts, "The marriage was not consummated owing to the wilful refusal of the Respondent to consummate it".'

'I wonder why?' asked Jane.

Dixon turned the page.

'Part 6, Statement of Case. It's handwritten so it looks like her dearly beloved didn't use a solicitor. "The Respondent has failed to consummate the relationship and continues to live with her father. She has not stayed in what was supposed to be the matrimonial home with me once since the marriage and has now left for Kenya with her father. I have no idea when or if she is intending to return".'

'Daddy's girl,' said Jane. 'I wonder why she bothered to get married in the first place.'

'Daddy's girl indeed,' replied Dixon. 'Look at this. He even had to get an order allowing service of the petition by email because he had no address for her. I wonder what became of Mr Taylor?'

'I'll find out.'

'What about her medical records?'

'Here they are. Not much use, though. They begin nine years ago, presumably when she got back from Kenya.'

'It's time I had a proper word with Rowena, I think,' said Dixon. 'Where's Chard?'

'Gone home.'

'Whatever time she's being charged tomorrow morning, get it put back. Set up an interview for 10 a.m. but don't tell her it'll be me interviewing her. She'll need Dunn here too, don't forget.'

'She's in the Custody Centre at Express Park.'

'That's fine. They'll be bringing her over anyway to be charged.'

'Chard's gonna love this.'

'Get him to ring me if you have to. And get DCI Lewis here as well.'

'Lewis?'

'Someone of equal rank to Chard who's on my side . . .'

'I think you'll find he's on his own side.'

'Possibly, but that's better than nothing.'

'Let me try Chard now. Then we can go and get something to eat.'

'OK.'

Dixon waited while Jane rang DCI Chard.

'I've got DI Dixon with me, Sir. He'd like to interview Rowena Weatherly in the morning and I was wondering if we could put her charging back to the afternoon.'

Jane flinched, looked at her phone and then dropped it back into her handbag.

'What'd he say?'

'We'll worry about it in the morning, apparently. 8 a.m. sharp.'

'Tosser.'

'Let's go home,' said Jane. 'Nothing's gonna happen tonight. We can feed Monty and then nip over to the Red Cow.'

'Better not. If the birth certificate is genuine, then Gordon Patrick Lee is in that school somewhere, and that's where I need to be.'

'The Greyhound, then?'

'OK. Just let me send Lewis a text,' replied Dixon.

He took out his phone and tapped out a message to DCI Lewis.

*Taunton ps tomorrow 8am can u be there? it's going to hit the fan*

The reply came as Jane drove out of Taunton towards Staple Fitzpaine.

*that was quick! yes will be there*

---

Monty was sitting at Dixon's feet in the corner of the public bar with his lead looped around Dixon's leg. He had stopped tying him to the table in pubs after an unfortunate incident with a cocker spaniel in the Red Cow that had ended in a horrible mess, another round of drinks and empty stomachs. Monty had just wanted to play, of course, but it had been after 9 p.m. and too late to order more food. Dixon would not make the same mistake again.

'So, what's the plan for tomorrow?' asked Jane.

'The first thing we've got to do is make sure Rowena is charged with the right offences.'

'Which are?'

'The murders of Clive Cooper and Derek Phelps.'

'And the attempted murder of DI Nick Dixon?'

'I'm not too fussed about that. She'll get life, anyway, so . . .' Dixon shook his head.

'I'm guessing you want Lewis there because it'll come out about Fran?'

'It will.'

'Chard'll go nuts.'

'Possibly. But I'm relying on Lewis to calm him down. After all, Chard's the one who's going to look a prat.'

'So, what if Rowena clams up?'

'We've got to hope she doesn't,' replied Dixon. 'Time's running out and we haven't got the DNA results on the lock of hair yet, so I'll be breaking my golden rule.'

'Golden rule?'

'Never ask a question you don't know the answer to.'

Jane rolled her eyes.

'Anyway,' continued Dixon, 'I can tell you who she's protecting right now if you want.'

'Really?'

'I can even tell you his name.'

'Go on, then.'

'Gordon Patrick Lee.'

'You really are a twat.'

'Thank you, Constable.'

Jane dropped Dixon back at the school on her way home to feed Monty and give him a run in the field. It was just before 10 p.m. and all was quiet apart from a few sixth formers still in the library. The masters' common room was empty and dark. Dixon felt for the light switches and turned them on. Then he walked along the lines of pigeonholes on the table to the left of the door, looking at the names of the teachers one by one.

Griffiths had no pigeonhole of his own but several envelopes addressed to him were in Haskill's. Otherwise, Dixon spotted nothing untoward apart from a sealed envelope in Rowena's. He opened it to find a memo informing her that the governors had decided to end the term a week early. Term would, therefore, finish this coming Friday morning, after the carol service on Thursday evening.

It came as no surprise, given Dixon's conversation with the headmaster earlier that day. What it meant, though, was that he had a little over two days to find Rowena's father.

He walked up to his rooms, unlocked the door and switched on the hall light. There was a note on the floor.

'Could we have a chat when convenient, please, Sir? Ben Masterson.'

Dixon folded it up and put it in his pocket. He wondered what it was that Ben wanted to talk about. Tomorrow afternoon would be the earliest he could speak to him, unless he could catch up with him at breakfast, perhaps.

He lay down on the bed, set his alarm for 7 a.m. and closed his eyes. He imagined himself taking Monty for a walk on the beach on Saturday morning. It would all be over by then, one way or the other.

# Chapter Thirteen

'Where the fuck have you been?' said Chard. 'I said 8 a.m.'

Dixon had been to breakfast at the school in the hope of catching Ben Masterson, but he had not turned up or, at least, had not done so before Dixon had to leave.

He looked around the room. Jane was sitting at her temporary desk in the far corner. DCI Chard and DI Baldwin were standing in front of the whiteboard talking to DCI Lewis, who was sitting on the corner of a desk. Dixon had watched them through the small windows in the door before he walked in. They had been engaged in an animated conversation, with lots of gesticulating by Chard at various photographs pinned on the board. You didn't need to be an accomplished lip reader to get the gist of what he had been saying.

'What's this all about, Nick?' asked Lewis.

'Where's Rowena Weatherly?' asked Dixon.

'On her way here,' replied Baldwin.

'Good. I need to speak to her about the murder of Clive Cooper, amongst other things.'

'The friend of Derek Phelps?' asked Chard.

'That's right. On or about 7th March last year, Rowena staved in the back of his head, possibly with her hockey stick, and pushed him into the River Taff. He was found floating face down in the water just along from the Millennium Stadium. Coroner's verdict was open.'

'Why?' asked Baldwin.

'Blackmail.'

'Jolly fucking hockey sticks,' said Chard, with a sneer.

'Best get on with it, then,' said Lewis.

'Thank you, Sir. There are other matters arising, so I suggest you watch the interview on the TV?'

'Sounds fine to me,' replied Lewis.

'Has someone spoken to her solicitor?'

'He'll be here at 9.30 a.m.,' said Baldwin.

'And nobody's told her or the solicitor it'll be me interviewing her?'

'No.'

'Let's keep it that way, please.'

'What's the big deal?' asked Chard. 'She knows who you are from the school, anyway.'

'She knows who I am and she knows what I know. That's what frightens her and it's why she tried to kill me.'

'What the hell's that supposed to mean?'

'You'll find out.'

---

'How much longer are we going to be kept waiting?'

Stephen Dunn and Rowena Weatherly were sitting in an interview room. Opposite them DI Baldwin was sitting next to an empty chair. Chard, Lewis and Jane were sitting in an adjacent room watching the scene unfold on the television screen.

'Where the bloody hell is he?' asked Chard.

'I don't know, Sir,' replied Jane.

'Don't give me that. You know full well where he is.'

He was right. She did. But taking his dog for a walk in Vivary Park was almost certainly not the answer Chard would have been expecting. 'It's about composure,' Dixon had said, 'mine and Rowena's.'

'I should imagine he's doing it deliberately, if I know Nick,' said Lewis. Jane smiled. Maybe Lewis was on his side, after all.

Rowena was picking at her fingernails with the top of a BIC biro, pushing back the skin at the base of her nails with it and then running the thin end along underneath them. No doubt Dunn would not want it back. She was wearing blue jeans and a black polo neck sweater. Jane and DCI Lewis watched her intently. She did not look up, even when the interview room door opened.

'Who are you? We were expecting DCI Chard,' said Dunn.

'My name is Detective Inspector Dixon. I will be interviewing Miss Weatherly this morning.'

That got Rowena's attention. She looked up sharply, dropped the pen top and glared at Dunn.

'This can't . . . this is not right . . . do something!'

Her face was flushed red and she was shaking.

'An interesting reaction,' said Lewis.

Chard nodded.

Dixon sat down opposite Rowena. He placed a thin green file on the table in front of him, looked at DI Baldwin and nodded. She started the tape. Dixon confirmed the date, time and place before introducing those present and asking each of them to acknowledge their presence for the record. Then he reminded Rowena that she was under caution.

'My client knows she is to be charged with the murders of Derek Phelps and Isobel Swan. She has made a full statement confessing to both and has nothing further to add,' said Dunn.

'I don't intend to ask Rowena anything about the murder of Isobel Swan.'

'Why not?'

'She didn't kill her, so what would be the point?'

'I did kill her,' screamed Rowena. 'I cut her throat.'

'My understanding is that Miss Weatherly is to be charged with her murder,' said Dunn.

'New evidence has come to light that calls into question Rowena's involvement in the murder of Isobel Swan,' said Dixon, matter of fact and without looking up.

'You can't,' shouted Rowena. 'I . . .' She placed both hands over her mouth and began breathing hard.

'What about Phelps?' asked Dunn.

'Your client made a full and frank admission that she killed Derek Phelps and we have evidence corroborating that.'

'So?'

'I may wish to ask about her motive and the timing of his murder but we'll come back to that later, perhaps. Let's talk about Clive Cooper first.'

'Who is Clive Cooper?' asked Dunn.

'Do you want to tell him, Rowena, or shall I?' asked Dixon.

'He was a friend of Derek's.'

'And why did you kill him?'

'He was blackmailing my . . .' Her voice tailed off. 'No comment.'

'Nearly had her then,' said Lewis, grimacing.

'How did you kill him?'

'I arranged to meet him on Fitzhamon Embankment, opposite the stadium. There's no CCTV there. And I hit him with my hockey stick. He went into the river and that was that.'

'When was this?'

'March last year.'

'How many times did you hit him?'

'Three.'

'What time of day was it?'

'Nineish. I wanted it dark for obvious reasons.'

'What was he wearing?'

'A coat. Jeans. I can't remember.'

'Was he carrying anything?'

'No.'

'That's right. He wasn't. He'd left his belongings behind a bush.'

Rowena looked nervously at Dunn and then back to Dixon.

'You get used to hiding your stuff when living rough,' continued Dixon. 'How did you get in touch with him?'

'He wrote to me and I had to ring a payphone number at a certain time.'

'He wrote to you?'

'Yes.'

'Are you sure he didn't write to someone else and you intercepted the letter, perhaps?'

'No.' Agitated again.

'What did he want?'

'Money, of course.'

'Was this the first time?'

'Yes.'

'Why not pay up, then? You'd been paying Phelps for years.'

'He was a down and out. No one would miss him.'

Not even his own mother, thought Dixon.

'What about Phelps, then? Why kill him now, after all these years?'

'He said he recognised you. He was going to tell you everything.'

'What does Colossians 3:25 mean to you?'

'Sounds like a Bible reference,' said Rowena, shaking her head.

'What does it say?'

'I don't know.'

Dixon opened the file on the desk in front of him and took out a piece of paper.

'This is a photocopy of the flyleaf from a *New World Translation* of the Bible found in Clive Cooper's rucksack.' Dixon pointed at it. 'What does that say?'

'Colossians 3:25.'

'Whose handwriting is that?'

Rowena hesitated. 'I don't know.'

'I think you do, Rowena.'

She shook her head and looked at Dunn but he kept his head down, writing notes.

'Let's wind it back a bit, then. How did you first meet Clive?'

'He was a friend of Derek's and I met him when he came to Brunel.'

'Wrong,' said Dixon. 'Try again.'

'I don't . . .'

'Try harder.'

'I can't . . .'

'Let me refresh your memory, then. He was a kitchen porter at St Dunstan's. You and I both know that because we were both there, weren't we?'

'Yes.' Rowena had her head bowed.

'They were at school together?' said Chard. 'For fuck's sake.'

Lewis looked at Jane and raised his eyebrows.

'You've known him a long time, haven't you, Rowena?' continued Dixon.

'Yes.'

'And Derek Phelps. Remember, it was a standing joke, wasn't it? Derek and Clive?'

'Yes, yes, I remember.'

'So, what do you think we found in amongst Derek's belongings?'

'I don't know.'

'I think you do.'

'A Bible?'

'That's right. A *New World Translation* identical to the one we found in Clive's rucksack.' Dixon took another piece of paper out of the folder and put it on the table in front of Rowena.

'What can you tell me about the *New World Translation*?'

Rowena shook her head. 'Nothing.'

'Are you a Jehovah's Witness, Rowena?'

'No.'

Dixon pointed at the copy of the flyleaf. 'What does that say?'

Rowena craned her neck forward and read aloud.

'Colossians 3:25.'

'Let's have another go, then, shall we? What does it mean?'

'It's about revenge. I can't remember the exact words.'

'Revenge. For blackmail, perhaps?'

'Yes.'

'Do you recognise the handwriting on this one?'

'No.'

'I think you do.'

Rowena was shaking her head from side to side violently. Tears began falling off her cheeks onto the table in front of her.

'Look at it, Rowena.'

She looked up slowly and stared at the handwriting in front of her.

'It's your father's, isn't it?' asked Dixon.

Rowena began sobbing and buried her face in her hands again.

Dixon waited.

'Whose writing is it, Rowena?'

'No comment.' The reply came through deep sobs and sharp intakes of breath.

'Take your time.'

'No comment.'

'OK, here's what I think happened. Phelps is blackmailing your father. We'll come onto why in a minute. That's when you and he go to Kenya, perhaps? Or was it back to Kenya?'

'How d'you . . . ?'

'Had you been to Kenya before, Rowena?'

'How do you know about Kenya?'

'The divorce petition filed by your ex-husband, or should I say annulment. Your dearly beloved paints quite a picture of a real daddy's girl, doesn't he? Couldn't bring yourself to leave your father, even on your wedding night, it seems?'

'He's all I've ever had and . . .' More sobbing. 'You'll never understand.'

'Try me.'

No reply.

'OK. Now, where were we? Poor old Clive can't stomach it, hits the bottle and loses his job.'

'No comment.'

'Then when you come home the blackmail starts again, doesn't it?' Dixon paused. 'Phelps even moves to Brunel so he can be near you. Must've been difficult, that?'

'No comment.'

'And as if that wasn't enough, Clive Cooper finally decides he needs some money. And we know where he ends up, don't we?'

Dixon opened the file in front of him and took out a piece of paper.

'Let's move on, then. For the tape, DI Dixon is placing a photograph on the table in front of Miss Weatherly. Who is that, Rowena?'

She stopped crying, wiped her eyes and leaned forward.

'Isobel Swan.'

'It is. Well done.'

He took another piece of paper out of the folder.

'For the tape, DI Dixon is placing another photograph on the table in front of Miss Weatherly. Who's that?'

'I don't know.'

'I'll give you a clue. You told me the other day that she'd been a good friend of yours, but we know that wasn't true, don't we?'

'What the fuck is going on?' asked Chard.

Lewis looked at Jane and raised his eyebrows. She shrugged her shoulders.

Rowena looked away.

'Let me ask you again. Who is that?'

'Fran Sawyer.'

'It is. Well done.'

'Who the hell is Fran Sawyer?' asked Chard.

Lewis turned to Jane. 'Do you know?'

Jane nodded.

They turned back to the television screen when Dixon spoke again.

'And what happened to Fran Sawyer?'

'I don't know.'

'Derek Phelps and Clive Cooper knew, didn't they?'

No response.

'One more, then. For the tape, DI Dixon is placing a third photograph on the table in front of Miss Weatherly. Now, who is that?'

Rowena peered at the photograph. Dixon looked for any reaction but there was none.

'Who is it, Rowena?'

She sat back in her chair, looked at Dunn and then back to Dixon.

'You know who it is.'

'I do. But I need you to tell me.'

'It's my mother.'

'What was her name?'

'Charlotte. Charlotte Sampson.'

'What do you notice about all three photographs, then?'

Rowena spoke without looking at them.

'They all look the same.'

'Who do?'

'The people in them.'

'Describe them for the tape.'

'You can see them for yourself.'

'I want to know what you see.'

'Blonde hair tied back in a ponytail. Smiling.'

'What happened to your mother?'

The question caught Rowena off guard. She closed her eyes and took several deep breaths. Dixon watched and waited.

'She . . .' Rowena hesitated. 'She abandoned me. Disappeared.'

'When?'

'Just after I was born.'

'Disappeared where?'

'We never knew.'

'Who never knew?'

'My father and I.'

'I think your father did know, Rowena, don't you?'

Dixon watched the tears falling slowly down Rowena's cheeks, his facial expression blank.

'He told me she didn't want me and left.'

'Did he.'

'Yes.'

'And you believed him?'

'Yes.'

'Your mother told your father she didn't want him, not you.'

Rowena was shaking her head violently.

'That's why he killed her,' continued Dixon.

Rowena threw herself forward onto the desk, her tears falling onto the picture of her mother.

'And why he kills anyone who looks like her.'

Dunn opened his mouth to speak but decided against it when Dixon glared at him.

'Fran Sawyer seventeen years ago. Isobel Swan. How many others are there we don't know about, Rowena?'

'I don't know.'

'And you're protecting him. The man who killed your mother.'

'He didn't. He couldn't have done.'

'He cut off her ring finger and then killed her. Just like he did to Isobel.' Dixon paused. 'And just like he did to Fran.'

Lewis and Chard were watching Rowena on the television screen. Jane watched Dixon. He reminded her of a shark hunting its prey, no expression in his dark, blank eyes. She knew it was an act. He was dying inside with each question, just a little. And she was dying for him too.

Rowena sat back in her chair and looked up at the ceiling.

'Let's assume your birth certificate is real . . .' said Dixon.

'It is real.'

'How do you know?'

'My father told me. He got it for me.'

'They weren't married, were they? So, he asked her to marry him, and she said no. Rejected him. So he killed her. He cut off her ring finger so no one else could have her. That was your expression when you confessed to killing Isobel, wasn't it? Then he killed her and dumped her body somewhere. Took you to Kenya and told you she disappeared when you were old enough to understand.'

'It wasn't like that.'

'How old were you when you first came to England?'

'Seven.'

'Really? So, it was like that?'

'No.'

'What was it like, then?'

'No comment.'

'You saw all the other kids with their mummies so you asked Daddy where your mummy was?'

'No.'

'What did he say when you asked him, Rowena?'

Her eyes glazed over. Dixon waited.

'He said she didn't want me and abandoned us. That's when we went to Kenya.'

Dixon nodded.

'Kenya? Becoming a bit of a routine that, isn't it? A girl disappears then you and Daddy go to Kenya. It happened after Fran disappeared, didn't it?'

'Yes.'

Dixon waited.

'He said Mummy left us.'

'And you believed him?'

'What choice did I have?' asked Rowena, screaming now.

'None,' said Dixon, shaking his head. 'None. But you did have a choice when you killed Phelps and Cooper. And you have another choice now. You're protecting the man who killed your mother. Aren't you?'

'No.'

'You're going to prison for life to protect the man who killed your mother.'

'He didn't.'

'Two men have died so you can protect him.'

Rowena shook her head.

'How many more girls are going to die, their only crime being that they looked like your mother? How many, Rowena?'

'None.'

'Good. So, let's start at the beginning. Did you kill Isobel Swan?'

'No.'

'Who did?'

'My . . .' Rowena was shaking violently. Her eyes were bloodshot and tears were streaming down her cheeks, dripping onto the photographs on the table. A small drop of blood appeared under her left nostril. Dixon waited. '. . . father.'

'What's his name? Give me his name.'

Rowena shook her head.

Dunn spotted the blood trickling down Rowena's face. 'I think that's enough for now, Inspector. My client needs medical attention.'

# Chapter Fourteen

'What just happened in there?' asked Chard, storming into the CID Room with Jane and DCI Lewis close behind him.

Dixon was standing in the window, looking down at Jane's car and watching Monty asleep on the parcel shelf. Any last hope that Fran was still alive somewhere had just vanished and he was hurting all over again. He had known it all along, of course, but now, for the first time in seventeen years, it had been confirmed. He thought about a long and difficult conversation that he knew was coming. Still, her parents had to know. He turned around and walked over to the coffee machine.

'Rowena admitted that her father killed Isobel Swan,' he said.

'And who the hell is Fran Sawyer?'

'She was a seventeen year old student at St Dunstan's who disappeared seventeen years ago.'

'And Rowena's father killed her too?'

'He did.'

'Where's her body?'

'We don't know yet.'

'Let me get this straight. You were at St Dunstan's when that happened?'

'I was. That's why I was sent in there, don't forget.'

'So, you knew the cases were connected . . .'

'Not until now, no.'

'But you suspected . . . ?'

'Yes.'

'And you never thought to mention it?'

'I'm mentioning it now. And if you'd done your job properly you'd know about it . . .'

'You cheeky little . . .'

'Dixon has a point, though, Simon,' said Lewis. 'Perhaps he should have told you about it before now, I don't know, but you'll need to be able to explain why you don't know about it anyway. Have you checked for previous cases?'

'Murders, yes, of course.'

'But not missing persons?'

'Where's Margaret Baldwin?'

'Her fault now, is it?' asked Dixon.

'It's not a question of fault,' replied Chard.

'It will be when the shit hits the fan.'

'This is getting us nowhere,' said Lewis. 'What happens now, Nick?'

'We find her father.'

'How?' asked Chard.

'Rowena was born on the second of July 1979, as far as we know, so we DNA test every male in that school old enough to be her father. Anyone born on or before second July 1963 should cover it.'

'We'll need authorisation for a test like that.'

'Get it,' replied Dixon. 'There are several teachers who were at St Dunstan's seventeen years ago, so start with them. Griffiths . . .'

'Who's he?' asked Chard.

'The supply teacher. Haskill and the headmaster.'

'The headmaster?'

'He was only there for one term but check him all the same. And the driving instructor. Don't forget the driving instructor.'

'Was he at St Dunstan's?'

'He taught Fran Sawyer to drive.'

'How do you know that?'

*Because I waited for her with a bunch of flowers when she took her test.*

'I interviewed him,' replied Dixon.

'Haskill's in the Far East, isn't he?' asked Lewis.

'A man holding Haskill's passport was spoken to by Malaysian police. That's all we know for sure, Sir.'

'We can have another go at Rowena this afternoon too,' said Chard.

'You can try but I doubt you'll get very far.'

'Looks like you've got your work cut out, Simon,' said Lewis.

'Don't think this is over, Dixon. You've got some serious explaining to do . . .'

Dixon turned his back on Chard and walked towards the door.

'Where the fuck are you going?'

'Back to school,' replied Dixon, without turning round.

---

Dixon was sitting in his Land Rover looking up at the front of Brunel School when a beep coming from his pocket announced the arrival of a text message. He checked his phone.

*Monty's claws need clipping J x*

He wondered what on earth had made Jane think of that, while he switched the SIM cards over. Another text message arrived seconds later.

*Chard getting Fran file out of store*

He tapped out a reply.

*inevitable. how long*

He looked at his watch. It was just before 1 p.m.

*tomorrow morning x*

He nodded. Things had to happen fast now, or not at all. And a few risks needed to be taken.

Dixon spotted Ben Masterson sitting on the far side of the dining room with three other boys he had not seen before. He walked over and stood next to him, holding his tray of food in both hands.

'You all right, Ben?'

'Yes, thank you, Sir.'

Dixon noticed him look nervously at his friends.

'Only you pushed a note under my door yesterday.'

'Oh, it's nothing, Sir, really,' replied Ben, blushing.

'Well, if you're sure?'

'Yes, Sir, I'm fine now.'

Dixon put his tray on the table and took a business card out of his pocket. He handed it to Ben and watched him reading it.

'So you can find me, if you need a chat.'

Ben looked at Dixon and then back to the card. Then he slipped it into the top pocket of his jacket.

'Yes, Sir,' replied Ben. He smiled at Dixon and nodded.

Dixon sat down at an empty table to eat his lunch and wondered what it was that Ben had wanted the day before. Whatever it was, he was clearly too nervous or embarrassed to discuss it in front of his friends. Dixon also wondered whether and if so how long it would be before everyone in the school knew he was a police officer.

It was just before 2 p.m. when Dixon walked into the masters' common room. It was largely deserted apart from Clarke, the English teacher of French, and McCulloch, the Scottish teacher of English. Mercifully, Clarke spotted him first.

'Robin was looking for you. He's gone down to his lab, I think.'

'I thought Wednesday afternoon was sports?' asked Dixon.

'Cancelled. We're running Thursday afternoon's timetable, given that we shut up shop tomorrow.'

'Thanks.'

Dixon walked down to Phillips' chemistry lab and peered in through the small window in the door. It was empty, so he opened the door and then looked in the small office at the back. Phillips was sitting at his computer with his back to the door.

'Come in, Nick. You need eyes in the back of your head in a place like this.'

'Or a small mirror stuck to your computer.'

'Quite,' replied Phillips, spinning round on his chair. 'How're you getting on?'

'Fine.'

'Where've you been?'

'I had to nip into town.'

'What for?'

'Some parts for my car.'

'And you get those from the police station, do you? I drive past there on my way in every morning and saw you.'

Dixon hesitated.

'Who are you?'

Dixon shut the door. Then he took his warrant card out of his pocket and handed it to Phillips.

'I knew it,' said Phillips, smiling and nodding at the same time. 'All that farting about in the old convent chapel. And there was me thinking the local plod were useless.' He handed Dixon back his warrant card. 'No one'll hear it from me.'

'Thank you.'

'How's it going?'

'We're making progress.'

'What have you . . . ?'

'I really can't say.'

'No, no, of course not. I quite understand. So, what happens now?'

'I need to speak to Mr Griffiths, the supply teacher. D'you know where can I find him?'

'Jack Griffiths? He's not mixed up in this, is he?'

Dixon raised his eyebrows.

'No, sorry, of course, you can't say,' continued Phillips. 'He's here now, actually, teaching . . .'

'Can you get me in there? As a trainee teacher to sit in, perhaps?'

'Yes, we'll give it a go. He can't really object, can he? Follow me.'

Dixon followed Phillips down the steps and along the cloisters. He watched Phillips walking in front of him and wondered whether he really had seen him by chance or whether he had followed him.

At the far end, on the left just before the doors of the chapel, was a flight of two stone steps that led up to a small classroom.

'One question before we go in,' said Dixon.

'What?'

'Is he a Jehovah's Witness?'

'No idea. Sorry.'

Phillips knocked on the door and went in. Dixon counted three rows of four desks, two of them empty, such was the popularity of the classics these days.

'Jack, can Nick here sit in with you? He's a trainee teacher. I thought he might like to see an old master at work.'

'Literally,' said Griffiths, rolling his eyes. 'What do you teach?'

'Law and history, hoping to anyway,' replied Dixon.

'Yes, well, come in and sit down. Latin will bore the pants off you but so be it.'

'It does us.'

'I heard that, Smallwood.'

'Sorry, Sir.'

Griffiths was a small man with thinning grey hair and his love of the classics clearly extended to his clothes; suede shoes, corduroys, a tweed jacket and a yellow and black waistcoat that wouldn't have looked out of place on Rupert Bear. Dixon thought him to be in his late sixties and hoped he had long since retired by the time he reached that age. If he reached that age, as Roger would no doubt remind him.

Dixon listened to the lesson unfold. He had forgotten about Latin declensions long ago and, judging by his exam results, what little he had learned had been picked up from *The Life of Brian*. It had been a subject he had dropped at the first opportunity, at much the same time as he had abandoned any pretence of learning physics.

A loud bell at 3 p.m. signalled the end of the lesson. Griffiths wished the class a happy Christmas and reminded them about the essays to be written over the longer than usual school holidays, before letting them go. Dixon waited behind.

'Did you enjoy that?' asked Phillips.

'Yes.' Dixon lied. 'It was interesting to see how you keep their attention with such a dry subject.'

'I have the advantage that they've all opted to take this subject but it doesn't always work that way.'

'What else do you teach?'

'Ancient history, mainly, but Latin and Greek as and when required.'

Dixon watched him stacking a large pile of books into a box.

'Can I give you a hand with that?'

'If you wouldn't mind carrying it out to the car, that'd be very helpful.'

'Not at all,' replied Dixon.

Griffiths was carrying a briefcase in each hand. Dixon walked behind him carrying the box.

'We'll take a shortcut. My car's round the back.'

He went into the chapel and then out of the back doors, which were open. Dixon followed him around the side and along to the car park by the kitchens.

'There are no deliveries in the afternoons, so it's usually all right to park here, but they can get quite sniffy about it,' he said, opening the boot of the car.

Dixon placed the box in the boot and then stood back to allow Griffiths to put his briefcases in. Then Griffiths slammed the boot, shook hands with Dixon and got in the car, before winding down the window.

'Good luck.'

'What with?' asked Dixon.

'Your teaching career.'

'Yes, thank you.'

Griffiths drove off. Only then did Dixon get a clear look at the rear window of his car. In the bottom right hand corner was a sticker. It was a stencilled image of Jesus Christ, identifiable by his beard and crown of thorns, against a background of blue sky and white clouds. Underneath it was the message 'John 3:16'.

'For God so loved the world that he gave his one and only Son . . .' said Dixon under his breath.

He took out his phone and sent Jane a text message.

*The Greyhound 7.30 bring what we've got on Griffiths N x*

---

'What happened about the school play?' asked Dixon.

'*Sweeney Todd*, the musical,' replied Phillips, 'the head cancelled it. No time for it anyway, what with the term ending early.'

Dixon nodded.

'And Geldard's house play went the same way. *Arsenic and Old Lace*. Cancelled.'

'Shame.'

'Not really. I saw the dress rehearsal,' replied Phillips. 'They'll inflict it on us next term instead, I expect.'

Dixon was looking at the timetable on the wall in the masters' common room and noticed that the headmaster had a law class starting at 3.15 p.m.

'Where's room U7?'

'Underwood Building. Ground floor on the right.'

'Thanks.'

Dixon looked over his shoulder as the door closed behind him and saw Phillips examining the timetable, no doubt trying to work out where he was going.

He arrived outside the classroom just as the lesson was getting under way, knocked and opened the door.

'Come in, Nick. Everyone, this is Mr Dickson, a trainee teacher who's going to sit in.'

The whole class watched him as he took a seat at an empty desk at the back of the room, clearly welcoming the interruption. There were far too many of them and they were too young to be studying law A Level so this was going to be another of the head's general knowledge classes.

'We were talking about crime last time, weren't we,' said Hatton. 'What are the two elements of any crime?'

A hand went up at the desk in front of Dixon.

'Tom.'

'The actus reus and mens rea, Sir.'

'Good.'

Dixon watched the headmaster. He appeared distinctly uncomfortable, glancing across at Dixon at regular intervals. Either he was nervous because there was someone in the room who knew far more about the subject than he did, or it was something else altogether.

'What do they mean?' continued Hatton. 'Anyone?' His eyes scanned the room. 'Yes, Clare.'

'The act and the mind, Sir.'

'And what do we mean by the mind?'

'Intent, Sir?' The voice came from the front of the room.

'That's right. Intent. Someone give me an example.'

'If you hit someone in a car, Sir. You could say it was an accident, then it's death by dangerous instead of murder.'

'You've been watching *The Bill* again, haven't you, Craig?'

Hatton waited for the laughter to subside.

'It's a good example, though,' he continued. 'To prosecute for murder, the Crown would have to prove you intended to kill the victim, drove at him deliberately intending to kill him rather than just injure . . .'

'What about if you slit someone's throat, Sir?'

Stunned silence.

'Get out, Welham,' shouted Hatton.

Dixon watched the boy get up from his desk and trudge towards the door. His shirt was hanging out and his top button undone. How he got away with that Dixon would never know. He was a scruffy individual, of that there could be no doubt, but maybe he knew something.

'Wait outside and don't move.'

'Yes, Sir.'

'Right, we'll talk about theft instead, I think,' said Hatton.

Dixon waited until the discussion got going again. Then he got up and walked out of the classroom, avoiding eye contact with the headmaster as he went. Welham was sitting on the window ledge opposite, kicking his heels against the wall.

'Welham, is it?'

'Yes, Sir.'

'First name?'

'Richard, Sir.'

'What was that all about, then, Richard?'

'Nothing, Sir.'

'There was a point to your remark. What was it?'

'There wasn't, Sir.'

'What did you think he was going to do? Give you a gold star?'

'I don't know.'

Dixon took his warrant card out of his pocket.

'Do you know what this is?'

'Yes, Sir.'

'Then you are privy to some very important and highly confidential information.'

Welham nodded.

'Now, you were making a point. What was it?'

'Just rumours, Sir.'

'What rumours?'

'That he was having an affair with a girl at the school.'

'The headmaster?'

'Yes.'

'And it was Isobel Swan?'

'I don't know, Sir. It was just a rumour.'

'When did you hear it?'

'A few days ago.'

'Had you ever heard this rumour before Isobel was murdered?'

'No.'

Dixon shook his head and sighed. He looked at his watch. It was nearly 4 p.m. and the lesson would be ending within minutes.

'Sounds like schoolboy mischief.'

'Yes, Sir.'

'This little situation you've got yourself into is going to end in one of two ways, Richard. Either you go in there and beg for forgiveness or you're likely to spend your Christmas holidays explaining to your parents why you've just been expelled.'

'Yes, Sir.'

'And who do you tell that I'm a police officer?'

'No one, Sir.'

'Good lad.'

The bell went.

'Right, now get in there and get grovelling.'

# Chapter Fifteen

Dixon tore the blue tape off the door frame.

'Should you be do . . . yes, of course you should, sorry,' said Phillips. 'Here's the key. Drop it back down to Mrs Weston in the kitchens when you've finished.'

'Thanks.'

Dixon waited until Phillips had gone and then opened the door. Derek Phelps' room was small and cluttered. There was a single bed, now stripped to the bare mattress, with a bedside table on one side and an armchair on the other. Opposite the end of the bed was a cheap pine wardrobe and then a sink in the corner. Every inch of wall space above the dado rail was covered with Beatles pictures and, in amongst them, Dixon recognised the photo cards and collage poster from the *White Album*. Originals too, by the looks of it.

He sat down on the edge of the bed and opened the top drawer of the bedside table. There was a pair of Bose headphones, a tube of Bonjela and a new tube of toothpaste that was still in its box, but apart from that nothing except empty sweet wrappers and several packets of paper handkerchiefs. The next drawer down seemed to be the tobacco store. There were several pouches of rolling tobacco, three Zippo lighters and a tin of lighter fluid. Dixon lost count of the packets of red and green Rizlas. Derek Phelps was a man who liked smoking and listening to the Beatles, possibly at the same time; that much was clear.

The cabinet underneath contained a pair of carpet slippers and, on the shelf, a wooden cigar box. Dixon picked it up and shook it. It was light and felt empty, but he heard a single piece of paper or card rattling around inside it, so he took it out of the cabinet and opened it. Inside he found a single business card. It was a few years old, judging by the state of it, and his logo had changed but there was no mistaking 'Arnold Davies, Driving Instructor'. Dixon slipped the business card into the top pocket of his jacket before putting the cigar box back in the cabinet.

He noticed a CD player on the tiled windowsill and pressed the 'Eject' button. The lid popped up to reveal *Help!* so he closed it again, which started the disc spinning. He quickly switched it off at the wall and watched the disc slow back down again, but the song started in his head all the same. Dixon nodded. He needed help, perhaps, but Phelps was way beyond it.

Dixon was surprised to find that all of Derek's clothes, apart from one jacket, had been thrown into a large black bin liner, which was sitting in the bottom of the wardrobe. He was tempted to open it but the smell persuaded him that this was not such a good idea. He checked the jacket pockets and found nothing.

Next, he pulled an obviously empty suitcase off the top of the wardrobe and threw it onto the end of the bed. He unzipped it and checked the elasticated pockets in the base, finding only three old style ten pence pieces, one euro and a pair of tweezers.

When Dixon reached into the largest pocket in the lid of the suitcase his fingers closed around what he knew to be a single photograph from the feel of the paper. He took it out and stared at it for several seconds before he recognised the man standing in the foreground.

The photograph had been taken in summer, if the leaves on the trees and the weed in the river were anything to go by, but, more importantly, Clive Cooper was just as Dixon remembered him from St Dunstan's seventeen years ago, which dated the picture to within a year or two, perhaps. He wondered if Derek Phelps had taken it.

Cooper was smiling at the camera but Dixon thought it odd he was standing so far away. Maybe photographic composition was not one of Derek's strong points? He turned it over, hoping for some caption or note on the back, but there was nothing.

Dixon slid the photograph into his inside jacket pocket, zipped up the suitcase and threw it up onto the top of the wardrobe. Then he locked the door behind him, stuck the blue tape back across the frame and went down to the kitchens to return the key to Mrs Weston.

The sound of organ music coming from the chapel caught Dixon's attention as he walked back along the corridor towards the masters' common room. He stood at the end of the cloisters listening to it for several minutes, wondering whether Derek Phelps had been learning to drive or whether it was something more sinister than that. Why else might he have a business card belonging to Arnold Davies? Jane would need to check. And the photograph. What was the significance of the photograph?

Dixon heard the sound of keys jangling behind him and looked round to see Robin Phillips locking the door of his chemistry lab. He spotted Dixon straight away.

'Find anything interesting?'

'Nothing much. I dropped the key back to . . .' Dixon's voice tailed off when a crowd of boys and girls ran around the corner and down the steps straight towards him. He stepped back just in time as they turned into the cloisters, some of them jumping down the small flight of stone steps in one leap. They drowned out the organ music as they raced along the cloisters towards the chapel.

'What the . . . ?'

'The choir,' replied Phillips. 'Evensong's at 6 p.m.'

Dixon looked at his watch. It was just after 5.30 p.m.

'You coming?' asked Phillips.

'I think I will,' replied Dixon. 'I've not been to a chapel service yet.'

'It's going to be a Eucharist rather than an evensong, though, with prayers for Derek too.' Phillips noticed the surprised look on Dixon's face. 'Headmaster's orders. It'll be the last Communion of the term now that everyone's going home before Sunday.'

Dixon nodded. He had not been a regular churchgoer since Fran had disappeared. Births, deaths and marriages only, and there had been precious few of those in the years since her memorial service. He had been warned that his faith would falter and it had. He had not taken Holy Communion since then either.

'I'll catch you up,' said Phillips. 'I've just got to nip to the . . . er . . .'

Dixon walked along the cloisters, sat down at the back of the chapel and switched his phone to silent mode.

The music teacher, Christopher Nelmes, was still playing the organ, although given that Dixon was the only one listening, he thought it more for practice than anything else. The chancel was a hive of activity with pupils coming and going, filling incense burners and lighting candles. Then the choir appeared from the Lady Chapel all dressed in flowing white robes over red gowns. Dixon could see Father Anthony, wearing white robes and a red stole, reading from notes in the pulpit.

By the time that Phillips arrived there were fifty or so boys and girls sitting near the front of the chapel. Phillips tapped Dixon on the shoulder.

'Not compulsory, this one, so we tend to sit nearer the front.'

Dixon followed Phillips to a pew halfway down the aisle and adjacent to the old altar stone. He looked down, half expecting to see a Ouija board.

He sat down in the aisle seat and watched the pews in front of him filling up. He thought about the last time he had attended a chapel service at St Dunstan's, Fran sitting next to him. He could see, even now, the boy to his left playing a key ring sized Rubik's cube. Another reading a small war comic. And then there was . . . Dixon shook his head. He couldn't remember his name. Whoever it was had been listening to the radio through a small earpiece up his sleeve. And he got caught. Faces, voices, memories. More of them came flooding back. Scenes he thought he had blotted out but they were still there, just beneath the surface, waiting for the slightest chance to jump out at him.

The layout of the chancel at St Dunstan's had been different but only marginally. There had been no Lady Chapel and the organ was on the right with the choir sitting opposite. At Brunel both were on the left, opposite the Lady Chapel. It was a familiar scene and it felt like only yesterday since he had last watched it unfold.

The sound of heavy and deliberate footsteps behind him brought Dixon back to the present. He checked his watch. It was exactly 6 p.m. No doubt this would be the headmaster, whose arrival would signal the start of the service. He looked over his shoulder and watched Hatton sit down in the aisle seat of an empty row behind. The organ music stopped and Father Anthony walked out from behind the altar to the top of the three stone steps leading up to the altar.

'Welcome, everyone, to this the last Holy Communion of the term.'

He raised his arms.

'In the name of the Father, and of the Son, and of the Holy Ghost.'

Dixon listened to the congregation reply.

'Amen.'

'*It will return to you, one day, my boy. Your faith will return.*'

Maybe it would. But Dixon knew then that day still lay ahead of him.

He listened to the greeting and then the congregation singing a hymn he didn't recognise. He could hear the headmaster singing behind him and Phillips to his left but, whilst he followed the words in the hymn book, he could not bring himself to sing.

Phillips leaned across and whispered in his ear.

'You don't sing?'

Dixon gave a pained smile.

'Long story.'

The look on Dixon's face convinced Phillips not to press the issue.

Dixon looked along the pew to his left. There were several teachers he recognised: Whitmore, McCulloch and Griffiths, the supply teacher. In the pew behind sat Clarke, Small and the maths teacher, Keith Foster. Dixon looked at him closely. If he was Rowena Weatherly's father Dixon would find himself eating a large slice of humble pie. On the other side of the aisle were several more teachers, some he knew and, in the row in front of them, Ben Masterson, Emily Setter and Susannah Bower. Dixon smiled. Perhaps Ben would be all right after all. He wondered what it was that Ben had wanted to talk to him about when he left the note and decided to tackle him about it again after the service.

He looked over his shoulder at the headmaster, sitting alone and aloof at the back of the congregation. One thing he could be sure of was that Hatton was not old enough to be Rowena's father. Her brother, possibly, but not her father.

Dixon was deep in thought when he heard the familiar words of the Lord's Prayer.

'Thy will be done.'

*Why was it your will that Fran die?*

'As we forgive those who trespass against us.'

*Sorry, Lord, no can do.*

'But deliver us from evil.'

*That would be good, if you get a minute.*

He spoke the last sentence aloud.

'For thine is the kingdom, the power and the glory, for ever and ever. Amen.'

He took his wallet out of his pocket and pulled a passport photograph of Fran from the zip compartment at the back. It was the first time he had looked at it for at least five years. Then he looked up at the cross on the back wall of the chapel, behind the altar. He thought about the crucifix that Fran wore on a gold chain around her neck and wondered if he would be seeing it again. And if he would get the chance to return it to her mother.

He noticed the boys and girls at the front of the chapel getting up, walking forward and kneeling on the top step in front of the altar. It was time for Communion. One row at a time. First the Body of Christ then the Blood of Christ, the bread and the wine. Dixon watched the pupils going up in an orderly fashion. As each row returned to their seats, so the next one would get up and walk forward.

Within a few minutes the more senior pupils at the back of the congregation were beginning to get up and file out of their pews. Dixon saw Ben Masterson stand up and join the back of the line walking down the aisle, so he followed him. Ben looked over his shoulder and saw Dixon behind him. He smiled.

As he shuffled along at the back of the line, Dixon asked himself why he had followed Ben. Had he just wanted him to know he was still there or was there more to it than that? He shook his head. He really didn't know and before he had a chance to think too much about it he found himself kneeling next to Ben on the top step. He waited, trying to remember what he was supposed to do.

Dixon heard footsteps in front of him and looked up. It was Father Anthony. He made the sign of the cross with his right hand and then took a small white Communion wafer off the silver tray he was holding in his left, placing it in the palm of Dixon's hand.

'The Body of Christ.'

Father Anthony repeated the process along the line of pupils kneeling in front of him. Then he walked over to the altar, put down the tray and picked up a silver goblet.

'The Blood of Christ.'

Holding the goblet in both hands, Father Anthony held it to Dixon's lips. He took a sip and then watched Father Anthony work his way along the line giving each pupil a sip from the goblet. When Father Anthony reached the far end of the line, Ben Masterson nudged Dixon and gestured towards the aisle. Dixon got the message, stood up and walked slowly back to his seat.

Another hymn that Dixon did not recognise and service was over. He looked at his watch. It was just after 7 p.m. and he was due to be meeting Jane in half an hour at the Greyhound. He waited in the cloisters, hoping to catch Ben Masterson leaving the chapel, but felt a hand on his shoulder before he got the chance.

'Enjoy that?' asked Phillips.

'Bit of a trip down memory lane.'

'I bet.'

They walked side by side back along the cloisters, occasionally being jostled by the lines of younger pupils pushing past them on either side.

'Where are they off to in such a hurry?' asked Dixon.

'Supper.'

'That explains it.'

'I gather we're all going to be DNA tested on Friday morning?'

Dixon nodded.

'Ask me no questions, I'll tell you no lies, I suppose,' said Phillips.

'Is that the time?' replied Dixon, looking at his watch. 'See you tomorrow.'

Dixon drove out towards the Greyhound Inn at Staple Fitzpaine with the heater and fans on full blast. It was a clear night, crisp and cold, and it had taken the last of his de-icer to clear the windscreen.

He thought about the DNA test that he now knew would be taking place on Friday morning. It occurred to him that if Phillips knew then so did Rowena's father and only he would know or suspect the real reason for it. The rest would think it was purely standard procedure. Still, at least they would know who they were looking for if he did a bunk. Dixon shook his head. That would not do at all. Watching him being interviewed on a TV screen or looking through the slit in a cell door was not enough. Not by a long way. Dixon wanted to look him in the eye when he arrested him, assuming he decided not to kill him, of course. Try as he might, Dixon still had no real idea how he would react when he came face to face with Fran's killer. What concerned him more was that it was still an 'if' rather than a 'when' he came face to face with him.

He parked next to Jane's car and checked for any sign of Monty. Shame. She must have left him at home. Then he thrust his hands as deep as they would go into his pockets and walked across the car park listening to the ice crunching beneath his feet. Each crunch was followed by a splash as he broke through the thin layer of ice that had formed on the puddles.

Monty spotted Dixon first when he walked into the public bar and almost pulled Jane off her chair trying to get to him before she let him go. He ran over to Dixon and began jumping up at him while he was waiting at the bar.

'You got a drink?'

Jane held up what looked like a Diet Coke.

Dixon picked up a menu, walked over and sat down opposite Jane.

'We're gonna be all right, aren't we?'

'What d'you mean?' asked Jane.

'You and me. When this is all over.'

'What makes you say that?'

'It must be difficult for you . . .'

'Don't be silly. Of course we'll be all right.' Jane smiled at him. Then she stood up, leaned across the table and kissed him. 'And I'm with you every step of the way.'

'Thank you.'

Jane looked down at Monty curled up on the floor at Dixon's feet. 'I gave him a run on the beach and he's been fed.'

'Thanks. Tell me about the DNA test.'

'It's fixed for Friday morning.'

'Whose idea was that?'

'The headmaster's. Tomorrow is the last day of term now and they'll all be too busy, apparently.'

'There's a rumour going round that he was having an affair with Isobel and he killed her,' said Dixon.

'Hatton?'

'It's just schoolboy mischief.'

'How d'you know?'

'I was one once, don't forget.'

'Shouldn't we look into it?'

'No time left. Chard can follow it up later if needs be.'

Jane nodded.

'What about the driving instructor?' asked Dixon.

'We've got a sample from him.'

Dixon took the business card out of the top pocket of his jacket.

'I had a rummage in Phelps' room and found this in a cigar box in his bedside table,' he said, handing it to Jane.

'Why would . . . ?'

'Exactly. Ask him, will you? First thing in the morning.'

Jane took her notebook out of her handbag and began making notes.

'Maybe he wanted to learn to drive?'

'Quite possibly,' replied Dixon. 'And it's reasonable to assume he'd ask an instructor he saw coming to the school regularly.'

'I'll speak to him in the morning.'

'And don't go alone.'

'OK, OK.'

'Take someone from Bridgwater, if you're stuck. Louise Willmott.'

'I get it.'

'Have you found anything else on Rowena's father?' asked Dixon.

'No. There's no record of a Gordon Patrick Lee appearing anywhere after Rowena's date of birth, but then we knew that. And that's assuming it really is her date of birth.'

'She was Rowena Abbot at St Dunstan's.'

'I checked for a Gordon Patrick Abbot. Nothing.'

'So, he kills Rowena's mother,' said Dixon, 'takes her to Kenya for five years and then comes back with a new identity.'

'Makes sense.'

'And it's all hunky dory until he meets Fran . . .'

'Possibly not.'

'What'd you mean?'

Jane opened the file on the table in front of her and handed Dixon a photograph.

'Lynnette Margaret Peters. Aged eighteen. Reported missing in 1983.'

'She's the spitting image of Fran,' said Dixon, staring at the photograph.

'And Isobel.'

Dixon shook his head. 'Where?'

'Wells. She went to a local school.'

'The Cathedral School?'

'No. Chard's getting the files out now.'

Jane watched Dixon's eyes glazing over the more he stared at the photograph and could see he was no longer focussing on it. She waited. Suddenly, he slammed the picture down on the table with his left hand. Monty woke up and started growling.

'What's he doing about it?'

'Who?'

'Chard.'

'Tracking down all the staff at her school and interviewing them, I think.'

Dixon picked up the menu and passed it to Jane. 'Hungry?'

'Er, yes,' replied Jane, frowning. 'What's going on?'

'It's right in front of me, Jane. Right in front of me. So close I could reach out and touch it.' Dixon grimaced. 'But I can't see it. I just can't see it.'

'What?'

'If I knew that, we'd be home and dry.'

'You've lost me.'

'It's like doing a huge jigsaw puzzle and finding the last bit's missing.'

'Jigsaw puzzle?'

'Only you've seen it, lying around somewhere, you just can't remember where . . .'

'You know who it is?' asked Jane.

'No,' said Dixon, shaking his head. 'But it's there. The last piece of the jigsaw puzzle is right there.'

'So, what do we do?'

'We eat.'

'You can eat at a time like this?'

'I have to. I'm diabetic, don't forget. And what do we do when we can't remember an actor's name?'

'Google it.'

'If you can't google it,' said Dixon, rolling his eyes.

'Think about something else . . .'

'Exactly. Now what d'you want to eat?'

They both ordered the curry and then sat in silence watching Monty lying fast asleep in front of the fire. It was at least ten minutes before Dixon spoke again.

'What about Haskill?'

'He left Malaysia on a flight to Shanghai this morning. Chard's onto the Home Office and the request's gone in to see if the Chinese will pick him up.'

'And Griffiths?'

'Squeaky clean. Here's a copy of what we've got,' said Jane, handing a plastic document wallet to Dixon.

'Is he a Jehovah's Witness?'

'No.'

'I'll read it later,' he said, putting the file to one side. 'What happened after I left this morning?'

'You mean apart from all the cursing and swearing?'

'Yes.'

'There was a lot of shouting and yelling, barking of orders, that sort of thing. Lewis managed to calm him down, though, I think.'

'What worries me most of all is that it'll be Chard making the arrest and not me.'

'He'll have you off the case when Fran's file comes out tomorrow. You know that, don't you?'

'Yes.'

The smell of curry distracted them both and several minutes passed before Jane spoke again. Dixon had cleared his plate before she was even halfway through her own meal.

'You were hungry,' she said.

'School food.'

Dixon reached into his inside jacket pocket and took out the photograph. He handed it to Jane.

'I found this in a suitcase in Phelps' room. Where is it, d'you know?'

'It's Clive Cooper.'

'I know that, but where is it?'

'Looks like the King's Sedgemoor Drain to me. Too wide to be anything else and the banks are that steep, I think. D'you want me to check?'

'No, don't bother.' Dixon slid the photograph back in his pocket.

'I thought Derek Phelps' room had been searched?' asked Jane.

'It had but they didn't know what they were looking for, did they?'

'I suppose not.'

Dixon was staring at his empty glass.

'Another drink?' asked Jane.

No reply. Jane waited.

'Wasn't Phelps illiterate?'

'He was,' replied Jane. 'Couldn't read or write.'

'Yet he managed to write the letters 'KF' in the mud . . .' Dixon frowned. 'Email me the photo of his murder scene, will you. The letters in the mud. Zoom in so I can see them. Nice and clear.'

'Will do.'

Jane added it to her list of things to do. 'So, what happens now?' she asked.

'I don't know. I really don't know. But it's shit or bust tomorrow, one way or the other.'

It was nearly 10 p.m. by the time Dixon parked in front of the school. He had spent the last ten minutes sitting in the car park at the Greyhound waiting for his windscreen to clear and Jane was well on her way home by then. The heated windscreen in her red VW Golf had done the trick for her in less than thirty seconds and it was yet another reminder that Dixon had bought the wrong car.

He walked along the main corridor, the silence broken only by the slow and deliberate click of his heels on the tiled floor. The notice boards on either side were emptier now, evidence of cancelled meetings and activities now that the term was ending a week early. Good news for some, bad news for others. Dixon could certainly have done with a few more days. He was still no nearer to finding the missing piece of the jigsaw puzzle, although it would be found by a process of elimination on Friday morning. And by someone else. That was the bit that hurt the most. The prospect of being thrown off the case and languishing at home while Chard arrested the man who had killed Fran. Or, worse still, let him get away.

He made a cup of tea and then sat down on the small sofa in his rooms to read the file that he had pulled out from under the mattress. It was the only place the missing piece could be or, at least, it was the only place he had left to look. Either way, it felt better than doing nothing and he was unlikely to sleep. He read the witness statements again and then Isobel Swan's post mortem report, before taking a sip of tea that was by then stone cold.

It was going to be another long night.

# Chapter Sixteen

Dixon was shivering violently when he woke up just after 5 a.m., slumped on the sofa with Isobel Swan's post mortem report lying on his chest. He sat up, rubbed his eyes and began fumbling for the plug on the wall next to him, eventually finding the switch. Then he sat in the dark listening to the oil fired electric radiator clicking and cracking as it warmed up.

He thought about the day ahead. It would be the day the full extent of his personal involvement in the case would be laid bare for all to see. And it could well turn out to be the day his police career came to an abrupt halt. Shit happens, he knew that only too well, but it would be a price worth paying.

He waited until he could feel the warmth from the radiator and then got up to make a cup of tea. If he had been at home, he would have taken Monty for a walk around the lanes, but today he would have to make do with tea. Shame. He did his best thinking when he was out with his dog. He sat down on the edge of the bed, holding the mug of tea in both hands and with his feet resting on the radiator.

He was hunting a man who had killed four women. The mother of his own child and then three girls he encountered who looked like her. Dixon shook his head. He knew exactly who he was looking for and where to find him but he was missing one last piece of information to complete the puzzle. A name. He thought about having another go at Rowena in interview but he couldn't risk a visit to Taunton Police Station and another run in with Chard. Not when Chard would have Fran's file on his desk. No, the longer he could stay out of his way, the better. He would have to leave Rowena to Chard or Baldwin now.

It would end today, one way or the other. Dixon just had to hope that Rowena's father made one mistake to give himself away. That's all it would take, just one mistake. Unless he had made it already and Dixon had missed it. Fuck it. That feeling hit him again. The missing piece of the jigsaw puzzle. Dixon gritted his teeth and nodded. The mistake had been made. He knew that. And he had seen it, whatever it was. He just had to hope the true significance of it hit home in time.

The smell of burning socks got the better of him before the pain and he took his feet off the radiator. Time for a shower. A quick glance in the mirror told him that a shave was out of the question, but at least his stubble was starting to cover the cuts and scratches he had picked up on the Quantocks. A shower would have to do, then down to breakfast nice and early.

Dixon was listening to the excited chatter in the dining room while he checked his email on his phone. The most recent was from Jane and attached a photograph of the letters in the mud next to the body of Derek Phelps. Dixon opened it and stared at the picture for several minutes. There was a clear mark adjacent to the second letter that looked to be the beginnings of a third, but Phelps had died before he could complete it. Dixon was frowning as he tapped out a reply.

*which bloody idiot thought that was KF?*

He was surprised that so many pupils were there at that time in the morning but no doubt the excitement of the last day of term would account for that. A morning of lessons to endure, an afternoon spent packing and then the carol service at 5 p.m., followed by Christmas dinner.

Dixon was sitting alone at the top table, watching all the comings and goings and picking at a bowl of lumpy porridge. A food fight started on a table in the far corner but stopped before he felt the need to intervene. Anybody would think he was a real teacher but then it might have looked a bit odd if he hadn't stepped in.

'Nobody warned you about the porridge, then?'

Dixon looked up. It was Ben Masterson.

'No, sadly not.'

Ben smiled and moved to walk away.

'Sit down, join me. I'd like to have a word with you, if you've got a minute.'

Ben looked nervously around the dining room and then sat down opposite Dixon.

'You all right?' asked Dixon.

'Yes, Sir. Thank you.'

'Less of the "Sir". In any other setting I'd be calling you Sir, don't forget.'

Ben smiled.

'I wanted to ask you about that note . . .'

'That was nothing, really. But I did just want a chat about . . . well . . . there's a rumour . . .' His voice tailed off.

'About what?'

'It's probably nothing.'

'Mr Hatton?'

'You've heard it?'

'Yes,' said Dixon, nodding.

'Is it true?'

'I don't think so.'

'Well, at least you know about it.'

'I do.'

Dixon watched Ben prodding his cornflakes with his spoon.

'Did they offer you counselling?' he asked.

'Matron mentioned it but I said no.'

'Me too. The British stiff upper lip and all that.'

'I suppose.'

'Did Isobel have an unusual relationship with any of the other teachers?' Dixon asked.

'What d'you mean?'

'I'm not sure I know, to be honest, Ben. I'm just looking for anything out of the ordinary.'

'Not that I can think of.'

'Was she worried about anything in particular?'

'Not really. Her driving test, perhaps.'

'When was that?'

'It would have been on the Wednesday afternoon.'

'What did she say about it?'

'Just that she didn't feel ready. She was getting stressed out about it.'

'What did you say?'

'I told her to take it anyway. What was the worst that could happen?'

'Was she going to?'

'I think so.'

'Did she say anything else?'

'No.'

'Well, I'll leave you . . .'

'Tell me about your girlfriend,' said Ben. He was looking down, still pushing cornflakes around his plate with his spoon.

'She was my fiancée, technically,' replied Dixon. 'We were at St Dunstan's, seventeen years ago.'

'You were engaged?'

'We were. We hadn't told anyone, but we were.'

'D'you think it's the same killer?'

'I do,' replied Dixon. 'But that's between you and me.'

'You'll get him, won't you?'

Dixon got up to leave.

'We'll get him, Ben, don't you worry.'

Dixon walked back along the corridor, past the cloisters towards the masters' common room and up the flight of steps at the end. He stood looking along the main corridor. There were several groups of pupils walking towards him, no doubt heading for the dining room and breakfast. He felt a blast of cold air as another group came in through the door behind him.

The door of the masters' common room was open, so he went in and spent the next five minutes looking at the notice board. There was a large notice about the DNA testing the following morning and a sealed envelope in each of the male teachers' pigeonholes, no doubt a personal memo from the headmaster on the same subject.

He was distracted by a commotion in the corridor outside and looked at his watch. It was just before 8.15 a.m. so it was probably the late rush for breakfast. He went outside and watched the last of the pupils sprinting down the corridor towards the dining room and was surprised that he could still hear running and shouting even now that the corridor was empty. He spun round when he heard a loud crash followed by raucous laughter. It was coming from the library.

He pushed open the right hand door in time to watch the baton changing hands in what appeared to be a relay race over the bookshelves. A line of girls was waiting in front of the shelves on the left and a group of boys were on the right. Dixon shook his head in disbelief as he watched a boy climb the shelves in front of him, drop down on the other side and then reappear on top of the next set of shelves, each book that hit the floor in the process being greeted by a loud cheer. A girl was doing the same over the left hand set of shelves and it was impossible to tell which team was winning.

Both groups were so intent on cheering on their teammates that they failed to notice Dixon's arrival, so he let go of the door and waited for it to slam behind him. The effect was immediate.

'Who's winning?'

His question was greeted with stunned silence by both groups. The girl racing over the shelves on the left saw him and stopped but the boy on the right seemed oblivious to Dixon's arrival and kept going, much to the amusement of the girls. His moment of triumph was shattered only when he arrived on top of the last shelf and spotted Dixon. He tried to stop himself, lost his balance, and fell from the top shelf, landing in a heap on a pile of books lying on the floor.

Dixon watched him get to his feet, mercifully none the worse for his fall.

'And you are?'

'Bromfield, Sir.'

'Take a tip from me, Bromfield.'

'Yes, Sir.'

'Don't take up mountaineering.'

'Yes, Sir.' He was blinking furiously and rubbing his eyes.

'Are you all right?' asked Dixon.

Bromfield stopped blinking and looked up at Dixon.

'I've lost a contact lens, Sir.'

'Well, you'd better look for it, then.'

Dixon stood back and watched Bromfield and the other boys searching for the contact lens. He turned to the group of girls.

'And you lot can make a start getting those books back on the shelves.'

'Here it is,' said Bromfield, holding up a copy of *The Battlefields of England* by Alfred Burne. Dixon could see the lens stuck to the cover of the book and watched Bromfield peel it off. He held it up to the light on the end of his index finger and then put it back in his eye.

'That's fine,' he said, blinking again.

'Good. That means you can see to put these books back on the shelves.'

'Yes, Sir.'

'And make an effort to get them in the right order. I'll be back to check in twenty minutes.'

'Yes, Sir.'

Dixon looked over his shoulder to check that the boys and girls were putting the books back on the shelves before he opened the door. Suddenly, the image of Bromfield's contact lens stuck to the cover of *The Battlefields of England* flashed across his mind. He closed his eyes and took a deep breath.

'That's it,' he muttered.

Then he left the door to slam behind him and sprinted up the stairs opposite. Leaving the key in the door of his rooms, he ran in and pulled the copy of Isobel Swan's file from under the mattress. He took out her post mortem report and flicked through the pages until he found the passage he was looking for.

'Left eye missing contact lens, soft, possibly disposable. Right lens retained for comparison.'

Dixon sat in his Land Rover and rang Jane. It was several rings before she answered and he grimaced when he heard the sound of a car engine in the background.

'Where are you?'

'On my way to see the driving instructor. Why?'

'I needed you to see if we had Isobel's contact lens prescription on file.'

'Sorry.'

'Are you on your own?'

'No. Louise is here.'

'Good. Let me know how you get on.'

'Will do. You sound . . .'

Dixon had already rung off. It took him less than five minutes to get to Musgrove Park Hospital, stopping at the only set of traffic lights that had a camera installed on them. The others he ignored.

It was not quite 9 a.m. and the pathology lab was still closed, but he could see Roger Poland's car in the car park, so he started banging on the window nearest his office. The laboratory assistant inside turned around and shouted through the window at Dixon.

'What do you want?'

'Where's Roger Poland?'

'In a meeting.'

'Get him, will you? Tell him it's Nick Dixon.'

He waited under the canopy by the front door and listened to the rain hammering on the roof. Then he heard the sound of the door being unlocked behind him.

'What's going on?' asked Poland.

'Isobel's contact lens. Have you still got it?'

'Yes. It's in the store.'

'Can I see it?'

'Er, yes. Come in.'

Dixon followed Poland through to his office and sat down on a chair in front of his desk.

'Give me a minute,' said Poland.

He reappeared a few minutes later carrying a small vial of clear fluid. One side was covered by a label but Dixon could see a small blue tinted contact lens suspended in the liquid. He held it up to the light and flicked it, watching the lens turn over and over in front of him.

'Makes you wonder what the last thing she saw through this was, doesn't it?'

'It does,' replied Poland. 'What's your interest in the contact lens, then?'

'I know where the other one is.'

'The other one?'

'I've seen it, or at least I think I have. Can I borrow this?'

'What for?'

'I need to get it identified by an optician and get some exactly the same.'

'You'll bring it back?'

'In half an hour. Then we'll see if I'm right.'

Dixon parked on the pavement outside Richard Firth Optometrists in East Reach, switched his hazard lights on and then ran in.

'Is there an optician available, please?' he asked, showing his warrant card to the receptionist. 'It is rather urgent.'

'I'll just check.'

He watched her get up and walk through to the back of the shop, then he turned to look for traffic wardens out of the window.

'Can I help?'

Dixon spun round to see a man in his early fifties with a pair of spectacles resting on top of his head and another pair hanging round his neck on a cord.

'I'm Richard Firth.'

'Thank you,' replied Dixon. He took the vial out of his jacket pocket. 'I need you to identify this lens for me, if you can.'

'Can I take it out?'

'No.'

'Hmmm . . .' Firth held the vial up to the light and began turning it. 'It's an Acuvue, I think. Possibly their Trueye daily disposable. No telling the strength, of course. Hang on a sec.'

He handed the vial back to Dixon and then disappeared to a room at the back of the shop before returning a minute or so later with another lens in a clear plastic pot. He held them up to the light side by side.

'Yes. They look pretty much identical to me. Here, see what you think,' he said, handing them to Dixon.

'They're both stamped "UV". Does any other manufacturer do that?'

'No. Bausch & Lomb stamp theirs "B&L", from memory.'

'Have you got a sample I can take?'

'Yes, of course.'

Dixon raced back to Musgrove Park Hospital with a strip of five contact lenses in his jacket pocket. He parked behind Poland's car, blocking him in, and then ran into the pathology lab.

'Dr Poland's expec . . .'

Dixon was already through the swing doors before the receptionist had finished her sentence.

'Any luck?' asked Poland.

'Yes. According to Richard Firth they're Acuvue Trueye daily disposables,' replied Dixon, handing Poland both vials. 'See what you think.'

Poland walked into his office holding both vials up to the light. Dixon followed.

'They certainly look the same.'

'They do.'

'Now what?' asked Poland, sitting behind his desk.

Dixon shut the door behind him and then sat down opposite Poland. 'The acid test,' he said, taking off his left shoe.

He placed it on the desk in front of him and then took out the strip of new lenses. He tore the seal off one and took it out, balancing it on the end of his index finger. Then he gently placed it on the outside of the shoe, just above the heel.

'Now we wait.'

'Is there a coffee machine in this place?' asked Dixon.

'We've got a kettle and a jar of instant.'

'That'd be lovely, thanks, Roger. No sugar in mine.'

Poland sighed loudly and then left the room. Dixon sat watching the contact lens on the side of his shoe.

'So let me make sure I've got this right. You're saying that Isobel's other lens, the missing lens, is stuck to her killer's shoe?'

Dixon turned round to see Poland standing behind him with a mug in each hand. He passed one to Dixon.

'Yes.'

'But it would have come off, surely?'

'Not necessarily.'

'Let's hear it, then,' said Roger.

'No one heard a scream so we can assume she went willingly with her killer. She knew him and trusted him. Right?'

Poland nodded.

'He would've been dressed as usual so as not to arouse her suspicions.'

'He would.'

'So, let's assume you've drugged her and cut off her ring finger. Now you've got to dispose of her body. Or maybe before you cut off her finger, even? What's the first thing you're gonna do?'

'Get changed,' replied Poland.

'Exactly. You take your shoes off. And it's not likely to be until the following day that you put them on again, which is plenty of time for a soft contact lens to dry out.'

'What happens when it does, I wonder?'

'We'll see, won't we, but I'm guessing it'll stick like glue.'

'You'd see it, surely?'

'Not if you were short sighted. And when was the last time you looked at the heel of your shoe?'

'I'm not sure I ever have.'

'Exactly.'

'So, how did her lens come out?'

'Maybe she fell heavily or just rubbed her eyes, something like that,' said Dixon.

'It doesn't take much for them to come out, that's for sure,' replied Poland. 'I'm always having to stop the clock so some twit can put a lens back in.'

'I forgot you referee rugby matches.'

'Keeps me fit.'

Dixon picked up his shoe and examined the contact lens. It was shrivelled at the edges but still only stuck to the shoe in the very centre of the lens.

'That's not it at all,' said Dixon. 'And you'd see that.'

'Try another one the other way round,' said Poland.

Dixon tore the seal off another contact lens and placed it on the side of his shoe, this time facing outwards. The edge of the lens formed a seal of sorts to the leather.

'That's more like it. It'll stick flat to the side when it dries out, you watch.'

'It'll take a while,' said Poland.

'Time for another coffee?'

'I've got to check on a post mortem. I'll bring one back with me.'

'OK.'

Dixon picked up his shoe and watched the contact lens stuck to the side gradually drying out. He prodded it with his finger and it moved but not much. It hadn't taken long for a seal to form around the rim of the lens and only a direct hit would shift it now.

By the time Poland returned with two more mugs of coffee the lens was stuck flat to the side of the shoe.

'Forty-one minutes it took,' said Dixon, holding the shoe out to Poland.

He took it and examined the lens.

'That's not coming off in a hurry. It looks almost vacuum sealed.'

'You could even polish over it and wouldn't come off.'

'Then you'd never see it.'

'Only I did see it,' said Dixon. 'Plain as day. And so close I could reach out and touch it.'

Dixon sat in his Land Rover and listened to the rain hammering on the roof. He looked at his watch: 11 a.m. He turned out of Musgrove Park Hospital and then drove north-west out of Taunton. It had been seventeen years since he had last been to St Dunstan's and he had always sworn that he would never go back. Still, needs must, he thought.

He looked down at the school from the bridge over the railway line before turning right into the main entrance. It was a grand building, almost Gothic in its appearance and very much like Brunel, built of grey stone with a central tower over the front entrance.

Dixon parked across the front door and ran in. He knew exactly where he was going. He turned right along the main corridor and then left along the corridor leading to the assembly room. He was looking at the photographs on the walls either side as he ran. School teams going back in time the further along the corridor he went. Rugby, football, hockey, cricket and tennis. He slowed as he went further back and stopped at the team photographs from seventeen years ago. He stood in front of the girls' tennis team looking at the picture of Fran. She was sitting in the middle of the front row of three, with three teammates standing behind her and the coach standing on the left. Mr Adrian Saunders, according to the names printed beneath the photograph.

Dixon shook his head. He could not remember an Adrian Saunders at all.

'Dixon, isn't it?'

He spun round and recognised his housemaster from all those years ago. A bit greyer, perhaps, but otherwise he had hardly changed a bit.

'Mr Hopkins,' said Dixon, holding out his hand.

They shook hands, as Mr Hopkins looked him up and down.

'You look well. What're you up to these days?'

Dixon took out his warrant card and handed it to him.

'Oh,' said Hopkins, rolling his eyes. 'Are you here on business?'

'Yes. What can you tell me about Adrian Saunders?' asked Dixon, pointing at the photograph of the girls' tennis team.

Hopkins peered at it.

'Not a lot, really. I seem to remember he was a postgraduate teaching assistant or a trainee here for a year or two, perhaps. I think. But it didn't work out so he just left as far as I . . . d'you want me to ask? Someone may remember him.'

'No, it's fine.'

'I never forget a face. Pupils, that is; teachers and staff are a different matter. I don't know half the ones here now.'

Dixon looked at the picture mounted on the wall. It was in a brown wooden frame screwed to the wall with brass brackets on either side.

'You're gonna have to bear with me, Mr Hopkins. I'll be back to pay for the damage later.'

'What damage?'

Dixon smashed the glass with the edge of his phone. Then he pulled the photograph out from behind the cardboard mounting and ran back to his car. It wasn't the first time that Mr Hopkins had been left to pick up the pieces.

# Chapter Seventeen

Dixon sped north up the M5. He had his foot down hard on the accelerator and his old Land Rover was creaking and rattling in protest. Not only that, but he could hardly hear himself think over the roar of the engine. He needed to get the photograph blown up and then the subject, Adrian Saunders, aged.

He tried hard to remember Adrian Saunders. A trainee teacher, according to Mr Hopkins. Dixon shook his head. It had been a week of memories flooding back at every opportunity, but the last one, the vital one, eluded him. Still, whoever he was then, Dixon knew damn well who he was now and they would soon be face to face.

Taunton Police Station had not been an option so he had driven to Bridgwater and arrived at Express Park just after midday. At least there he would be out of Chard's reach, for the time being. He would need to stay out of DCI Lewis' way too.

It was his first visit to the Bridgwater Police Centre at Express Park. Concrete blocks and glass, lots of glass. He ran in the main entrance, waved his warrant card at the receptionist, and then continued up the stairs to the open plan CID Room on the first floor. It looked more like a call centre than a police station. Still, it was his first visit and likely to be his last too, so there was no point worrying about it.

He spotted WPC Louise Willmott sitting at a desk at the far end.

'Where's Jane?' he asked.

'She dropped me off and then went back to Taunton. Said she might pop home first, though.'

'You saw Arnold Davies?'

'Yes.'

'What'd he say?'

'He was approached one day by a kitchen porter who said he wanted to learn to drive. He gave him a business card but heard no more about it.'

'Did he give a description?'

'Yes. Jane's got my notes. She said it fitted with Phelps.'

Dixon handed the photograph of the tennis team to Louise.

'I need this photo blown up to focus on the coach. This man,' he said, jabbing his finger at the man standing on the end of the back row. 'Then we need to age him.'

'When d'you need it done by?'

'Now.'

'Oh. Right. I'll be back in a minute.'

Louise got up, taking the photograph with her, so Dixon sat at her desk. He looked along the line of desks in front of him, all of them white, with black partitioning, and shook his head. He didn't recognise a single officer either, until he spotted DCI Lewis at the far end. He ducked down behind Louise's computer and hoped for the best.

'Hiding from anyone in particular, Sir?'

Dixon looked up to see PC Cole standing over him.

'The DCI, down the far end.'

'He's gone now, Sir.'

'Thank you, Cole,' said Dixon, sitting up.

'Saw you on the telly the other day. At Taunton Racecourse.'

'Not you as well?'

'We all did.'

Dixon was about to respond when he saw Louise standing behind PC Cole. She was leaning on the corner of the desk opposite, breathing hard.

'Did you sort out the photo?' he asked her.

'We can blow it up easily enough,' replied Louise, 'But you'd need to go to HQ Portishead for the age progression software. It's not same day either.'

'Shit.'

'Know anyone who can use Photoshop?'

'No.'

'You could try SCAT.'

'You, Louise, are a star,' said Dixon. 'Is there a back way out of this place?'

'Follow me, Sir,' said Cole.

Dixon sat in his car and rang Jane. He tried three times but got no reply. Maybe she was at home. He just had time to get there and then get to the Somerset College of Arts and Technology before 2 p.m. Perfect.

Monty started barking when he heard the sound of Dixon's engine outside the cottage but there was no sign of Jane. He tried her mobile phone again. Still no reply. So he put Monty in the car and sped south on the M5, back to Taunton.

As he raced past Express Park, which was visible from the motorway, he wondered if he would have a chance to get his mileage claim in before he was fired.

Dixon parked in the loading bay directly outside the Arts and Design Centre at the Somerset College of Arts and Technology. It was nearly 2.30 p.m. More concrete and glass but the rusting steel statue on the lawn caught his attention as he ran up the path. It reminded him of Icarus, with his wings outstretched and full of holes. No chance of wax melting on a day like today, he thought, running with his hands in his pockets.

He rubbed his hands together and blew on them as he waited for the receptionist to finish her telephone call. He looked around at the pictures on the walls, spinning round when he heard the call end.

'Can I help you?'

Dixon placed his warrant card on the counter.

'I need to find someone who can use Photoshop. And quickly, please.'

'Photoshop?'

'Yes. It's software for editing photogra . . .'

'I know what it is. Why do you need it?'

'It's a murder investigation and I don't have time to go through the proper channels.'

The receptionist turned round and shouted towards an open door behind her. Dixon had thought the room was empty.

'Jan, who would use Photoshop?'

'Try Peter Bailey. He teaches photography.'

'Where would I find Mr Bailey?' asked Dixon.

'He'll be in the canteen now, I expect. Down the corridor on the right.'

'Thanks.'

Dixon ran along the corridor, through the swing doors and into the canteen. The serving area was directly in front of him as he went in and a large queue of people waiting patiently with their empty trays turned and stared at him. To his left were perhaps twelve or so round tables, all of them occupied by six or more students.

'Peter Bailey?'

'Over there,' replied one of the students in the queue, pointing to a table on the far side of the canteen occupied by older diners. Dixon ran over to it.

'I'm looking for Peter Bailey.'

'That'll be me.'

He had curly ginger hair and looked suitably casual in a white collarless shirt, open at the neck, under a threadbare brown corduroy jacket.

'Is there somewhere we can have a private word, please, Mr Bailey?'

'Now?'

Dixon handed him his warrant card.

'Oh, right, yes, through here.'

Dixon followed Peter Bailey through a door at the far end of the canteen, into the corridor and then along to an office at the far end, his own, judging by the name on the door.

'How can I help?' he asked, sitting down behind his desk.

'I'm told you use Photoshop?'

'Yes, I do.'

'Would you be able to age a photograph for me?'

'Don't you have access to age progression software these days?'

'We do but I don't have time . . .'

'What's it all about?'

'It's a murder investigation.'

'Oh, God. Have you got the photo with you?'

Dixon handed Bailey the team photo.

'It's the man standing back left. Can you blow it up and age it?'

'Shouldn't be a problem.'

'How long will it take?' asked Dixon.

'An hour or so. Depends how accurate you want it.'

'Just a general idea will do.'

Bailey stood up and lifted the lid of a scanner on the table next to his desk. He placed the photograph face down on the glass, closed the lid and then pressed a large green button.

'There we go. It'll be in my email right about . . .' The computer on the table in the corner of his office made a soft ping sound. '. . . now.'

He took out the photograph and handed it back to Dixon. Then he sat down in front of his computer.

'You can stand behind and watch if you want. You get used to people doing that in my line of work.'

'I suppose you do,' replied Dixon.

Bailey opened his email and then clicked on the attachment to the first email in his inbox. The photograph opened in Microsoft Picture Viewer then he clicked on an icon bottom right, which closed that programme and opened another called Paint.

'Now we can cut out the subject.'

Dixon tried to follow the clicks of the mouse. He watched Bailey draw a square around Adrian Saunders then right click on the mouse and select 'Cut'. Saunders disappeared from the photograph, leaving a small square hole. Seventeen years too late, thought Dixon.

The mouse clicks began speeding up now and Dixon was soon lost. He watched Saunders reappear in a new picture, this time all on his own.

'What shall we save it as?' asked Bailey.

Dixon was miles away and did not reply.

'"Untitled one" will do,' said Bailey. 'Now we can import it into Photoshop.'

Dixon nodded. He watched Bailey open Adobe Photoshop and then import the small photograph of Saunders into the middle of a large screen with a bewildering array of toolbars either side and above.

'It'll get a bit grainy when we blow it up but I can soon fix that, don't worry,' said Bailey. 'D'you want me to explain to you what I'm doing as we go along?'

'It won't mean anything to me if you do, I'm afraid,' replied Dixon. 'You've lost me already.'

'Photoshop does that to people, particularly if you're not used to it.'

'I've never seen it before,' said Dixon.

'OK, I'm just going to blow it up as large as I dare, then tidy up the edges . . . just refining the mask . . .'

Dixon looked out of the window. The sun had come out and was reflecting off the windows of his Land Rover parked outside.

'Right, how old do you want to go?'

'Let's make him sixty-five. Can you do that?'

'Yes.'

'I'm just gonna use the patch tool to add some wrinkles first . . .'

Dixon shook his head and looked back out of the window. Monty was sitting on the passenger seat of the Land Rover looking around and sniffing at the small opening Dixon had left in the window.

'What about the hair?'

'Same style but grey.'

'That's easily done.'

Bailey began humming as he worked. Dixon closed his eyes and counted to ten. It was a small price to pay.

'I'm just gonna drop in some similar ears off an older subject. OK?'

'Yes, fine.'

Dixon watched Bailey scrolling through photographs of older men.

'Those look about right, don't they? Same shape.'

'Look fine to me.'

'We'll use those.'

More humming.

'Now for the eyebrows. I just need to create a brush first.'

Dixon checked his phone. He had missed a call from Jane, which was odd because he didn't remember hearing it ring. Perhaps it had been drowned out by the noise of his diesel engine out on the motorway?

'There we go. How do they look?'

'Fine.'

'What else?'

'The nose is thinner, somehow?'

'Maybe he's had a nose job. Do you want me to . . . ?'

'No, don't bother. Can you make the hair whiter?'

'Yep.'

Dixon looked at his watch. It was nearly 4 p.m. He looked back to the computer screen. His eyes narrowed as he started to recognise the face looking back at him.

'Anything else?'

'Glasses. Black, horn rimmed.'

'Coming right up.'

Dixon was breathing heavily now. His pulse was racing and a sick feeling was rising from the pit of his stomach.

'They're sitting nice and central. Anything else?'

'A beard. Give him a beard.'

'White?'

'Yes.'

'How long?'

'Three inches or so.'

Dixon tried to follow the last few clicks of the mouse as Bailey created a brush and then drew a white beard on the image of an older Adrian Saunders. But Saunders was long gone.

'D'you know him?' asked Bailey.

'I do.'

*She parked in the car park at the back of the school and looked up at the sports hall. Only a few days before, she'd been standing behind it, shivering in the cold, looking down at the body of a kitchen porter with the back of his head bashed in.*

*Violent places, these boarding schools. Maybe she hadn't missed out after all?*

*She got out of her car, locked it and then walked along the side of the Bishop Sutton Hall.*

*Where the bloody hell are you?*

*And why aren't you answering your effing phone?*

*She was standing in front of the Underwood Building wondering what to do when a small boy sprinted around the corner and crashed into her, almost knocking her to the ground.*

*'Sorry, Miss.'*

*'It's all right,' she said, straightening her coat and pulling the strap of her handbag back over her shoulder.*

*'D'you know where I can find Mr Dixon?'*

*'Who?'*

*'He's a trainee teacher?'*

*'Don't know him, Miss. Sorry. You could try the masters' common room.'*

*'Where's that?'*

*'Along the main corridor. Just round there.'*

*'Thank you.'*

*She watched the boy running off across the grass towards the sports hall. She knew where the masters' common room was, or at least she thought she did. She'd been there, after all, and if he wasn't there, someone else might know where he was.*

*She walked along the main corridor, the noise of her heels making her feel conspicuous. She tried walking on her toes but soon gave up.*

*Apart from the small boy who had nearly knocked her over, she'd seen no one. Odd, that. She checked her phone. Thursday 8th December.*

*Definitely the right day.*

*Where was everybody?*

*She was halfway along the corridor when she heard footsteps coming down a flight of stairs behind her. She turned when she heard a man's voice.*

*'Can I help you?'*

*'Yes, thank you. I'm looking for Nick Dixon.'*

*'He's in the Lady Chapel, sitting in on a confirmation class. It's the last of the term. I'm on my way there now, if you'd like to follow me.'*

*'Thank you, I will.'*

*What harm can it do? He's a harmless old duffer.*

*She followed him along the main corridor, past the masters' common room, which she recognised, and then into the cloisters. He paused to unlock the chapel door.*

*She frowned. How did Nick and everyone get in for the confirmation class?*

*Maybe there's another way in?*

*She heard the sound of keys behind her. The door being locked.*

*A sharp intake of breath caught by a hand over her mouth.*

*Then a scratch on the side of her neck.*

*Her legs went from under her. She looked up. The roof was spinning.*

*Hyperventilating now.*

*Going to be sick.*

*She closed her eyes. When she opened them again she was looking down at a man carrying a woman over his shoulder, her blonde ponytail hanging down.*

*Who's that he's carrying down the aisle?*

*Wake up . . . please wake up . . .*

*More keys.*

*The war memorial. I remember that.*

*Another door.*

*An alleyway. Where am I?*

*Darkness.*

*Then nothing.*

# Chapter Eighteen

Dixon arrived back at Brunel just as it was getting dark and parked in front of the school. He ran upstairs to his rooms and fumbled under the mattress for the floor plans of the school. He unrolled them on the bed and looked at the key in the bottom left corner. Room 23 was the one he was looking for and it took him several seconds to find it on the third floor, directly above the front entrance. He left the floor plans on the bed, slammed the door behind him and ran downstairs.

Boys and girls were filing along the main corridor towards the chapel with Dixon running against the flow. He kept to the left, hugging the wall, and only once did he have to push someone out of the way. He arrived at the bottom of the first flight of stairs and looked up. Several pupils were coming down them so he took hold of the rail in his left hand, put his head down and started running up the stairs, using his right arm to clear a path.

Seconds later, he was leaning on the handrail at the top, trying to get his breathing under control. A small boy ran out of a door at the far end of the corridor and turned down the flight of stairs further along.

Dixon was staring at a large carved oak door on the far side of the landing. A small nameplate was fixed to it at waist height with a name written on it in ornate gold lettering. He walked across the landing and tried to listen at the door, but all he could hear was his own breathing and the sound of his heart pounding in his ears. He tried holding his breath but that gave him the urge to cough.

He waited until he was sure that no one else was around and then tried the door. Locked. It was a Yale lock, level with the door handle. Dixon smiled. One sharp kick should deal with that but there was a quieter way. He reached into his back pocket for his wallet and took out his Police Federation membership card. He probably wouldn't be needing it soon anyway. Then he inserted it in the crack between the door and the frame adjacent to the barrel of the lock and pushed, at the same time turning the door handle. The door swung open.

Dixon peered into the hallway, which was dark apart from the first few feet lit by the lights on the landing. He fumbled for the light switch, found three and turned them all on at once. Against the wall on the left was a large radiator cover with several ornaments arranged along the top. The light had come on in the small kitchen opposite and it was empty.

Dixon followed the passageway. It was almost identical in lay-out to Haskill's rooms, which Dixon had been using. He crept past a small bathroom, also empty, and into the living room. He heard the door close behind him, which was no bad thing. He didn't want to be disturbed.

He looked around the room. The bed was against the wall to his left and at the far end of the room was a desk with a leather swivel chair behind it and a leather sofa in front of it. His eyes returned to the bed and the two suitcases lying on top of it.

*Going somewhere, are we?*

Dixon opened the first suitcase and emptied the contents out onto the floor. It was all clothes. Then he unzipped the second suitcase and opened it. Several jackets were folded flat and lying on the top so he threw those on the floor, revealing toiletries and personal items underneath. Dixon looked down at them. Something was out of place. He began taking the items out one by one and throwing them on the floor. Hairbrush, wash bag, alarm clock. Then it hit him. A black plastic box with the Philishave logo on it. He picked it up. It was light, far too light to have a shaver in it and it rattled when he shook it. A soft rattle.

Suddenly, the realisation of what he had found hit him. And what he was about to see. His hands were shaking as he pressed the black plastic clip and lifted the lid.

The shaped plastic liner where a shaver would once have sat had been removed and replaced with a flannel that was lying in the bottom of the small box. Its corners had been carefully folded in to cover the contents, so Dixon folded them back, one by one. He grimaced. It had been some years since he had studied biology A Level but he knew human finger bones when he saw them.

Three of them were white, recently boiled to remove the flesh. Those would be Isobel Swan's. The rest were older and grey. He closed his eyes.

*I was supposed to put a ring on your finger. Not this. It wasn't supposed to be like this.*

He couldn't bring himself to count the remaining bones. That could wait. He folded the flannel back over them and closed the box. Then he ran downstairs and locked it in the glove box of his car.

He took his mobile phone out of his pocket to ring Jane and saw that he had missed two calls and three text messages. He frowned. He must have forgotten to switch the alerts back on after the chapel service the previous evening.

He looked at the text messages, the first of which came from her.

*where are u j x*

The other two both came from his voicemail service alerting him to messages waiting. The missed calls were both from Jane. Dixon listened to the messages.

'Hi, it's me. Where are you?'

He deleted it and listened to the next message.

'Chard's read Fran's file and is on the warpath. I'm coming over there now. Keep an eye out for me. Bye.'

*Oh, shit.*

Dixon looked around the car park and could see no sign of Jane or her car.

*Where the fuck are you?*

He dialled her number. No reply. He rang Louise Willmott.

'Have you heard from Jane?'

'Not since this morn . . .'

Dixon had already rung off. He ran along the main corridor towards the chapel. He was breathing through his nose and listening to the click of his heels. He paused at the top of the cloisters. The carol service had begun and the full congregation were on the first verse of 'Hark! The Herald Angels Sing'.

'Peace on earth and mercy mild.'

*Sorry, Lord, not this time.*

Dixon jumped down the stone steps and ran along the cloisters. He slowed to a walk as he entered the chapel. The teachers sitting at the back turned to look at him, the headmaster included, but he avoided eye contact. He stood at the end of the aisle looking up at the chancel. Father Anthony was standing behind the altar, singing.

Dixon began running down the aisle, pupils turning to watch him as he ran past them. He had reached the old altar marker before

Father Anthony looked up, saw him coming and bolted towards the Lady Chapel. Dixon could see him fumbling in his pockets as he ran.

'Hark! The herald angels sing,

Glory to the newborn King.'

When he reached the steps at the foot of the chancel Dixon turned right and ran into the Lady Chapel just in time to see a door at the back slam shut.

'Where does that go?'

'The Memorial Quadrangle,' replied a boy sitting at the back of the Lady Chapel.

Dixon tried the door. It was locked. He remembered the alleyway that came out by the kitchens.

*Fuck it.*

He turned and ran back down the aisle. He tried the handle on the door at the back of the chapel. It was open so he ran out into the darkness, down the side of the chapel and round to the alleyway by the kitchens. He spotted two kitchen porters smoking in the dark.

'Have you seen Father Anthony?'

'He went that way,' said one, pointing to the right.

Dixon sprinted along the service road at the back of the school. He could see Father Anthony two hundred yards ahead of him, in the lights of the Underwood Building. He disappeared around the front, heading towards the Bishop Sutton Hall.

Dixon was sprinting around the front of the Underwood Building when his phone rang. He put the phone to his ear as he ran but could hear only screaming and crying. Hyperventilating too. He stopped.

'Jane, is that you?'

Then he heard her vomit.

'Where are you?'

She sounded as if she was gasping for air.

'Dark . . .'

Sobbing now.

'Can you hear anything?'

'An engine . . . moving . . .'

'Stay on the line,' said Dixon. He ran in the back door at the end of the main corridor and along to the front entrance, getting to his Land Rover just as Jane's car disappeared down the drive from the Gardenhurst car park. Father Anthony was behind the wheel. Dixon jumped in his car and sped after him. West Road was long and straight and he could see Father Anthony's tail lights in the distance when he arrived at the bottom of the drive. He turned after them and put his foot flat on the accelerator.

'Jane, are you still there?'

Dixon got no reply but he could hear her sobbing in the background. Not easy over the noise of his old diesel engine but he had the phone clamped to his ear as tight as he could get it.

'I'm gonna ring off and get help. I'm right behind you. All right?'

Still no reply.

He followed her car left into Stoke Road and then left again onto Chestnut Drive. Dixon knew then that Father Anthony was heading for the motorway. He dialled 999.

'This is 3275 Inspector Dixon. I'm in pursuit of a red VW Golf north along Chestnut Drive. The driver, Father Anthony Johns, is wanted for murder and Detective Constable Jane Winter is in the boot of the car. Is that clear?'

'Er, yes, Sir.'

'I think he's heading for the M5. See if you can get a car to block him off. And get the helicopter.'

'Yes, Sir.'

'I'm in an old Land Rover so he's going to pull away from me when we get out onto the motorway. We must have the helicopter.'

'Leave it with me, S . . .'

'Right, right, into Blackbrook Way,' said Dixon. 'That's the M5 junction next.'

'Stand by.'

Dixon went the wrong way around the roundabout at the end of Blackbrook Way, narrowly avoiding a collision, and then jumped the lights at the motorway roundabout. He followed Father Anthony's tail lights up the northbound slip road onto the M5.

'We've got Traffic on their way, ETA twelve minutes. Heading south now.'

'Too late, we're northbound on the M5. Have you got that?'

'Yes, Sir.'

'Where's the helicopter?'

'Diverting to you now. Will be with you in eight minutes.'

'If we lose the connection ring me back immediately and keep trying till you get me.'

'Yes, Sir.'

Two sets of blue lights flashed by on the opposite carriageway, heading south. Dixon managed to keep track of Father Anthony's tail lights in the distance. He was five hundred yards ahead and pulling away slowly, or so it seemed. Dixon was in the outside lane and had his foot down hard on the accelerator. He was getting just over 80 mph out of the old Land Rover but it was not going to be enough.

'This fucking car!' he screamed, venting his frustration on the steering wheel with his fist.

'What about the slip road at Bridgwater South?'

'Stand by,' replied the controller.

Dixon waited.

'A local car is blocking that now, Sir. And the helicopter is overhead. They have the red VW in sight.'

'Thank God for that,' muttered Dixon.

He glanced up the slip road as he sped past and spotted the patrol car blocking the exit. He looked up and could see the red tail light of the helicopter above and in front of him.

'Bridgwater North is blocked and we've got a car coming up behind you. ETA three minutes. There's another waiting on the slip road at Burnham.'

Dixon peered in his rear view mirror but saw no sign of blue lights. He spotted the wicker man in a field on the nearside. Bridgwater North was less than a mile away now. He checked his rear view mirror again. Still no sign of the police car behind him.

'Left, left,' said the controller. 'He's got off at junction 23.'

'Oh, shit,' muttered Dixon, through a mouthful of fruit pastilles.

He swerved across all three lanes and sped up the slip road. Father Anthony up ahead mounted the offside kerb and tried to squeeze through the gap on the grass verge. He rammed the front wing of the patrol car blocking the exit in the process but got through and sped off around the roundabout.

'East, east on the A39,' said the controller.

Dixon aimed at the same gap but hit the front of the patrol car, sending it spinning. Then he raced around the roundabout and turned east on the A39. Not good. The long climb up Puriton Hill from the M5 would allow Father Anthony to pull away still further, but the helicopter was overhead keeping track. Dixon changed down and floored the accelerator again.

'Where the fuck is he going?'

Dixon managed to get his old Land Rover up to 90 mph going down the hill on the other side and was able to pick out Father Anthony's tail lights in the distance, trying to get through the traffic lights at the bottom of the hill. Off to his right, several sets of blue lights and sirens were screaming out of Bridgwater towards the bridge over the King's Sedgemoor Drain, which shimmered in the moonlight.

He thought about the photograph of Clive Cooper standing by the Drain. Then the letters in the mud, written by an illiterate and dying Derek Phelps. What had been so significant that Phelps would use his dying moments to give it away? Then it hit him. It wasn't 'KF', it was 'KS'.

'It's the King's Sedgemoor Drain,' screamed Dixon. 'He's going for the King's Sedgemoor Drain.'

Dixon crossed onto the wrong side of the road to avoid the queue of traffic at the lights, sending two cars swerving into the nearside kerb.

'Right, right into New Road,' said the controller.

'Can anyone cut him off?'

Dixon looked up and saw the helicopter hovering off to the right of the A39. He turned into New Road too fast. It was a narrow country lane and the back of the Land Rover swung round and hit the hedge. He suddenly remembered Monty, and glanced over his shoulder to see him curled up in his bed under the nearside bench seat.

'Right, right, into Bradney Lane.'

'Am I the nearest car?'

'Yes, Sir.'

Dixon saw houses flashing past on either side of the narrow lane.

'Where am I?'

'Bawdrip, Sir,' replied the controller.

Dixon looked up and saw the searchlight come on underneath the helicopter. It was hovering much lower now with the beam of light pointing straight at the ground beneath it.

'What's happening?' screamed Dixon.

'Stand by.'

Dixon oversteered on the bend by the church and the back of the Land Rover swung out and hit a parked car. He kept going.

'The car's gone into the Drain. Left before the bridge into the field. You can see the light.'

'What the . . . ?'

Dixon threw his phone onto the passenger seat. He spotted too late the five bar gate that Father Anthony had driven through and was going too fast to make the turn anyway, so he aimed at the fence just beyond it instead. His Land Rover crashed through the wooden fence, bouncing over the rough ground behind it where the cattle congregated. He changed down into first gear and accelerated out of the mud and across the field.

He could see Jane's red VW floating nose down in the water about thirty yards away. He slammed on his brakes and skidded to a halt. Then he jumped out of the Land Rover, opened the passenger door and reached into the back. He tipped up an old cardboard box in the rear passenger footwell and picked up the car jack. Then he ran down the bank and launched himself into the river.

The cold water hit him exactly as he knew it would but he was able to suppress his gasp reflex. He surfaced only two or three yards from the back of Jane's car and swam towards it. The searchlight in the belly of the helicopter lit up the scene, the downdraft from the rotor blades sending spray high into the air.

Monty was running up and down the bank barking at the car but Dixon could hardly hear him over the noise of the helicopter.

He reached up and tried the boot of Jane's car. It was locked. The car was sinking now, the weight of the engine taking it down nose first. He swam round to the driver's door and looked in. Treading water, he could see Father Anthony unconscious and slumped forward over the steering wheel. Dixon swung the car jack at the window, smashing it with the first hit. Then he dropped the jack and reached in for the car keys. Water started pouring in, making the car sink even faster.

His breathing was speeding up but his movements were becoming slower. He managed to swim round to the back of the car, which had reared up still further out of the water as the passenger compartment was swamped. His fingers were cramping and he needed to use his left hand to line up the key properly in his right. Then he pulled himself up on the bumper and inserted it in the lock. He turned it and the boot popped open.

The car began sinking fast, the boot getting lower and lower in the water. Suddenly, Jane was right in front of him. She was unconscious, so he reached in and grabbed hold of her coat just as the car sank from underneath her. He held her head above the water and managed to kick out towards the bank.

Blue lights were flashing all around him now. Dixon looked up at the bank. There were several police cars and an ambulance in the field.

'Whose is that damn dog?'

'It's the inspector's.' Dixon recognised Louise Willmott's voice.

Suddenly, he felt hands lifting Jane clear of the water. He paused.

'Put her here . . . she's still breathing . . .'

An outstretched hand appeared in front of Dixon. He looked up. It was Louise.

'Tell 'em she's had ketamine. They'll know what to do,' said Dixon. Then he turned and swam out to where Jane's car had sunk. He stretched down with his legs and could feel the roof of the car under his feet. He took a deep breath and dived down.

The searchlight penetrated the murky water to a depth of five or six feet and Dixon could just about make out the roof of the car beneath him. He reached down and took hold of the driver's door, pulling himself down the rest of the way. The cold was clawing at his flesh, every second he spent in the water making movement more difficult.

He fumbled in the darkness for the door handle, found it and pulled open the door. The pain in his fingers was excruciating. Then he grabbed Father Anthony's arm, pulled him out of the car and kicked out for the light above.

Gasping for air as he broke the surface, Dixon turned to see Louise in the water swimming towards him. A second officer took off his hi-vis jacket and jumped in. It was PC Cole. He took hold of Father Anthony and, keeping his head above the water, made for the bank.

Louise tried to help Dixon but he was spent. All feeling in his legs and arms had gone and Louise was fighting to keep his head clear of the water.

'Help me, someone,' she screamed.

PC Cole passed Father Anthony to the paramedics, who lifted him onto the bank. Then he swam back out to help Louise. Together they dragged Dixon to the bank and lifted him out of the water.

He lay on the grass listening to the helicopter and the sirens all around him. A blanket was thrown over him.

'Well done, Sir.'

Louise was standing over him with a blanket wrapped around her shoulders.

'Is she . . . ?'

'She's going to be fine, Sir.'

Dixon lay back and closed his eyes. Then he felt Monty licking his face.

Dixon watched the paramedics working on Jane. She was on a stretcher, wrapped in foil blankets with a mask over her mouth.

Louise helped him to his feet.

A second helicopter, this one yellow with a green stripe, was landing in the field behind them.

'It's the air ambulance, Sir,' shouted Louise.

'Father Anthony?'

'Going to Frenchay Hospital, Bristol.'

'Is he . . . ?'

'He'll live, Sir.'

Dixon nodded.

*He's got some explaining to do.*

'You'll get a medal for this, Sir.'

'I doubt that, Louise,' replied Dixon. 'I doubt that very much.'

# Chapter Nineteen

Jane woke slowly. It took several minutes for her eyes to focus on a nurse standing at the end of her bed.

'Where am I?'

'Musgrove Park Hospital.'

'What happened to me?'

'You were drugged with ketamine and thrown in the boot of a car. You've got a broken collar bone and your right arm's in a sling, but apart from that you'll be fine. Once the ketamine wears off, that is.'

Jane raised her left hand and looked at it, first the palm and then the back.

'It's still there.'

'What is?' asked the nurse.

'My ring finger. I thought for a minute it might . . .' Her voice tailed off.

'You may need it one day,' said the nurse, nodding in the direction of the armchair next to Jane's bed. 'He's been here all night.'

Jane turned her head on the pillow to see Dixon, fast asleep next to her. She smiled.

'I remember water . . .'

'The car went into the King's Sedgemoor Drain. He dived in and got you out.'

Jane reached over with her left arm and tapped Dixon on the knee. He woke up.

'You're awake?'

'I am,' replied Jane.

'How d'you feel?'

'Bit of a headache but fine, really.'

Dixon smiled. He stood up, leaned over and kissed her.

'This is becoming a habit.'

The voice came from behind them. Dixon and Jane looked up to see DCI Lewis standing in the doorway.

'Three times in as many weeks I've visited one of you in hospital and I hate these bloody places.' Lewis turned to the nurse, who was still standing at the end of Jane's bed. 'No offence.'

'None taken,' she replied, walking to the door, 'I'll leave you in peace. Give me a shout if you need anything.'

'I will, thanks,' replied Jane.

Lewis turned to Dixon. 'I thought I'd find you here.'

'Where else would I be?'

'Where's Father Anthony?' asked Jane.

'Frenchay Hospital. He's on a life support machine, but he'll live,' replied Lewis. 'And his precious daughter has become very talkative since he was arrested.'

'What's she got to say for herself?' asked Dixon.

'Swears blind she never knew he killed her mother. And she only found out about the Peters girl after Fran was murdered and the blackmail started.'

'I can believe that. She was just a kid then, don't forget,' said Dixon.

'Phelps saw him take Fran and they must have followed him in Cooper's car. Next thing they know they get a photograph of

Cooper standing on the riverbank and it's the usual story from then on. Paid them once. Then Phelps came back for more. That's when they buggered off back to Kenya.'

'So Nick was right about everything?' asked Jane.

'Pretty much. It started again when Phelps caught up with them at Brunel but it was little and often, and they could cope with that, apparently. Till Cooper decided to stick his nose in the trough and Daddy met Isobel Swan.'

'What's his real name, then?' asked Dixon.

'She said she doesn't know, he's changed it that many times. You were right about the Jehovah's Witness thing too. He was one. Went to Kenya a Witness and came back an Anglican Priest.'

'Is there a real Father Anthony?'

'There was. Kenyan police are looking for him but they don't hold out much hope of finding a body. Hyenas and vultures don't tend to leave much behind.'

'How did you know it was him?' asked Jane, looking at Dixon.

'You get a bloody good look at the priest's shoes when you take Communion.'

Jane frowned.

'I'll explain later.'

'What about Chard?' asked Jane.

'Just keep out of his way for a while, Nick,' replied Lewis. 'I'll see what I can do but he's gonna want the book thrown at you. And it's a large and very heavy book.'

Dixon nodded.

'And I am sorry about Fran,' continued Lewis. 'Sorry you had to go through that.'

'Don't be,' replied Dixon. 'It's done now.'

'We've still got to find her though, haven't we?' asked Jane.

'Well, we do at least know where to look,' replied Lewis.

'We do,' said Dixon. 'The King's Sedgemoor Drain.'

---

Dixon was driving north on the M5 three hours later when his phone rang. He passed it to Jane, sitting in the passenger seat.

'Jane Winter.'

Dixon listened to her side of the conversation.

'Yes, he's driving.'

'OK, I'll tell him.'

'We're on our way.'

'Yes, fine, thanks, Louise.'

'That was Louise. She says we need to get over to Bawdrip. There's something she thinks you ought to see.'

Dixon turned off the M5 at Bridgwater North, avoiding the broken glass on the motorway roundabout where he had smashed into the patrol car less than twenty-four hours earlier. He was driving down through Bawdrip before he spoke.

'Louise saved my life last night.'

'What happened?'

'I was in the water too long. The cold. She jumped in and got me out.'

Jane smiled and nodded.

Dixon turned into the field just before the bridge over the Drain. Louise was standing there waiting for him with a man in blue overalls and a hi-vis jacket. Dixon parked next to a patrol car and helped Jane out of the Land Rover.

'This is Keith Bates, Environment Agency, Sir,' said Louise. 'I thought you should see what they've found.'

'Well?'

'We've lowered the water level to recover the VW and . . . well . . . see for yourself,' said Bates.

Dixon walked over to the top of the bank and looked down at the water. The roof of Jane's VW Golf was sticking out of the water right in front of him. Ten yards to the left was the roof of a small white van and then, further left, two more cars were visible. One red, one blue. They were covered in sediment and looked as if they had been in the water for some time.

Dixon closed his eyes and took a deep breath. He felt Jane put her arm around his waist and pull him close to her. Tears began streaming down his cheeks. His bottom lip trembled when he spoke.

'We've found her.'

'I know,' said Jane. 'I know.'

---

Dixon parked across the drive and looked up at the large detached house on the edge of Minehead. He had been back only once since Fran died.

'I'll wait in the car,' said Jane. She had insisted on coming with him even though she still felt a bit groggy.

Dixon looked at her, unable to speak. He blinked, releasing the tears in his eyes. He wiped them away with the palms of his hands before reaching across and putting his hand on Jane's thigh. She held it in her free hand and squeezed it.

He got out of the car and stood in the middle of the gravel drive. The wisteria had gone and the large square Volvo estate had been replaced by something sleeker, but apart from that, nothing much had changed.

It took him several minutes to summon up the courage to knock on the door. It was answered by a woman in her late sixties. Her grey hair was tied back in a ponytail and Dixon doubted they were laughter lines on her face. Otherwise, it was like mother, like daughter.

It took Mary Sawyer a moment to recognise him.

'Nick?'

He nodded.

'Michael, Nick Dixon's here.' She shouted over her shoulder without taking her eyes off him.

He heard the sound of a broadsheet newspaper being folded up in a hurry and thrown onto a coffee table. Then Michael Sawyer appeared in the doorway next to his wife. Neither of them had changed very much.

Dixon put his hand in his jacket pocket and his fingers closed around a gold chain with a crucifix on it.

'It's lovely to see you, Nick,' said Mary. Then she noticed his bloodshot eyes. 'Is everything all right?'

'What are you doing here?' asked Michael.

Dixon handed him his warrant card.

'You're a policeman?'

Dixon took a deep breath.

'Can I come in?'

# Acknowledgements

There are a number of people without whom this book would not have been written and I want to record my gratitude to them while I have the chance.

Thinking about it, their help has been invaluable throughout the series and I would not have got this far without them.

First, my thanks to Andy White of Avon and Somerset Police, based in Bridgwater, whose invaluable advice on technical and local policing issues has been pure gold. And for the guided tour of the new police facility at Express Park, Bridgwater. Thanks, Andy!

To Emilie Marneur and Katie Green. Thank you for your support and advice and for bringing a professional edge to my writing.

To my dear friends and unpaid editors, in no particular order, Monica Dyer, Charlie Szechowski and Rod Glanville. Thank you for your constructive and kind criticism, as always.

I should also like to express my particular thanks to my parents, Michael and Diane. Thank you for your support and encouragement along the way.

And lastly, to my long suffering wife, Shelley, who has lived every page of every book with me. Thank you!

# About the Author

*Photo © 2013 Damien Boyd*

Damien Boyd is a solicitor by training and draws on his extensive experience of criminal law, along with a spell in the Crown Prosecution Service, to write fast-paced crime thrillers featuring Detective Inspector Nick Dixon.

Made in the USA
Columbia, SC
03 June 2020